Stained

This is the first novel by James A. Lewis, who lives near Ann Arbor, Michigan. James grew up in Milwaukee, and drawing on his Catholic school heritage and his experience of being part of a close-knit family, he takes his character's childhood beyond the boundaries of the typical family, where things go terribly wrong.

A graduate of Cleary University and Central Michigan University Graduate School of Business, James is married and has grown children.

Stained

James A Lewis

ISBN: 0615982077
ISBN 13: 9780615982076
Library of Congress Control Number: 2014904446
LCCN Imprint Name: James A Lewis, Brighton, MI

Acknowledgments

No work of art is a solo performance. Whether story, painting, dance, or musical composition, the artist is shaped by the world around him, tempered by the experiences that change him. Without the interactions of life, the artwork would never reach its full potential. So I would be negligent if I didn't acknowledge the people who helped this novel develop. I am first grateful for the stable childhood provided by my parents and siblings.

I would like to express my appreciation to my initial readers and editors, who helped shape this book. To Jonna Holt, my primary editor, I owe a debt of gratitude. I asked her to read and edit what I thought would be a short story, and she stayed with me as a novel developed. I thank my sister, Mary F. Lewis, and my close friend Julie Woodruff, each of whom read an early draft and offered support and input.

Finally, I thank Kimberly A. Lewis, my best friend and the love of my life. Her acceptance, support, and encouragement in all things allow me the freedom to be who I am and explore expression of thought from which this novel has sprung.

"A man is a slave to whatever has mastered him."

—2 Peter 2:19

Prologue

Only when it was too late did Anthony realize that going back to a place that once held meaning is almost never a good idea. What was his reality he had been able to change into happiness in the years since. It was in going back that the reality crushed him, as touching a hardly noticeable crack in a mirror can cause it to shatter. During the warm summer of 1988, when he was thirty-one years old, Anthony found that he had been completely destroyed years earlier. It simply took a while to fall.

One

At fourteen, Anthony wasn't a winner. He was short for his age—shorter than many of the boys in his class and shorter than the already-maturing girls. He wasn't ugly, but he had his liabilities. His sandy hair tended to stand up in unfortunate places, a violation of the code of conformity required of all teens. Skinny—wimpy really—he was slow to develop, with puberty only beginning its march across his body. An average student, he occupied that no-man's-land between the truly admired kids and the really nerdy ones. Those groups had camaraderie—they were cohesive. Anthony stood in the middle, too "normal" to hang with the nerds, too deficient to really connect with the alpha males. Noticeable for his unremarkability. He typically hung around the fringes of the popular circle, looking for the scraps of validation that might be thrown his way. The group sometimes included and sometimes bullied him.

Anthony was flat. Two-dimensional in a three-dimensional world. Living behind a window, nose pressed up to the glass, seeing depth around him but having no way to get inside. Bonds formed between others that were deep and connected. Connections with breadth. With context. An elusive third dimension.

Even as he knelt to pray at Sunday Mass, he somehow felt counterfeit. Like the other parishioners would be able to tell that his faith was forged—a clever duplication of the authentic. Pretty but ultimately worthless. He secretly prayed each night, gripping the wooden-beaded rosary he'd received for his First Communion. Reciting a decade of Hail Marys with the concluding Our Father before lying awake wondering who, if anyone, was listening. Even without trying, he could see the reflection of the streetlamps of Wright Street on the slanted walls of his attic bedroom. Yet the God he sought appeared eclipsed, visible only peripherally, if at all. God, though, if He existed, had certainly discovered Anthony's doubts.

He did the things that other boys did. Neighborhood baseball games, bike rides to the public swimming pool in the summer, skating on the frozen pond off Sixty-Fourth Street in the long winter months. But transparently. Artificially. Tentatively, as if the surfaces he tread were continually yielding. A life unsupported by realizable structure.

It was as he skated ovals around the perimeter of the pond that winter near Joan, perhaps the prettiest of the eighth-grade girls, that Anthony first realized that he felt more kinship than attraction. It wasn't even quite so much a realization as it was an awareness that he felt different. But enough awareness so as to be cathartic. The fear that his feelings of being different might apply to his sexuality began to terrorize him early. If anyone found out, his life was over. He could think of few things worse than being a homosexual, even as he saw it as a confusing possibility. He was sure, though, that he had thoughts that the other boys did not.

Joan caught up to Anthony on a straightaway. "You're not like the other guys." His cringe was shrouded by the darkness of the unlit rink. Even if this was meant as complimentary, these were the exact words Anthony never wanted to hear. Joan continued, "I mean, other guys never just want to talk. I can talk to you. I think you are the sweetest boy in our class."

With that, she turned and kissed him on the cheek. A peck only, but for Anthony, a moment significant enough to stick. He detected the scent of Juicy Fruit on her breath. The feel of her soft, Carmex lips was to be forever imprinted on his otherwise numb cheek. The spectacle happened in full view of the other popular girls, and by lunch period the next day, the story was all over school. Anthony felt himself temporarily slide into the center of the circle—admired, perhaps even accepted. He wondered if his prospects were looking up. The answer came in the form of a punch in the stomach by Brian, purported to be Joan's boyfriend. The fact that the kiss was most certainly a sisterly show of affection didn't matter to Brian. For Anthony, having the wind knocked out of you by a bully's punch was far preferable to having the emotional breath taken from you by the fact that you are "just a friend" to the prettiest girl in school.

Joan apologized to Anthony later that day, saying that she wanted to be friends even if other people didn't understand. But Anthony distanced himself from her for the rest of the school year, not so much in fear of Brian's misplaced jealousy as in the fear that Joan did indeed understand him.

Anthony wondered as he opened his Christmas gifts that year if his parents might know that he wasn't confident they loved him. It was a feeling unsupported by objective evidence. He received gifts clearly chosen with care, in the same quantity as his siblings. Yet the feeling was unquenchable. He was the emotional runt of the Conway litter: always welcome to nurse from the font of family support yet often displaced by the stronger of his pack. He simply *always felt different.*

He was sure he was unique in his misery, that other boys in better families, in nicer neighborhoods, and in more glamorous cities, had none of his problems. In reality, he had a good family, and Milwaukee was a fine place to spend a childhood.

A gritty, polite town, where men got dirty at work but lived on tidy streets in clean houses. Anthony grew up in the shadow of the Miller Brewing Company. On summer days, he would walk through the hilly industrial complex politely called Miller Valley in order to sit in the bleachers at County Stadium for a Brewers day game. The stadium smelled like all stadiums—of hot dogs and beer. But Anthony always associated the Brewers with the yeasty smell of Miller Valley. He did more than breathe the tangy fumes; he *absorbed* them. Bathed in the fermenting hops as he walked the two miles to the stadium for the dollar-fifty bleacher seat, he couldn't wait to drink beer. His father always drank Pabst Blue Ribbon, but Anthony was sure he would like Miller High Life better.

The city's population reached its zenith at 741,324 in 1960, two years after he was born, and grew to become America's eleventh-largest city by the time he was a boy. But Milwaukee was always regarded as "the city north of Chicago," its identity elusive. Even the national weather maps on black-and-white TV always showed Chicago and Minneapolis—Milwaukee was noticeably missing in the space between them on the map. Anthony could relate.

It was during his early education, courtesy of St. Veronica's Catholic School, that the seeds of disbelief were sown. Every lesson, every lecture, every function at the school was laced with the grace of God and the authority of the church. God could take care of you but only with the permission of the church. Love was earned through obedience, and nurture was fleeting. One wrong move, one errant word, and damnation!

When his sister Kathleen died, Anthony was eight years old. Searching for logic, for spiritual truth, he found none. She was one year Anthony's elder and had leukemia in the days when the prognosis for recovery was dim. Two years of futile treatments had rendered her frail, bald, and pale. On the few days when she could come outside to play, she mostly stood silently with her eyes closed, facing the sun, as if soaking in what life was left. Seeing her, Anthony thought she resembled a corn shock overlooked in last season's harvest: standing tall but wilted in countenance and clearly past her prime—a figure who could not be taken for anything other than that which had been accidentally missed in the previous year's cutting.

"What will you do after I die?" she asked Anthony one breezy summer afternoon. Her few wisps of hair floated down her forehead as if to help the averting of her eyes.

"I won't do anything," he replied. "None of us will. We won't be a whole family anymore. We'll be like the Larsons."

The Larsons were the only divorced family in the neighborhood. Mrs. Larson, it was rumored, had run off with one of the men who roofed their house. Mr. Larson was a ghost. Talked about but only seen through the opaque curtains late at night when the house lights were on. He worked long hours and was rarely seen in daylight. The Larson children never played outside, preferring to sit in their house on the warm days of summer and watch television game shows. They didn't have bicycles. They didn't play Little League. They simply *didn't do anything*. Day after sunny day, the neighborhood children would ride past the Larson house on their bikes, heading for the city pool, or the railroad tracks where nickels could be crushed, or to the asphalt baseball diamond on the playground at the public grade school. They would hear the clapping and laughter of the audience during another episode of *Truth or Consequences* or *What's My Line?* blaring through the torn window screens. The children inside were only spectators of life. Outside the circle of anything interesting. Stunted in development by a rending of their family.

"We'll be like that. We won't be a whole family without you." Anthony was sure of it.

Kathleen missed an entire year of school and died on Mother's Day. It was clear from the tearful words of everyone Anthony knew that nothing would ever be the same. The grief of his parents made clear the love they'd had for his sister. Yet, just two days after the funeral at which Kathleen had looked surreal and plastic, with a poorly fitted adult-size wig on her head and a First Communion rosary entwined in her folded, ghostly hands, Keith Conway returned to work, and Annie laid out dough for a batch of white bread. The other three Conway children went back to school, the birds of spring chirped, the Saturday-morning cartoons continued on the television. After resisting for nearly a week, Anthony rode his bike. In the end, it seemed to Anthony that life did go on, remarkably the same as before.

That life went on was brought home to him the following fall as the school year began. The Conway family had made a habit of coordinating schoolbook purchases with the Lehner family across the alley. They had five children, none in the same grades as the Conways. Thus, the families would trade schoolbooks year to year. Although only in the second grade when his sister died, Anthony had already learned that when he received his books for the first day of the new term, the inside front cover would bear the names of the eldest Lehner, Rose, followed by Alan Conway, Marie Lehner, William Lehner, Lynn Conway, and finally Kathleen. Anthony would place his name under Kathleen's, knowing that next year Leonard Lehner would add to the list by writing his name under Anthony's. But as Anthony entered the third grade, his name was to be placed directly under Lynn's. Kathleen had not attended a day of school the previous year, although Mrs. Lehner had held the books out of respect. As Anthony wrote his name in each book, he felt himself changing. If life was a race, he had built an insurmountable lead over someone he had said he would never leave behind. Reading Fundamentals, New Concepts in Math, World Geography, Wisconsin History, Spelling and Grammar, Religion. He passed her in school. Passed her in life. It had been only four months since she was gone, and she wasn't spoken of very often. Mother would cry on the next Mother's Day and would continue this honorarium for many years. But Kathleen was gone, and in spite of the oaths taken that life would never be the same, it was.

Anthony wondered if feelings of love could have lasting depth when the object of love was so easily dismissed. Forgotten. A vapor. Months after her death, he would suddenly stop his bike and stand in the road, making sure he still remembered her name and what she looked like. He was certain that without disciplined attention to the details, Kathleen would vanish completely.

Completing grade school, his parents enrolled him at Central Catholic High, while most of his classmates were going to Sacred Heart High School or St. Mary's Academy. But Mrs. Conway had gone to Central Catholic, as did Anthony's older sister and brother. During the summer before starting high school, Anthony joined the newly formed youth choir at St. Veronica's on Haley Street. His parents required weekly attendance at Mass, and singing in the choir meant sitting in the choir loft—a place perceived to be far more interesting and at least removed from parental scrutiny. Additionally, Patty Larinski from across the street was joining, and Anthony thought it would be nice to be seen walking to and from rehearsals with such a pretty girl. He wasn't sure he could sing, but he wasn't opposed to the idea.

Ron Wilcox had just been hired as the choir's director, and the still-gawky twenty-two-year-old quickly pronounced Anthony a tenor, a slap in the face of the manhood to which he aspired. His older brother, Alan, was placed in the bass section, his sister Lynn an alto. The three Conways were among twenty-three teens to join the St. V's Youth Choir. Even years later, Anthony was not sure what had motivated him and his siblings to join. It seems that when the eventual result of a decision is monumental beyond all expectations, the reason for the initial choice pales until forgotten. But in 1972, he began a journey that changed everything about him.

St. Veronica's was a cavernous church built in 1946. It was not the ornate kind of church of earlier times. Rather, it was a midcentury interpretation of the Romanesque style, a soaring tan brick building with large, vertical planes. It was one of the modern churches of the 1940s and the first church in the archdiocese to cost more than one million dollars. The building's architecture lay in the void between the ornate steeples and gargoyles of the 1800s and the low-slung buildings with fan-shaped seating of the 1960s. It was grand in scale but plain in its features, except for incredible stained-glass windows that depicted favorite saints of the church. Anthony's mother had grown up in the parish before the massive sanctuary was built. As was the tradition of the Catholics, St. Veronica's built the school first, holding the weekly services in the church hall. Once the congregation reached critical mass, the centerpiece—the permanent place of worship—rose. And rise it did. St. Veronica's was as tall as it was wide, the ceiling a soaring eighty feet over the main aisle. There seemed to be acres of stained glass, including a rose window over the altar.

As was the custom of the times, the church was open during the day to accommodate the troubled passerby. Anthony would sometimes wander into the church to sit and watch the light move through the windows. He loved the soft colors and gradually built silent relationships with the figures held captive in the glass. They were there for him. Reliable. Attentive. Present. Oftentimes, his only company on these clandestine visits was an elderly woman found in one of the white oak pews, rosary in hand, praying as if cramming for some divine final exam. She alternately sat and knelt, her tired body doing its best to support what was perhaps an uneasy soul. Anthony wondered what dark deeds of the past would require this daily supplication.

Each of the wide sanctuary windows depicted a saint that St. V's children learned about throughout grade school. Cool, deep blues were dominant in the scenes. Accented by purples, reds, and golds, the windows were spectacular. Anthony remembered being told that stained-glass windows dominated by blue panes indicated a wealthy congregation, because the compound needed to create blue glass—cobalt—was one of the most expensive. An expanse of blue glass was a statement on the blessings of God upon the people of that church. He loved the windows and came to love the saints they held in custody.

The building was oriented such that the morning sun illuminated the left side of the sanctuary—bringing Thomas, Paul, Barnabas, Joshua, and Moses to life. The afternoon sun favored Peter, James and John, Joseph, Elijah, and Abraham. As the light played through the saints, their faces changed in expression. Moses seemed angry about the golden calf in the morning but serene on the mountain of God's presence by afternoon. Joseph moved from gentle and fatherly to exhausted by a destiny not chosen. Although the movement of light never betrayed sibling rivalry, Anthony always wondered if James and John felt slighted that they had to share a window.

He had once had the foolish nerve to ask Father Francis why the church grouped the brothers together even though each was a saint. The terse response was typical of church leadership: "The saints never once questioned the authority of the church in their lives, and neither should you."

The monstrance over the altar was covered in gold leaf, and everything from the rail separating the priest from his congregation to the rose window over the altar was Italian marble. The rose window was an amazingly intricate design of blues, greens, purples, and golds, with Jesus seated on his throne directly in the middle. Although the window was quite large, Jesus occupied a fairly small space at the center. Anthony thought it odd that, while he occupied the focal point front in the church, Jesus was the smallest cast member held in glass. The floors were edged in forest-green marble; the central floor under the pews was cream-colored terrazzo with flecks of green and gold. The altar itself was hewn of ivory-colored marble. There was a large choir loft at the rear, seating over one hundred and flanked by bronze organ pipes. Over the loft, on the rear wall of the church, was the largest single window. It featured St. Veronica, holding the towel with which she wiped the face of Christ as he was dragged to his death on the cross. Catholic tradition teaches that the face of Jesus was left imprinted on the towel, and this was depicted in gold and crimson glass. The church itself was deceivingly small in terms of capacity. With a center aisle of over 120 feet and a soaring ceiling, the building actually seated a little less than a thousand. It was built for impression, not practicality. In the 1970s, it was still impressive. Anthony loved the church building most when it was empty, cool, and quiet. God, if He lived there—if He lived at all—seemed more likely to be discerned when His house was emptied of the coughing, sighing, and distracted faithful.

Like all good Catholic children, he was terrorized by nuns and intimidated by priests, beaten with the rod of Catholic doctrine each school day. In fourth grade, an eccentric and elderly nun spun a tale of a Sister in the adjoining convent possessed by a demon. According to Sister Mary Lawrence, the afflicted nun required round-the-clock attention, lest she float off her mattress under the unction of Lucifer during the night.

"On the days when I don't return your homework, it is because I spent the night—*while you were sleeping*—serving our Lord Jesus Christ by sitting at the bedside of this poor Sister. Your life is easy compared to the lives of those who truly serve our Savior."

Anthony wanted to ask what the Sister did to invite the presence of evil right into her body and why the good Sisters could not prevail in casting it out. Instead, he raised his hand bravely and inquired, "Does she ever talk or eat?" Emboldened by the idea that the children were buying that story, the teacher began to elaborate.

"A few months ago, we sprinkled her food with holy water without her knowing it, and when she took her first bite, she screamed that her mouth was on fire!" Anthony could only wonder why, with all the priests and nuns and holy water and icons around, this demon had such free rein. It didn't add up, but it wasn't to be questioned.

In seventh grade, students were pressed into the service of the St. Dominic Savio Club. The club was formed by Sister Anne Marie to provide instruction to students on the ways of the apparently famous teenage saint. Meetings were spent in lessons about Dominic and in instruction about ways to raise funds for the club coffers, which were added to with weekly dues but never actually spent on anything, from what Anthony could tell.

According to the club's discussions, Dominic Savio was afflicted with tuberculosis as a boy of the same age as Anthony and his classmates. In spite of constant pain and suffering, he took extra measures to prove his faith and loyalty to God, including placing sticks and rocks under the blankets of his deathbed so as to add to the suffering he invited as an offering to the Most High. Anthony wondered why it escaped everyone's notice that perhaps the God that Dominic so faithfully served could have simply healed the boy and put all the energy the boy spent on suffering to use for the good of the community. He had learned from his earlier questioning of Father Francis on the topic of James and John that Catholic instruction was to be received without question, regardless of its preposterous logic.

Midway through the year, Sister Anne Marie challenged the students. "Each week, you children bring your club dues, which are really a sacrifice for your parents. These are their offerings, not yours. But Dominic Savio made his ultimate sacrifice for God when he was just your age. For next week, I do not want any of you to bring in money from your parents or anyone else. Next week's dues will be a love offering to God from you only. Bring in only your own money, children. If the offering is the biggest collection of the year, God will know how much you are willing to sacrifice for him. I will pray, children, for the gift of discernment to know if the offering you bring is truly your own money and if you've given all that God wants you to give." Throughout the next week, the students were updated on the prayers of the good Sister, and she repeatedly expressed her confidence that she would be able to tell if each child gave all that they personally had. Tension built as the meeting approached.

At the appointed time—the last hour of Friday afternoon—the club's meeting was called to order. As if to torture the children, who had been unusually quiet during that day, Sister put off the dues collection segment of the meeting until later in the hour. When it finally arrived, she came around her varnished oaken desk and leaned against it, ceramic offering bowl in hand.

"Each of you is to come forward individually and place your offering into the bowl. I want to see your eyes, so that through me God can look into your conscience."

The students held back, until Cheryl Anne, the winner of that week's spelling bee, walked forward. She smiled as she made eye contact with the imposing nun, then emptied her coin purse into the bowl. "Praise the Lord!" Sister Anne Marie exclaimed. "Our Lord is well pleased with you." Additional children began to line up with their offerings. Some were praised, others derided. Anthony hung back, watching. He had a dollar twenty-five—more than twice the normal dues. But it had come from his father, whom he had asked for extra cash for the club's annual fund drive for UNICEF. As he watched the students approach Sister Anne Marie, he noticed that their body language and eye contact clearly indicated their comfort with the process. By the tenth child in line, Anthony was predicting the teacher's reaction with absolute accuracy. He waited until late in the production and then took his place, second from last in the line of thirty-one students. Those who had hung back were by and large those who faced the wrath of God, the poor signals they sent out dooming them to chastisement.

"It would be better not to approach God than to do so with such guile and deceit!" she hollered at Rodney Shellenbacher.

"You shame Dominic Savio and your family!" she screamed out when Allison St. Croix dropped two singles into the bowl, tears streaming down her face.

"I don't get any allowance, Sister. I don't have any money for—"

"Enough!" Sister exclaimed, cutting the shaking girl off. "Dominic would have sold his very shoes to give to our Lord. Walked barefoot through the snow to school! Serving Jesus isn't about what you cannot do, Allison—it's about what you *will* do!" The girl returned to her seat, quietly sobbing.

Collecting himself, Anthony looked straight at Sister as he approached, forcing a smile on his face and holding her gaze as he emptied the five quarters into the bowl. "God loves you, Mr. Conway." She smiled as she patted his shoulder, turning him back toward his seat. As he walked away, he heard her rail against the last boy in line.

In the end, it was indeed the biggest offering ever—nearly fifty dollars. Sister got the opportunity to upset and bully her students, and the money was neither spoken of nor seen again. Anthony, however, learned that image is more powerful than integrity.

Each Conway child had been enrolled in piano lessons in the second grade. Alan had lasted a few months, never really learning the most basic musical concepts. Lynn and Anthony both took lessons throughout grade school and learned to read music with some proficiency. Anthony's first experience with singing, however, had come during music class in the fifth grade. Sister Novena was a new arrival at the school. She had the vocation to be a Notre Dame Sister but certainly not the talent and was given responsibility for music classes. She was tall and gangly, moving from classroom to classroom with huge, ungainly strides, like a robed praying mantis. Anthony always thought she was about to stumble over her large feet, perhaps because she didn't move at the hips like most adults. Her entire body seemed to turn from side to side as she strode through the hallways carrying her electric keyboard, rosary-bead belt swinging wildly. She was clumsy and disheveled, and Anthony often wondered if the worst of the nerds in his class would grow up to move like her. She couldn't teach, but she played the piano. The good Sisters knew that reading and arithmetic were nearly as vital as the religious instruction at St. V's. But music was a throwaway, and clumsy Sister Novena would do as little damage as one teacher could do if she stuck to musical instruction.

Anthony didn't much care about Sister's teaching style or lack thereof. He liked the break music class brought to the day twice per week—a class that required no preparation and demanded no homework. Never much noticed by any of his teachers, he was horrified one Thursday morning in seventh grade when Sister Novena stopped the class between verses of "O Come, O Come, Emmanuel" to express her pleasure at the vigor with which Anthony was singing. He hadn't intended to sing with any vigor—didn't remember doing so in the past—and wasn't really aware that he was singing at all.

"You're a singer!" Sister clapped her hands together in clumsy glee. Immediate was the snickering of the boys in the class. As Sister returned to her keyboard, Anthony heard Eddie quietly laugh. "Conway's a queer!" He tried hard to remember to never sing in class again. Even when his eighth-grade class sang at their graduation mass, he only mouthed the words, ensuring that he couldn't be heard. So it was with the hope that no bully would join the new youth choir that he put his name on the roster.

At the choir's first Thursday evening rehearsal, Anthony was surprised to see six other boys from his eighth-grade class in the choir loft, including the bully himself, Eddie. "Conway, I knew you'd join," Eddie chided when Anthony ascended the loft stairs. He felt good about his decision to walk with Patty

Larinski instead of riding in the family car with Alan and Lynn.
Eddie rose from his chair and came over to them as they followed directions and picked up music from the table. He
punched Anthony playfully on the shoulder to provide the
impression they were friends, then used the connection to
launch into conversation with Patty. Anthony was glad Eddie's
house was in the opposite direction from the church as his and
Patty's. There'd be no convenient way for him to join the walk
home. Anthony wondered as he picked up the sheet music if
a continued connection to the pretty girl would ultimately win
him acceptance from Eddie.

From the first hour of rehearsal, it was clear that it was to be
nothing like the music classes of grade school. The demands of
the music were more serious than those of the unison choruses
favored by Sister Novena. Ron was a true musician. Although
young, he was an accomplished organist who could fill the cav-
ern of St. Veronica's with the heaviest of classical organ music.
He had led his first choir at sixteen, and the story was that he was
good enough to play the organ for Mass at ten years of age, even
before his feet could reach the pedals. He insisted that the music
be sung as written, and he chose music that had never been
heard by these teens. No "Kookaburra Sits in the Old Gum Tree"
in Ron's youth choir. William Billings, Francis Poulenc, Ralph
Vaughan Williams. The idea that teens could learn and enjoy
the heavy sacred music of the church was not only novel—it was
radical. While the inner-city churches had gospel choirs and the
liberal suburban churches had guitar Masses, St. Veronica's was
to showcase a youth choir singing excerpts from Haydn's Mass
of Creation, Ralph Vaughan Williams's Mass in G Minor, and
William Billings's *Universal Praise*. It would quickly raise Ron to
hero status in the church. As the choir grew to its eventual eighty
members, the parents smiled, the priests bragged, and the nuns
admired. The members of the choir worshipped. St. Veronica,

there at every rehearsal, was the witness to Ron's ascension to deity status—a role he accepted and used.

In every way, Ron's style flew in the face of the typical church musician. He was reckless in speech and behavior. A spider weaving his web just over a spinning fan. One wrong move, and it was all over. But the spider is born to weave perfect webs. There aren't any wrong moves.

Anthony first heard the word *fuck* in church at a rehearsal after only two weeks with the choir. During a particularly difficult run of the soprano part, Ron became infuriated with some talkers in other sections. "What are you laughing about?" he screamed. "There's nothing funny in this fucked-up world!"

At the third meeting of the choir, Ron spoke to Anthony on a personal level for the first time. It was the end of the rehearsal, and music was being collected. Ron took a stack of tenor music from Anthony. "You read music, don't you?" Ron asked.

"I took piano lessons. I guess I can read a little," Anthony replied.

"I can see you following the music—turning the pages at the right places. It's nice to have a musician in the choir."

A musician? Anthony certainly didn't consider himself to be a musician, at least not before that night. Rather, it was Lynn who was the better pianist. But now a professional saw Anthony as a fellow musician. Just knowing he had been noticed made him proud. Ron smiled genuinely as he took the music from Anthony's hands. "Do you like being called Anthony, or should I call you Tony?"

It seemed inappropriate to impose his will on Ron, Anthony thought. Yet he hated being called Tony. "Everyone calls me Anthony."

"See you next week, Anthony." Ron smiled again and held eye contact as the two parted.

He felt less intimidated by Ron after that. In fact, he felt drawn to him. He studied the music carefully, looking for the places in a song—at the rests or time changes—when other choir members would be tripped up. He was sure to practice the correct reading of the music in his head so that, at the appropriate time, he could sing out correctly while others blundered. Ron didn't ever acknowledge his correct interpretations of the music, but he never directed his tirades at Anthony either.

At some of the rehearsals, Ron would stand irresponsibly on the loft balustrade to gain attention, walking across the ledge thirty feet over the terrazzo floor below. One Thursday evening, he slammed his fist on the light over the organ keyboard in a fit a rage, cutting open his hand. He finished the rehearsal bleeding, taking no notice of the cuts. The blood was neither a cause for concern nor a badge of achievement. It was entirely unnoticed by Ron, who seemed transfixed by the musical perfection he was demanding and gradually getting. As time went on, he drew perfect musical performance from this band of teens, as a glassblower uses heat to will sand into art. He was rude and often mean, singling out choir members for missed cues and imperfect notes and railing against the group for anything short of his expectations. But when the expectations were met, the reaction from Ron was not approval but ecstasy. At those moments, he held the countenance of a drug addict receiving his craved injection. The choir sustained Ron. He had no joy, no comfort, no high without perfection in the performance of the choir. Even during the most severe of beatings, the choir persevered with an eye on the prize of providing the salve to soothe the madman who beat it. The drive to meet the needs of the director was exceeded only by his hunger to receive. It was a symbiotic and unquenchable relationship.

Two

After only four weeks of practice, the choir began singing at the eleven o'clock Mass on Sunday mornings. Anthony had made it a habit of staying after the rehearsals and Masses to help collect and organize the music sheets. Patty Larinski would stay as well, which allowed them to walk home together. Eddie stayed with the pretense of assisting, although his help was generally not discernible. His interest was clearly in Patty.

Oftentimes Ron would be occupied with questions from members or with receiving accolades from parents who would climb the loft stairs to express admiration after Masses. One Thursday evening while the collection of music was under way, Patty mentioned, to no one in particular, although it was for Anthony's benefit, that she needed to use the ladies' room before they walked home. Neither Ron nor Anthony acknowledged the statement, but Eddie dramatically announced that he also "needed to whiz." Walking with Patty to the restrooms at the rear of the church allowed him precious moments with her. It allowed Ron and Anthony their first moments alone as well.

Searching for something interesting to say, Anthony was interrupted by Ron's words. "I think Eddie's moving in on your girlfriend."

"She's not my girlfriend. We just walk together because she lives across the street from me. I've known her since we were little, but she's not my girlfriend."

"She's pretty. Hopefully she sees through Eddie's foolishness." Ron chuckled and reached for the same piece of music as Anthony. Their hands touched briefly.

Anthony jumped at the touch, embarrassed. Ron didn't seem to notice. Anthony spoke quickly. "I think she has a boyfriend from Madison High. He's probably not Catholic, so he doesn't come around here. But I see a guy with a car pick her up at the house."

"Well, hopefully old Eddie doesn't get his ass kicked for sniffing around her. We need all our basses. It's the weakest section."

Anthony jumped at the opening. "I could sing bass if you want."

"Then the tenors would be the weakest section." Anthony looked up, and Ron was smiling at him. Anthony would wonder later that night if he'd ever gotten a more important compliment. They remained quiet as they finished sorting the mimeographed sheets spread on the organ console.

"You're important to this choir, Anthony," Ron said plainly, breaking the silence. Then he laughed lightly. "You're more than just a good music sorter!" Turning serious, he stopped stacking the completed piles and looked Anthony in the eyes. "I don't know too many people in Milwaukee yet. You and I may have a lot of common interests. It's lucky for me that you joined the choir. Perhaps you can be one of my first friends here." He held Anthony's gaze, still smiling. "We should hang out sometime. Just come by my place—anytime. I could play my favorite music for you."

Before he could say anything, Eddie and Patty bounded back up the stairs to the choir loft. Anthony didn't want to discuss the offer just made in front of Eddie. He didn't mind Eddie moving into his space with Patty, but he didn't want him to become chummy with Ron.

Seeing that the music was sorted and stacked on the organ console, Patty asked if Anthony was ready to go. "I'll walk part-way with you guys," Eddie offered. As they turned to exit the loft, Anthony looked back at Ron, who smiled and rolled his eyes in Eddie's direction.

By Christmas, the choir had swelled to forty. Just before the holiday, they performed at an inner-city music festival, singing two numbers. There were six youth choirs from area Catholic churches, including the event host, the mighty Holy Spirit Gospel Choir. Two things were clear at the end of the afternoon: The St. Veronica's Youth Choir was not in the same league as the sixty-voice host choir, whose hand-clapping power drove it. And Ron's pain at that realization was nowhere to be seen. Anthony expected a violent reaction from Ron after the concert—a chastising of the teens that would be both brutal and personal. But Ron did not seem bothered by the clear superiority of the other choirs. In fact, their performances did not even seem to register. The Holy Spirit Gospel Choir in particular seemed invisible to Ron.

Anthony was at the end of the back row on the risers during their performance, just behind one of the shorter sopranos. After singing its second number, the choir filed back to its section in the pews with him at the very end of the line, which put him in the pew next to Ron, who had followed the choir off the risers. As the Holy Spirit Choir sang their final number, Ron leaned toward Anthony and whispered, "That girl on the left looks like Aretha Franklin." Anthony knew the name but couldn't picture the famous woman in his mind. "They're really good," he replied. "Do you think we'll ever sound like that?"

"We'll never sound like that," Ron said, neither mournful nor envious. It was a statement of fact. Only later did Anthony realize that Ron's plans for his choir were so grand and so different that a popular choir like Holy Spirit was not on his radar. Perhaps the most disrespectful reaction to an enemy is no reaction at all. This powerful choir was certainly not an actual enemy, but it was clear that Ron did not feel competitive with them or any of the other choirs. He politely endured the kind and encouraging words of the other directors, who congratulated him on his new work at St. V's. He smiled but was clearly unmoved. He returned no compliments, engaged no one, and appeared to take no pleasure. He was there because it was a step—a learning experience for his choir. The other choirs were superfluous. While his members measured themselves against the other youth choirs, Ron saw the future. There were to be no rivals, no competitors. It was an exciting foreshadowing for Anthony, who was becoming addicted to the words and actions of Ron Wilcox. He found himself feeling superior by association with Ron and with this choir. While others at the concert may not have realized it, they had heard the greatest choir in the city sing when St. V's performed. They were simply hearing them early in their development. It was interesting to feel powerful when there was no outward appearance of power. The greatness of the choir, of Ron, was internal. The outward manifestation would follow. He was as sure of it as he could see Ron was.

He had wanted so badly to spend time with Ron after his invitation to listen to music. But he didn't have the nerve to call Ron, and Ron never called him. Anthony wanted it to be true that he was Ron's friend. To spend time with him. To be like him. Ron lived outside convention. It wasn't that he chose to ignore or break rules: he simply didn't see them as applicable. Anthony determined to imitate what was being modeled.

For the rest of his life, no figure, no event, compared to the force that was Ron Wilcox. As time went on, it was clear that many of the teens yearned for Ron's approval. It was as highly prized as it was rare. Ron started to invite groups of teens to his rented apartment to listen to music. Even as the choir grew to over fifty before the winter broke, a core group emerged as the more prized members of the choir. They were the more musical ones—those with the best voices. And the popular ones—the pretty girls and the boys who had cars. Anthony still couldn't explain it, but he was chosen as part of that group. So was his sister, although his older brother seemed uninterested in the commitment required to be a part of this inner circle. Alan had started at Marquette University and had developed other interests. College produced a new crop of girls for Alan. His time and attention were divided between the neighborhood life of St. Veronica's and the bigger world of the campus.

Ron paid no heed to the fact that his inner circle of choir members was composed of teenagers, with parents' rules and limitations. He would invite them over after rehearsals on Thursday nights, ignoring the fact that high school students weren't free for a beer at nine o'clock on a school night. There were a few eighteen-year-olds, but the rest were high school students. Anthony could not accept any of Ron's invitations. But simply being invited into the circle was a new feeling. He relished the fact that he was asked.

As the choir and its music developed within the parish, Annie Conway became enthralled by Ron Wilcox. Knowing he was living alone in a new city, she continually invited him to dinner. She asked about his favorite dishes, and upon learning that he liked scalloped potatoes, she vowed to him that not only did she make the best but that she wouldn't make them until he came for dinner. It was pitiful. She positively cooed over him. Finally, on a frigid winter weeknight in 1973, six months after his arrival, he accepted the invitation. He was there, in jeans, a dress shirt, and a square-bottomed knit tie when Anthony arrived home from school, numb from the five-block walk from the bus stop. Ron sat in the living room, talking with Annie about his vision for a choir that traveled, had matching outfits, and recorded albums. She ate it up. Lynn was not yet home from cheerleading practice, and Keith was working later than usual at the hospital pharmacy. Alan had no discernible schedule, home only unpredictably. When Annie left the room to tend to the dinner, Ron asked Anthony about the piano in the sunroom. "Are you the only one who plays piano?"

"Lynn and I have had lessons, and my dad plays sometimes."

"Play something." The statement was neither a request nor a demand. It was simply a logical next step in the conversation.

Anthony was terrified by the idea of playing for Ron. In his presence. Naked before him, musically speaking. Taking his place on the bench, he opened the music he'd been practicing for the week's lesson. He had mastered the right hand but still struggled with the left. It was a piece from *West Side Story*: "One Hand, One Heart." He knew from his grade school recitals that nervousness made him rush, and rushing made him sloppy. Taking a deep breath, he began to play the intro softly and slowly. Midway through the page, Ron sat down on his left and reached out to turn the music page for him. As he did, Anthony made what he knew had been his third discernible mistake in the left hand. He was about to stop the pain of his imperfect performance when Ron reached out and displaced Anthony's hand, playing the left-hand part as Anthony continued playing the right. They went on to the end of the music without talking. Both smiled as they finished, and Annie called from the kitchen, "That sounds great, Son!"

"You play well, Anthony," Ron offered. "You really are a musician."

"I always mess up in the same places with my left hand."

"Playing perfectly doesn't make someone a musician. It just makes them accurate. There are people with great voices and perfect fingering who aren't musicians—they are simply skilled. But you *feel the music.* I can tell. You feel what the composer is trying to say, what you want to say in playing the song. It's not just about right notes, at least during practice. It's about feeling the music. Understanding it. Making it your own expression. Accuracy is necessary and comes with practice. Then the emotion you feel when you first set out to learn the piece brings perfection in performance. To be a musician, a person needs to feel something when they sing or play. I can see the feeling in you—just release it."

Anthony felt flushed. This compliment was huge and seemed heartfelt. Ron maintained eye contact as he sat on the bench, their hips touching. This was the second time he'd been called a musician. And this time Ron went deeper in his description of his feelings about Anthony. This wasn't like receiving a compliment from a grandparent or doting aunt. These compliments were supposed to make you out to be more than you were. Those who love you are bound by a requirement to suspend honesty for your own good. Ron had no reason to lie.

"Thanks." It was all Anthony could say as Annie rejoined them, hoping to miss nothing.

Dinner was nice. Annie genuinely fawned over Ron and artificially fawned over Keith, who'd arrived just before dinner. Alan didn't show, but Lynn got home just after her father. Still in her practice-squad culottes and sweatshirt, hair up in a disheveled mass on top of her head, she seemed embarrassed and ran to change into jeans before coming to the table. Keith asked businesslike questions about the choir and Ron's work while Anthony and Lynn rolled their eyes at each other. Between answers, Ron directed his attention to Anthony numerous times, asking him in front of the family what he thought about certain songs the choir was learning. When Annie told Keith that Anthony had played beautifully just before dinner, Ron smiled and agreed, never mentioning his assistance. "If you ever need help with any of your music, just let me know."

Ron left shortly after the meal, explaining his need to review some music before a funeral scheduled for the next morning. Keith shook Ron's hand and retreated to his den. Annie chattered until the last moment, hugging him at the front door. As he turned from Annie, he caught Anthony's eye. "I'd enjoy helping you with any of the music that troubles you. I always make my mistakes in the same spots, just like you, but with my right hand. Perhaps we can help each other improve." Without awaiting an answer, he bounded down the three porch stairs.

"That's quite a compliment, young man," Annie said, turning to Anthony.

Lynn chimed in. "What ya do, wash his car for him? He *loves you*." Her tone was mocking, and she wasn't done. "Oh, Anthony, what do you think of this song? Oh, Anthony, do you think the choir should take a trip? Oh, Anthony, maybe you could help me play better." The sarcasm dripped from her sneered mouth. "Like *you* could help *him* play better. You can't even run scales without screwing up." There was a hint of playfulness in her voice, but it didn't mask her disdain for the idea that her little brother would be seen as being of any use to Ron.

"Lynn!" Annie countered. "Ron was being very polite and very complimentary to Anthony. He didn't hear you play. Don't think that he wouldn't have said the same things to you!" In one fell swoop, she moved to take the joy from Anthony. To minimize Ron's words by terming them *polite*. To minimize Anthony by assuming that the words could have been spent on

Lynn as well. That was Annie. If you succeeded, it was *because you were a Conway*. If you failed, you were on your own.

But she was too late. Ron's words were already rooted inside Anthony, even though there was no outward sign of the impact. Like a plant that digs deep first before showing the signs of producing fruit. Anthony could only hate his mother for minimizing the seeds planted. She was as jealous as Lynn was. He was sure of it. Anthony turned and left the room without a word.

—⁓—

Teen years are turbulent years. Anthony was fighting continually with his mother and siblings. His father seemed to have little interest in him or his struggles. Lynn the cheerleader and Alan the college man were deep into activities that interested their parents. Kathleen, who had occupied all her parents' attention during her illness, was gone. But Anthony sat on the fringe, this last child, this last obligation. The one who would ultimately stand between the parents and their independence from the chore of child rearing. And the one who had not yet exhibited any talents to which his parents could relate. At this point, Anthony was interesting to his mother only by association with the choir director she was coming to adore.

But Ron's visit put him in a different light, at least in Anthony's own mind. Ron was seeing him as a person, not just a kid. He seemed more interested in Anthony than in the other members of the family. That seemed incredible—probably to everyone in the family.

A week after Ron had been at the house for dinner, Anthony had a particularly strong battle with his mother. Like most of these arguments, the genesis was minor—the folding of laundry or the separating of cans and bottles from the rest of the trash. But it had escalated into waves of complaints and harsh accusations that had nothing to do with the original conflict. As had become his habit, Anthony stomped out of the room when he grew weary or had inflicted sufficient damage. Sometimes he went to his room; other times he ran out of the house. The latter was his route tonight. It was early evening but already dark, and after storming out of the house into the frigid Wisconsin air, he found himself walking toward Ron's apartment. Rounding the corner of Forty-Seventh and Nash Streets, he did the most uncharacteristically brave thing of his young life. He went to Ron's door and knocked. In spite of the fact that he had shown absolutely no evidence of having friends or connections outside of the teens of his parish, it never occurred to Anthony that Ron would be home. Startlingly, Ron answered the door and seemed genuinely pleased to see him. Anthony felt exhilarated as he stepped inside the house.

Three

Ron rented the first floor of a late-1800s two-family Victorian house. One family lived on each floor, and the peak roof housed a full walk-up attic of wasted space. Forty-Seventh Street was lined with nearly identical homes in various states of repair. If this neighborhood had been near one of the universities, the attic would have been converted into a valuable third-floor apartment. But this was a neighborhood in transition, not yet ghetto but destined to slide into the inner city. Except for some peeling of the white exterior paint, Ron's building was well preserved. Coming into the foyer, Anthony noticed the dusty, old smell of wood floors and oil heat. The apartment had a large L-shaped living room and dining room, plus two bedrooms, a turn-of-the-century kitchen with no cupboards, a small butler's pantry, and a bathroom with a claw-foot tub. The house was dark—thickly varnished oak flooring and woodwork dimly lit by a shaded lamp in the living room. Heavy scalloped draperies, probably belonging to the landlord, shrouded the windows. The apartment seemed to be hiding something. There were dark corners everywhere, even in the middle of the room. It was quiet as a funeral parlor. Built-in cabinets, deep windowsills, old mirrors so tarnished that they barely reflected what they saw. There was an air of secrecy there—a penumbra where what was seen was a sliver of what the space contained. But the apartment was warm, and Ron was smiling.

"Hey, I'm glad you stopped over." Ron offered cheerfully, turning toward the dark interior of the house. He followed Ron from the foyer through the somber living and dining rooms. "I was just listening to some music and making dinner."

The plaster walls of the front rooms were faded cream, and Anthony noticed twin breakfronts of dark wood flanking the archway between the two rooms. Each held shelves and terminated in a chest-high ledge. On the left side stood the only interesting furnishing thus noted in the apartment—a two-foot statue of Moses holding the two stone tablets of the Ten Commandments over his head. His hair and robe were frozen in a wild wind, and his face was full of fury. The statue captured the moment from the story when Moses descended the mount on which he had received the commandments to find the people of Israel worshipping around the golden calf they had erected in his absence. Anthony had learned in religion class that Moses had smashed the tablets in anger and had to return to the mountaintop to beg God for a replacement.

Whether the impressive statue was carved of real stone or merely cast of some plaster-like material was unclear to Anthony. It seemed to show the angry humanity of Moses and his spiritual position of leadership in the same captured moment. Anthony had seen depictions of a powerful Moses leading the children of Israel at the parting of the Red Sea. He'd seen the serene infant Moses in the basket afloat in the river. But he'd never seen him depicted as so completely human, with an imperfection as pronounced as a temper. The idea that this great hero of the scriptures should be seen in a tantrum of rage was startling. Moses, caught acting like a pissed-off CEO. Anthony didn't ask Ron about the statue. But it seemed appropriate that Ron, a respected and admired force within St. V's who was prone to rage and temper, would adorn his living room with a statue depicting Moses in the same behavior.

The dining room was that in name only. No table or chairs, only an old grand piano in the middle of the room and a stereo sitting on the built-in sideboard. The turntable was on, but the needle had been removed from the record, probably when Anthony had knocked on the door. He followed Ron to the more brightly lit kitchen. There, sizzling, was an electric frying pan containing a thick red-orange liquid. "I'm making some tomato soup. Want some?" inquired Ron.

Before he could catch himself, Anthony asked the obvious. "Tomato soup in an electric frying pan?" Although Anthony was rarely called upon to cook for himself, he was sure that soup was made on the stove.

"I don't have any kettles yet." Ron laughed. "I figure the frying pan gets hot, so the soup will get hot."

Anthony joined the joke, observing silently that even in minor tasks Ron had the ability to break the rules and yet get what he wanted.

"I've already eaten."

"Well, sit down. I'll just eat the soup from the pan then, since you don't want any."

Anthony sat at the metal and Formica table across from Ron as he scooped the soup from the pan to his mouth. Making an effort to appear as adult as possible, he explained that his mother was particularly bitchy this evening and he needed to take some time away from the chaos of home. Ron listened, offering few comments but affirming with body language. In the middle of Anthony's explanation and commentary, Ron dropped his spoon on the table and stood. Without fanfare, he offered some sweet pink wine from his faded white Kelvinator refrigerator—Annie Green Springs Strawberry Apple Wine.

Anthony had never tasted alcohol before. Other boys had drunk from the cruets of wine in the church sacristy, but Anthony had never had the courage to break a rule right in church. He accepted a wineglass from Ron, hoping he could drink without gagging or spilling. His hand trembled slightly as he took a small sip. With or without alcohol, it was intoxicating to be alone, unchaperoned, in a real adult home that had wineglasses. He felt his life changing as the wine touched his lips, giddy with the notion that he was with a real grown-up, with furniture and laundry and groceries—that Ron was *his host.* Anthony was being treated like a peer by an adult. And it was not just any adult: it was Ron Wilcox.

The wine, poison by the standards of any real wine drinker, turned out to be easy to drink. It was more like apple juice than alcohol, sugary and fragrant. Anthony immediately started searching his feelings for intoxication, expecting that the impact of alcohol would be immediate. Trying to focus on something in the room in order to evaluate his condition, he found nothing interesting. White, chest-high subway tile ran around the room, and there were no pictures on the mint-green walls above the tile. There were no cabinets, just a wall-hung farmhouse sink, the appliances, and the table at which he sat. There was a pull-chain light fixture above the sink and a harsh fluorescent ceiling fixture that had been added more recently. The fixture buzzed, and the single accoutrement in the room, an old white wall clock, ticked stoically. Refocusing on Ron, he found him pontificating on the topic of families and relationships.

"You have to grow beyond your family. You have a nice family, but they can't be there for you," Ron admonished. "That's not either good or bad, and it certainly isn't any reflection of you. There simply is no such thing as real commitment. No one can say they really commit to anyone. Your family can't really take care of you, and if there is a God, he's an asshole."

Anthony was stunned. No one had ever made such a blasphemous statement in front of him before, and this was coming from a church leader. He could only nod. Ron leaned away from his soup and went on. "Parents can only provide so much love for you—they're limited by their own shit. In the end, they rely on spreading the same threats and fears that they were raised with. The church does the same. The key to survival is to become independent emotionally. Connection is what creates complications, pain." He spoke with authority, directly to Anthony. Not like a teacher—like a friend. Clearly, his words were correct. Anthony wondered how Ron had known how he was feeling. He had, after all, always felt insufficient. The explanation was suddenly simple. God, parents, friends, and boyfriends and girlfriends could do nothing but let him down. It was not a specific insufficiency within him that caused the abandonment. It was the pursuit of care from others, even from God, that brought about the painful feelings. What Ron said rang true.

He considered the logic of the argument. To be abandoned, you must first be possessed. To be discarded, you must go from valuable to worthless—you must change in the eyes of the beholder. But if you're not possessed, if you're not valuable to others to begin with, then you've not been abandoned or discarded. You've simply always been alone. No one's *done* anything to you. You are simply all by yourself, in the company of others. That's what always plagued him—that feeling that he had somehow fallen from favor. Failed to measure up. But this was different. He wasn't discarded. He was simply alone. *No one is truly able to care for another.* It was a revelation. He hadn't been abandoned. He simply wasn't *connected.* Because *no one is connected.* Somehow, the idea of simply being alone was more comforting than that of having been rejected. It gave him power even if he had no outward appearance of control. With this idea already taking firm hold of Anthony, he realized that Ron was his Moses—the one who would lead him out of the wilderness of unobtainable connection to the promised land of independence.

He hung on every word, and this was evident to Ron. Philosophies on everything from God to sexuality were provided by the master and consumed by the student. "The universe would be so much better if there was no God, because then there would be no one to blame. You can only blame someone if you believe that he could have done better than he did. If there is no God, there's no order, no plan. So things could not be expected to work out better, because no one was responsible for making them better. To me, if there is no God, there is no one to blame for unfulfilled expectations. But God does exist, and He's defective. He could have done better, but He didn't. And now He can't face His failures, so He doesn't face us. He's here, all around, but His back is turned. Probably doesn't even know how much pain He created. People seeking God make Him feel even worse about His fuckup. So you have to stop seeking God. You don't want to be the focus of someone who can't get anything right. That's why it's best to acknowledge His existence and ignore His presence."

Yes, thought Anthony.

"Look at Job. He was all about God. The story says he was righteous and loved the Lord more than anyone. The devil comes along and says that he's only following God because he gets stuff from Him. That if he weren't rich, he'd curse God. So God takes a bet with the devil to see if Satan can torture this faithful follower enough to make him curse God. What kind of a sick bastard betrays his most dedicated follower like that? I would never betray my close friends, Anthony. I'd never leave them out there hanging or, worse yet, betray them just to see how they'll act. If God were truly secure, he wouldn't need to take bets on how much his followers love him. Job's story sure as hell makes me want to stay out of God's focus!"

Good point, thought Anthony.

Ron continued. "And they tell us we sin because we exercise free will. That God never violates our free will, so we do bad things and God doesn't stop them. That the starving children in the world and the people who get run over by drunk drivers—that it happens because people exercise their free will to be shitty, and God won't intervene. He *respects* us too much to violate our free will, so some sweet old lady gets shot in a bank robbery. But doesn't the story of Moses and the slaves in Egypt say that God hardened the pharaoh's heart so that he could bring more plagues? After the first few plagues, the pharaoh said the Israelites should leave, but God hardened his heart, and he reneged. Then God, who violated the pharaoh's free will, brings more death and destruction. Over and over. Frogs. Boils. Poison water. Until a bunch of kids are slain by the angel of death. Why? To glorify God? It's bullshit. The Bible itself says that God kept the pharaoh from following his heart. Seems like a violation of free will to me! But no one is supposed to question it. Well, I figure, why worry if what you're doing is right when you're probably just doing what you must anyway? Apparently God's going to fuck with fate only when it makes Him look good—so why try to do what you think is right? Didn't work out so well for Job and the pharaoh!"

Ron wasn't done. "The ultimate failure of the relationship between God and man is a template for the doomed relationships between people. We get so caught up in 'what's supposed to be' that we fuck everything up. You need to grab happiness where it can be found, without trying to define it as right or wrong and without trying to plan for the future. There is no happiness in the future; there's only what can be found today. To give up pleasure and happiness today because of some promise of the future is illogical." Ron leaned forward and took one last scoop of his dinner. The ticking of the clock interrupted Anthony's concentration. It was nearly nine o'clock.

Dropping his spoon into the metal pan, Ron stood, unplugged the frying pan, and put it into the cast iron sink. Anthony could not believe that he could behave so casually while imparting such wisdom. "You probably don't want to listen to my crap," Ron said at the sink, his back to Anthony. Cleary, he knew that Anthony had been his disciple since the beginning. The statement was delivered to enlist Anthony, not to check his feelings on the matter.

"No, I think you're right," Anthony quickly answered.

"It's just that people go so blindly about the day, saddled with wrongs and rights and definitions of what 'should be.' That kind of thinking doesn't ultimately bring any happiness or peace. It's when you realize that there is no ultimate happiness, no cosmic peace to attain, that you can sit back and grab bits of it that are around you all the time. People think that you shouldn't drink until you're an adult. What does that mean? Shouldn't each person be an adult in his own time? Is there an age for that? You and I are sitting here having a great conversation and a glass of wine. You seem pretty adult to me, so what does your age matter? People think you shouldn't have sex until you're married. That's crap—you miss the connection that you can have with so many people by binding yourself up with rules like that. If you want to get married, that's cool. If you only want to have sex with one person your whole life, that's cool, too. But why limit yourself with contrived rules if you don't feel that way? I mean, really, why limit sex with marriage? They have nothing to do with each other. Marriage is about physical coexistence. Sex is about pleasure. You don't have to commit to eating at one restaurant or to listening to one kind of music. Why should you make sex something more special than the pleasure of food or music? People get all bound up in 'the right person.' It just causes pain to think that way. Hell, I don't think you even have to define your sexuality. Black or white, guy or girl—if you want to have sex, have sex. You don't have to be gay to have sex with another guy; you just have to be open."

The rush Anthony felt was impossible to articulate. He had finished his glass of wine, but this was more than intoxication. He wasn't dulled by drunkenness; he was acutely aware. Ten years later, Anthony could recall the texture of this moment. The hollow sound of the ticking of the clock on the wall. It was more a clicking than ticking. The stark contrast between the harsh light of the kitchen and almost hazy look of the rest of the apartment. The feel of the crack in the Formica on the edge of the table to which he was clinging while on the ride of his life. His senses captured every nuance of the environment, but he could not articulate the sensation of terrified elation he was feeling. He wanted to cry and laugh at the same time. Ron's news was so pessimistic yet so reassuring and encouraging.

Why had no one who was supposed to love him ever told him this? Didn't his parents want him to be happy? Everything Ron said was so right, so logical.

Ron left the kitchen without explanation and sat down at the piano in his dining room turned studio. Anthony followed and could see little of the dimmed room, his eyes still accustomed to the bright kitchen. Ron started to play a somber, probably church-related song. On the piano, it sounded more classical than religious. The music was soft yet imposing, like the dark and foreboding house. As the melody floated into his head, so did the smell of dust and heat that would forever call this night to mind. Years later, he would enter a dusty room in an old library or college building and be reminded by the smell of this specific moment. Across the dim room, he could see the shadowed Moses, still windblown and furious, still determined to smash what God had granted unto him. "Is that what I am doing?" thought Anthony. "If I accept what Ron is saying, am I smashing the tablets on which all my rules are written?" Anthony, deep in thought, didn't realize that Ron was talking.

"...don't really play the piano that much, but it does something to me," Ron was saying. "I don't know; it's different than the organ. It gives me a hard-on—see?" Anthony moved to the side of the piano bench and saw that indeed the bulge in Ron's pants clearly indicated an erection. Frozen by the excitement and fear of being included in this observation, Anthony uttered only unintelligible syllables. The room raced. The bulge in Ron's pants was obtrusive, and he felt embarrassed staring. Yet something secret was being shared with him. He was captivated, not by the object of his gaze but by the gravity of the moment.

As quickly as Ron had changed the very fabric of the relationship between himself and Anthony, he changed the topic. Jumping up from the piano, he said, "Hey, I've got some new music for the choir to learn! Want to hear it?" Before waiting for an answer, he had moved around the piano and was searching through a disheveled stack of record albums stored in the oak breakfront. Long before Anthony had processed what had just happened, he was listening to an a cappella choral piece in Latin that Ron had already selected for the next year's Easter Vigil, even though it was not yet Christmas. The piece was entitled "Ecce Homo"— Latin for "Behold the Man." His mind whirred. The dust and oil scent. The clicking clock, the hush of a house under a veil of a secret not yet fully shared. It was all surreal.

Realizing now that he was completely undone, having no idea what to do, what was expected, or what was appropriate,

Anthony blurted out, "I should go and finish dealing with my mother."

"Ah, let her off the hook—she's just as fucked up as everyone else!" As Anthony turned to leave, it seemed that Ron was completely onto something else. The music was loud, and Ron was no longer in the room—at least not mentally. He smiled but barely responded as Anthony yelled, "See ya at practice." He certainly wasn't angry or disappointed. He was simply no longer part of the conversation. The music had him.

Four

The glacial blast that accosted Anthony as he raced down the four porch steps was a godsend. He took a circuitous route home so as to have time to think, but his excitement propelled him the mile in less than ten minutes. He was nearly running when he arrived at the back door. He quickly apologized to his mother for the earlier argument. "Let her off the hook—she's just as fucked up as everyone else" rung in his head. To his amazement, it worked. The apology was accepted with a comment about Anthony's maturity in returning to the scene to take responsibility for his action. He saw no reason to disagree. Knowing now that his mother couldn't help but be defective let him neutralize her words. Kindness was affordable. In fact, it seemed to cost him nothing. In five minutes, he was upstairs in his bedroom, having escaped without punishment, without even a lecture. Ron's ways were effective. "If I tell people what they want to hear, it costs me nothing because the words mean nothing." The voice spoke inside his head with ultimate clarity.

The analysis of the evening was complex. Everything Ron had spoken made sense. It was in the application of the teaching that Anthony struggled. Should God be acknowledged as existing but discarded as defective? Did sexuality need no definition? Was it really unimportant to know if one was straight or gay?

Did what Ron said indicate that he was neither straight nor gay? Anthony knew full well that Ron had a girlfriend—Judy—who often came from upstate to spend weekends with him. They had been high school sweethearts. He treated her as a girlfriend when she was around. Ron certainly wasn't gay. But he also was continually more and more unconventional. Why would playing the piano make you hard? And why would you point that out to someone? Clearly, you would only share such an intimate and embarrassing detail with a close friend. "I am his close friend," Anthony told himself over and over. As much as these philosophies were making perfect sense, Ron's actions were a mystery. Perhaps his action did make sense, because the philosophy was freeing. Therefore, actions did not need to follow convention. In accepting the freeing philosophy, he was completely captured by Ron. This man was a god. He was impervious to everything. Omnipotent. Omniscient.

Even as he wondered what the next move should be, Anthony knew he'd visit Ron again. Ron was offering a ride into uncharted territory that was exciting to Anthony. A preview of adulthood others his age weren't privy to.

He had not only been told that his parents could never truly love him but also that it was okay. He'd used this newfound revelation to manage his most recent battle with his mother to a peaceful end.

Lying in bed, his mind whirred with a limitless list of decisions and doubts. "Maybe I didn't understand. Ron may not mean that I should actually have sex with boys—just that I must not be shackled by fears about it." Anthony took comfort in that thought.

Five

There was no hint of any change in Ron's thoughts or attitudes at the next rehearsal. When Anthony found Ron alone during the ten-minute mid-rehearsal break and told him that things with his mother "were cool," Ron appeared to lack any idea of what Anthony was saying. It was clear that Anthony's disagreement with his mother, the disagreement that ushered him to Ron's door a week earlier, had no lasting impact on Ron's memory. Later in the rehearsal, there was another tirade—this time involving the altos, who were "scooping" to a high note. Slapping the page of the music against the organ console, Ron yelled, "You're in this choir to be in the one goddamn place where there's right and wrong! Insist on singing this passage the wrong way again, and we'll have to leave this piece for a more capable choir! Do you see a tie in that measure that gives permission to drag yourself up to that B-flat?" The sarcastic comment made perfect sense. "Right and wrong is wasted on the ethereal ideas of bigots," thought Anthony. "It's really found in the simple performance of music, where a tone is either universally right or universally wrong." Anthony smiled with pride. "I get it!" As he turned his eyes upward, he caught Ron's stare.

"Anthony, you read music. Sing the alto line to them!" It wasn't a request; it was an order. Anthony glanced down at his music and looked for the first time at the alto line printed above his own tenor part. The notes were in the treble clef, which Ron knew was more comfortable for Anthony. In an instant, he was able to make the assessment that the two-line passage generally followed the tenor part and was a third lower but sung in the alto octave. With less than the five seconds it took for him to make that observation, Ron was playing the first note on the organ and counting off the measure. Stretching to hit the alto octave, he sung the line, staring hard at each note and listening to the organ, which played the part with him. He was careful at the critical moment not to "scoop" into the high note. Instead, he left his normal singing voice and sang the note falsetto. Returning to his regular voice, he finished the line. Before he could look up from the music, Ron's voice startled him.

"There! Why does it take Anthony to sing your part? Because none of you goddamn altos are *musicians*! Now unless you want me to castrate Anthony so he can permanently join your section, sing it right!" There were a few giggles, mostly among the boys. Before any real reaction could be heard, Ron was leading the taciturn altos in a repeat of the lines.

As the teens left the choir loft at the end of the rehearsal, Ron called Anthony over. "Thanks for saving my ass. If you'd have gotten that alto part wrong, I couldn't have really blamed you. But I knew you'd be there for me." He smiled as Anthony beamed. "There's a recital at the Conservatory of Music tomorrow night. Wanna go and hear a chamber orchestra? They're doing Corelli's Concerto Grosso since it's Christmas." Anthony had absolutely no idea who Corelli was or why a concerto would be grosso, but he accepted the invitation without hesitation. "Be at my house by six." Anthony agreed and turned to leave, feeling like he'd just been asked for a date. A city bus apparently rounded the corner on Haley Street, its headlights piercing the middle window on the right side of the church. Joseph appeared more than exhausted as the bus lights passed through his eyes. He appeared concerned.

Anthony sprinted from the loft, three steps at a time. He forgot all about walking Patty Larinski home, dashing across the street through the steam cloud of diesel exhaust from the passing bus. "Rules apply only in the choir," Anthony noted. "Out here, there is nothing dependable and nothing rule bound. There is only me and what's right for me."

In school the next day, Anthony dutifully took notes on all the weekend homework assignments, and then absentmindedly left school without any of the books he needed. He had no thoughts other than of the evening ahead. His mother was perhaps as excited as he was. "How many from the choir are going?" Annie quizzed him.

"He just asked me." Anthony was irritated at the implication that this was a group activity. That Anthony wouldn't be enough for Ron. "He didn't make an announcement to the *whole choir*! God!" She ignored his tone, perhaps because she also was pleased by the idea that Anthony alone had been chosen for the concert. Her son. Ron's friend. The idea seemed a feather in Annie's cap. That made Anthony even angrier.

The questions went on and on as she prepared dinner, which Anthony couldn't wait for. He ate a peanut butter sandwich, then grabbed three Oreos and his coat and ran out the back door. Arriving at five-fifteen on Ron's street, he walked around the block, heading up the alley to kill time. Passing behind the apartment, he saw that the light was on in the rear bedroom—Ron's room. He had never seen the bedrooms. Didn't really even know what Ron used the second bedroom for. Looking into the yard, the window had its shade pulled, and no figure could be discerned through it. Anthony imagined that Ron might still be dressing and felt like an intruder into a private moment, even though none was evident. He walked through the darkened alley and then around the back side of the block. It was a cold night, the last weekend before Christmas. The sky was clear, and there was only a hint of movement in the air. Anthony had been outside since just after five. He hardly noticed his cold ears and toes. His mother had been excited to hear that he had been invited to attend the concert, giving permission without so much as a question. She even gave him five dollars so that he could pay for anything that was required. Anthony didn't tell his mother that according to Ron admission was free. At five fifty, he rang the bell. Ron opened the door and smiled as Anthony stepped into the doorway. But Ron barely moved aside, requiring Anthony to pass close to him to enter the house. He opened his mouth to curse the cold and then noticed that sitting in the dim living room was Joan, the most popular alto in the choir. Joan and her sister Carol had beautiful voices and large breasts. On a number of occasions, it was clear that Ron was attracted to both girls, perhaps for both reasons. Joan was three years older than Anthony and attended the larger, more expensive Sacred Heart High School in the North Shore suburbs. Anthony felt let down. He had been certain that this was to be an evening between Ron and Anthony, his new best friend. But Ron had invited Joan as well. And he was angry that his mother had been right—that others had been included in this now not-so-special night. To make matters worse, it was Anthony who had to sit in the backseat of Ron's Pontiac, since perky-breasted Joan wore a snug skirt and made it clear that she could not negotiate the backseat of the two-door.

The concert was in a historic mansion tucked just north of downtown on a bluff overlooking Lake Michigan. The lake was pitch black, giving the impression that they were on the edge of the world. Nothing beyond this place, this time. The

Milwaukee Conservatory of Music owned the prominent building, which was adjacent to the college. Students made up the string ensemble that was gathered around a harpsichord. There were about fifty tan folding chairs in a tandem semicircle around the instruments in what was undoubtedly the largest of the rooms in the three-story limestone home. No longer used as a residence, the building had been donated to the school some years earlier. Only the first floor had been restored. Period pieces dotted the perimeter of the soft cream room, the chipped metal chairs a gaudy intrusion. The high walls were interrupted on three sides by a dozen tall, narrow windows, the sills nearly meeting the floor. Each window was partially shrouded by scalloped and tied-back draperies. The heavy velvet was a deep royal blue. The furniture that belonged in the room was in various shades and patterns of light blue and gold. Anthony found it curious that this room, softly lit and quiet, was much less foreboding than Ron's home, in spite of similar heavy window treatments and dark wood.

The mimeographed programs announced that, indeed, Arcangelo Corelli's Concerto Grosso, Op. 6, no. 8 in G Minor—*Fatto per la Notte di Natale*—was to be performed. A description of the work stated it was written for a small group of soloists—two violins and a bass—along with an orchestra. It was originally composed for midnight Mass, perhaps at St. Peter's in Rome. The concluding movement, the "Pastorelle," was supposed to evoke images of shepherds in their fields. There was also to be a performance of two short pieces by Pachelbel, including the popular Canon in D.

The strings and harpsichord had amazing power—more than Anthony would have expected from an ensemble with no brass or percussion. This was an environment unimaginable before Ron. In accepting the invitation, it had never really occurred to Anthony that he would be listening to a musical

performance. His thought in accepting was that the focus of
the evening would be Ron. However, he now realized that they
sat in this parlor as peers—fellow attendees at a small concert.
A scan of the room confirmed that there were no other teens at
this concert. Clearly Ron was not old enough to be there with
his teenage children. No, they were three audience members,
and no one else in the room could know whether this music
was Anthony's passion or a distraction from his clandestine
interest this evening – spending time with Ron.

The musicians beautifully carried each piece, and the forty
in attendance clearly enjoyed the concert. According to the
program, he was listening to baroque music. He knew nothing of the style, but he genuinely liked the sound. The featured Corelli piece had a significant range of volumes and
paces, which the audience seemed able to anticipate. Anthony
could not see Ron's face, as he sat directly next to him. But
he assumed that Ron, likewise, was familiar enough with the
piece to anticipate and enjoy each movement's rise and fall.
The concert was over in about an hour. Anticipating a much
longer event, Anthony's mother would not expect him before
ten o'clock. Spending no time socializing with the musicians or
other attendees after the performance, it was eight ten when
they left the mansion.

Ron pulled up to Joan's house first, and she said her good
nights. He hugged Joan and thanked her for coming to the
concert, a clear indication that she was a friend with whom he
had spent time before this night. As they pulled away from the
curb, Ron asked, "Do you want me to drop you off, or do you
want to walk home from my place?" He hadn't given Joan that
option.

"I'll walk. I like to walk." Anthony nearly started an elaborate fabricated explanation of why he liked to walk when he
realized that no such diversion was required. Ron was already

turning the corner and heading in the direction of his house—
no questions asked.

"That was good," Ron stated flatly, assuming Anthony
would know the context.

"Yeah, I liked the Corelli piece the best," Anthony said.

"All the brides are asking me to play the Pachelbel Canon
these days, so it's overdone. The Corelli is better music. You've
got a good ear. Most of the people in the choir don't really
know music or even know *how* to know music. You have music
in you. Even though you haven't studied music in depth, you
know how to break the sounds apart and listen."

Anthony felt honored at the compliment, even though he
wasn't quite sure what it meant. After Ron parked the car in
the alley garage behind his apartment, he turned to Anthony.
"You're definitely not like other kids your age. I couldn't be
friends with most of the kids in the choir, because they're
not able to see the world as it really is. But you're definitely
friend material." Anthony felt his face flush from the heat of
the words. Ron asked, "Want to hear a recording of the Corelli
from tonight? The album I have is much faster than the way
they played tonight, but it's nice." As they entered the darkened
foyer of the apartment, Ron turned to his right to walk through
the living room. Anthony was surprised that Ron didn't flip the
switch to light the foyer and living room since the apartment
was lit only by the faint haze of the streetlamp light that struggled past the draped windows. But Ron walked into the living
room without hesitation. Then, pausing, he said, "Here, follow
me—the stereo is on the dining room hutch." With that, he
reached his hand back and touched Anthony's stomach. Ron
explained, "I don't want to turn the lights on because I like to
listen to the music in the dark. My eyes are already adjusted to
the dark, and if I turn a light on, it will make them readjust."
Anthony, unable to see the way, stepped forward to remain

in contact with Ron's hand. As he did, Ron's hand slid down to the front of Anthony's pants, and Ron giggled. "Hey, what are you trying to do?" Ron laughed again. With that, he gently tugged at the front of Anthony's pants. "You got a tennis ball in there?" It wasn't until Ron's question that Anthony realized, to his horror, that he was, indeed, erect. Before he could form a word of defense, Ron's hand was gone.

"Just sit on the floor there. I'll turn the record on." The moment was over before it would birth any real discomfort. Anthony, however, felt confused and excited at the impropriety of the moment just past. His mind flashed back to what he'd been thinking of when he'd walked through the alley earlier in the evening—Ron dressing behind the shaded bedroom window. In a few seconds, the opening of the concerto was playing, and Ron slid onto the floor of the dining room next to Anthony. For nearly five minutes, neither said a word.

"I think the choir is sounding really good," Anthony finally braved saying. "The music for midnight Mass is really great."

"Most of the choir doesn't really know how to sing," Ron answered. He let his head drift back against the wall and sighed. "I wish…" He paused, and they both waited.

Sensing that Ron had been about to share something personal, Anthony pursued.

"You wish what?" Another pause.

"Well, I was going to say that I wished there were more musicians like you in the choir, but I think that I don't wish that. If everyone in the choir were like you, my job would be simple, and that would be great. But you and I wouldn't be such good friends." Ron's tone was sober, almost sad. There was a trace of emotion in his voice that overwhelmed him, even as the rising movement in the music threatened to overpower his suddenly subdued voice. "We couldn't just sit and talk about things like this." He brightened. "The whole house would be filled with

Anthonys right now, and I think the world is better because there's only one Anthony!" He chuckled sincerely.

They both sat quietly until the Corelli had ended and the album advanced to another piece. Anthony was hot with emotion. He wanted to cry out with joy at the revelation that Ron really seemed to care about him. About him—personally. Like a friend. Like someone special. He couldn't believe he was being finally drawn so completely into the middle of an important circle. The most important one of his short life. He no longer felt on the fringe. His friends, his faith, even his family all paled in comparison to the allure of the center of Ron's circle. To be there was worth more than anything, and he would do anything to stay in that circle.

Finally Ron spoke again. "We sound okay, but no one knows how to sing from the diaphragm. Everything sounds throaty if you don't sing from there. You know what I'm talking about, since you sit next to William DeCello. His voice is so nasal he sounds like a foghorn!"

Anthony had no idea what a diaphragm was, but he liked the view from the middle of the circle. He could see William, there on the fringe. It was a new perspective for him, and it was funny how easy it was, once in the middle, to care nothing for those on the fringe. "Yeah, he sounds like shit most of the time." He felt only a passing guilt as he laughed at poor William's nasally voice. "I try to sing from there, but I am still practicing that."

Ron responded excitedly as he jumped to his knees. "It's easy to learn—you just sing lying on your back! It's impossible to sing from anywhere but your diaphragm when you lie on your back—try it." With that, Ron was up and removing the needle from the turntable. As he sat down in the dark at the piano, he ordered, "Lie down there and sing." He began playing the introduction to a Christmas hymn the choir had learned—"While Shepherds Watched Their Flocks by Night." Anthony lay back and, on cue, began singing the tenor part. After two lines, Ron stopped playing and sang along as he came around the piano to sit next to Anthony. He gently placed his hand on Anthony's stomach. "See, you have to sing from down here; you can't sing from the throat in this position." He slid his hand up to Anthony's upper chest, then back down to the abdomen. Then, quickly, as Anthony sang, his hand moved down over Anthony's crotch. This time Anthony was sure that he could feel Ron's hand through his pants. "Still got that tennis ball in there?" Ron said quietly. There was emotion in his voice—a sense of longing, of caring. Ron slid back across the wood floor and leaned against the wall. "I wish the choir could get rid of that throaty sound."

Ron and Anthony sat in silence and darkness, but Anthony had never felt more acutely aware of his surroundings. He could hear the ticking of the clock on the kitchen wall and was again aware of the scent of dust and oil. With the light of the dim mercury vapor streetlight trailing through the living room behind him, Moses seemed a shadow on the ledge between Anthony and the front windows. "I've still got some of that wine," Ron said as he stood, flipped the record over and dropped the needle onto side two, then vanished into the kitchen. Anthony saw the glow of the refrigerator light as the door opened, then heard the tinkling of glasses against the bottle. Ron returned, slid down the wall to the floor, and poured two glasses of wine in the dark. Handing one to Anthony, he asked, "How's your mom?"

"Crazy and bitchy," Anthony replied.

"Well, you can come here when you don't want to be at home."

Anthony heard the creak of the floor upstairs and realized for the first time that there was another occupant in the building.

"Who lives upstairs?" he asked.

"A little old grandma. I don't think she hears well because she never complains, even if I play the piano at midnight."

Anthony drank his wine and attempted to parrot back to Ron the philosophies that had been shared at the earlier visit. He wanted to express Ron's views, now purchased as his own. It was important for Ron to see that he also held the same dim view of people and relationships. But Ron seemed fairly uninterested in what Anthony had to say, though he did notice Anthony's empty glass and refilled it. On reflection, it made sense—Ron would not care that Anthony thought as he did. He required no accomplice to validate his opinions. Later in life, Anthony often noticed that when people shared opinions, they were not necessarily looking for a listener; they were often simply in need of an accomplice. Someone to support them. Ron required no such validation.

Anthony finished his second glass of wine and stood, slightly wobbly. "I should walk home." Ron stood, took the empty glass from Anthony's hand, and set it on the piano. "Wow, even though I only played the piano for a few minutes, it still gave me a tennis ball—see?" With that, Ron took Anthony's hand and led it to the front of his pants. Anthony touched the pants timidly. The bulge was apparent. Both of them giggled, and Ron reached over to Anthony's pants. "You still have your tennis ball, too." They went quiet, each touching the front of the other's pants. After a minute, Ron walked into the living room, switched on a dim lamp, and walked to the front door. "Don't freeze your tennis ball off on the way home!" he joked as he stood with the door open. Anthony laughed artificially.

"See ya," he called as he whisked past Ron and down the front porch steps.

Six

O nce again, there was no noticeable difference in Ron at the practices and performances that followed the Corelli concert. The midnight Mass on Christmas Eve was, in the opinion of the priest and the parents, spectacular. A few people from Ron's hometown had come to Milwaukee to sing with the choir for the service, including Ron's girlfriend, Judy. Apparently, most of the music the choir had learned had been performed by the choir Ron had left behind upstate. These extra choir members already knew their parts, and were able to add to Ron's performance. During the pre-Mass vigil, the choir performed excerpts of Benjamin Britten's *Ceremony of Carols*. Composed in 1942 for a boy's choir and accompanied by harp, the music ranged from the melodic "There Is No Rose" to the frantic "This Little Babe." The music had been adapted for a mixed-voice choir, and Ron had hired a harpist, who needed the help of two choir members to lug the gold instrument up the switchback stairs to the choir loft.

Since the Catholic Church rarely held evening services, only the rose window over the altar was lit at night, the saints of the church asleep in darkness. The light inside the church would, however, illuminate the figures to the passersby. This was a rare sight: the saints seldom got to peer outside. After the Mass, Ron seemed self-satisfied, almost pleased with the establishment of the choir as the premier force in the church community. His own mother was there and enjoyed the gushing of the elderly over her son. It seemed odd to Anthony that someone who occupied the center of the universe would have a mother.

After the Christmas Day services, Ron, his mother, and Judy came to Anthony's house for a family holiday dinner and open house, invited weeks before by Annie. She beamed at their arrival, knowing that Ron had passed on dozens of invitations from other doting mothers to come to her home. The reason for his acceptance could have been that this was the only family with three children in the choir. It could have been that Ron had become friends with Anthony. But Annie was sure that the heaps of sweet accolades she had lavished on Ron after nearly every Sunday Mass had been well invested. Ron had chosen her as his hostess for the holiday. She hovered over Ron and, to a lesser extent, his mother and Judy. She hardly acknowledged her own husband, who appreciated the music Ron had produced for the Sunday masses but didn't seem so completely enamored with the man. Annie didn't even notice her own children, other than to acknowledge them as bit actors in the master's production.

It amazed Anthony to see how effortlessly Ron had usurped Annie's own children as the center of attention at a family holiday celebration. He'd spent years looking for approval from his parents, and in a few short months, this man who didn't believe in relationships, love, or connection had captured his mother's complete admiration. Annie cooed over him, even *flirted* with him, right in front of his mother and girlfriend. It was difficult for Anthony to decide which was his stronger reaction: harsh resentment for the mother who so obviously found her own son unworthy of her love or awe for Ron, who had captured admiration he didn't require.

In the early evening, Anthony went up to his bedroom without purpose. His hope was that one of the people whose approval he craved would come seeking him. He lay on his bed, staring at the slanted ceiling, wondering just why he felt so bad. He was torn. He could be downstairs, close to Ron. He might draw him into conversation, perhaps even play the piano with him again. On the other hand, he'd probably be subjected to more of his mother's fawning over this outsider. In his mind, he plotted how he might move into the center of attention. Elaborate plans formed—a discussion of God in which he could stun his family with his newfound philosophy, after which Ron would support him. Or a musical topic where Anthony could discuss Corelli and whether the performance at the conservatory was a better-paced rendition than the faster-moving cut on Ron's album. No one but he and Ron could fully entertain that conversation. But as he played these and other scenarios in his mind, he also found ways in which his mother would subvert the conversation in order to take center stage. Each scene played out in his mind like the Corelli music—it would rise and fall as the story was told. But each would end with his displacement to the fringe of whatever conversation was playing in his mind.

Gradually he ran out of scenes to play and drifted into mindlessly staring at the ceiling, watching the melded light of moon and streetlamp wander through the bare maple branches and into his room. After forty-five minutes, he made his way down the rear staircase of the house into the kitchen, where his mother stood at the sink, hand-washing the pieces of crystal too fragile or valuable to trust to the dishwasher. The house was noticeably quiet, and the television was on in the adjoining den. Andy Williams stood arm in arm with his bear singing "Away in the Manger," the gray light of the black-and-white set outlining the profile of Anthony's brother, Alan. The earlier energy alive in the house was gone. Without needing to ask, Anthony knew that the guests had left.

"When did Ron leave?"

"Only a few minutes ago—didn't you let them out? Lynn must have. Where were you?" Clearly, Annie would have been at Ron's side to the final moment. She would have been there to see the guests out, and she would have known where each member of the supporting cast of her day was at the moment the curtain fell on her act. Although she feigned detachment, both knew better.

Anthony felt completely deflated. "I was upstairs. I didn't feel well." He left the room without awaiting the reply, which never came anyway.

Seven

The second week of Christmas vacation featured terse moments between Anthony and the rest of the family. He spouted off to his brother and got a fat lip as a reward. Annie suspended Alan's right to drive the family car as a punishment, which caused him to look for any opportunity to pick on his little brother when they were out of their parents' earshot. Lynn, who had just learned to drive, was delighted. Anthony's part in her good fortune didn't earn him any favor, however, and she'd plainly stated at dinner that she'd rather walk to the mall than be forced to drive Anthony as a condition for the use of the car.

"You bitch!" Anthony screamed. "If you weren't such a slut, no one at school would even care about you!"

His outburst resulted in a slap to his sore lip by his mother. "I will not tolerate that kind of verbal abuse in this house!"

Alan was about to point out the folly of his recent punishment in light of his mother's propensity to deliver a quick shot to the lip of the same family member but thought better of the risk he'd be taking. All in all, it was a miserable week for everyone, mostly at the hands of Anthony.

Two nights before the end of the school break, he had a fight—no, *picked a fight*—with his mother. Even as voices were raised over the topic of church attendance during the choir break, Anthony's attention was waning. The battle wasn't that interesting. It simply provided the opportunity to blow off steam and get out of the house. He stormed out the back door, grabbing his coat but forgetting his hat and gloves. With little thought, he set his course for Forty-Seventh Street. It was a cold night, a certain premonition of the long January to come. The snow on the few unshoveled sidewalks crunched under his feet, crisped by the windy chill of the night. In fifteen minutes, he stood on the creaky porch. His cheeks burned as he smiled when Ron opened his door.

"My mother is out of control again." Ron did not step aside to let Anthony in. Instead, he grinned. "Wait here. I'll be right out." Anthony was already frozen from the walk but stood patiently as Ron disappeared into the dark foyer. The frigid porch decking groaned as Anthony shifted back and forth from leg to leg to stave off frostbite. Winter in Wisconsin could be brutally cold, and this year was no exception. A few minutes later, Ron returned wearing a jacket and knit skullcap. "It's fuckin' freezing out," he gasped as he stepped onto the porch and pulled the heavy oak door closed. "I got my new car today—wanna see?" Ron skipped down the four stairs and started around the house to the backyard. Without a word, Anthony followed, suddenly unaware of his numb toes and aching ears. He caught up to Ron as he rounded the corner of the concrete block garage into the alley and, after unlocking the handle, heaved up the door. The light was diffused, the only source the single pole lamp near the middle of the block. The new car, a 1973 midnight-blue Camaro, sat backed into the stall. Anthony's initial thought was that Ron had a lot of guts to back a brand-new car into a darkened garage. "Let's go for a ride," Ron said, again awaiting no response. "I'll pull out so you can get in." With that, Ron moved into the darkness. As he opened the door, the dome light illuminated the car's shiny black interior and the smile on Ron's face. It was the first time Anthony had seen Ron excited by anything but music. He stepped out of the way as the car roared to life and pulled forward. Anthony got in. The car had the pungent aroma of newness, the styrene smell of vinyl and adhesive. Instinctively, he reached out in the darkness to feel the dashboard. It was mostly smooth, a pebbled finish in the plastic. Ron left the garage door open as he jerked the car up the alley. "I have to get used to this stick shift. My last car was a stick, but the clutch on this one is really touchy." They pulled onto Nash Street, and Anthony was thrust back as Ron popped the clutch and stepped on the gas. Leaning over, Anthony saw that the odometer read 22.4 miles. "You're my first passenger." Ron beamed. The vinyl upholstery was stiff and frigid, and Anthony loved knowing that he was feeling it first, ahead of any other passengers who would sit there. As the car began to warm, they merged onto US 41 heading toward downtown and the lakefront. The Camaro was low to the ground, and the dual exhaust growled in muscle-car fashion. Whether it was really fast or just built to look like a performer was not known. Ron was careful, keeping the car below sixty miles per hour on the freeway. They passed County Stadium, bearing left onto Interstate 94. As they passed other cars, Anthony was careful to look as nonchalant as possible, as if this were one of any number of new cars in which he could choose to ride. In doing so, he knew that he was again the passenger—not the center of the circle. Not on the outside fringe of the experience but not in control. He'd definitely moved up from the backseat.

In ten minutes, they were cruising down a nearly deserted Lincoln Memorial Drive, with the Lake Michigan shoreline to their right. The moon was just rising out of the water, huge and bright. It illuminated the silver waves that had been caught breaking onto the beach, now standing frozen solid at the shoreline. Unlike the salt water of the ocean, the Great Lakes freeze in the cold of winter. Ice forms as wave upon wave transgresses the line between the wet and the frozen. The ice gets thicker and thicker until a series of frozen stalagmites grow with each wave. Eventually the lake freezes out and away from the shore, leaving gray apparitions poised at the edge of the beach, somber and still. The lake was frozen halfway out to the harbor wall, leaving the beach eerily silent. The waves breaking against the ice two hundred yards from shore were nearly inaudible, a muffled sloshing heard in the distance behind the frozen militia facing east, awaiting some unseen and distant threat. The nearly full moon illuminated the spectacle in pale blue. In spring, the warm currents would erode this beachhead of intruders, and the sounds and smells of the water would return to the beach. Anthony loved Lake Michigan and would never live far from the shoreline.

After three miles along the lakeshore, Ron turned onto the snaking drive through the park opposite the shore and out onto the city streets, heading west back toward his house. During the forty-five-minute ride, he talked giddily about the car, its 350-cubic-inch V-8 engine, the cast aluminum wheels, and the extra wait he had endured for one in metallic midnight blue. "I don't like waiting for things," Ron said. "I like to take what's available—to find happiness when it's there. But I really wanted this color."

"Some things are worth waiting for," Anthony countered.

"No, they're not. You can choose to wait, but if you do so, you have to know that it may not ever come. And you have to know that when it comes, whatever *it* is, it may not be what you thought. You can wait for something that you want, but you can never say it's definitely going to be worth the wait. Most of the time, you have to take things when they come, enjoy them, and move on." It seemed like a rather in-depth lesson born of the simple desire for a blue car. But Ron went on, closing the loop.

"Like tonight—I didn't know you were coming over, but I was thinking about going for a ride. You came to the door, and I got the opportunity to share my new car with someone special. If you had said no, I would have taken my ride alone. It's better with you, but I would not have waited. One of the reasons you're a great guy, Anthony, is that you get that. You know that you need to grab things when they come; you get that nothing is reliable for the future. That's why this is a great night. You're here to ride in my new car with me." With that, Ron gently squeezed Anthony's leg, just above the knee.

Anthony could only drink in each moment, knowing that he and only he would ever be the first rider in the prized possession of his hero. He felt special. He would not even tell his mother about this night—ever. She would not be allowed to even share the story; she could have no part in this.

Ron pulled to the curb in front of his house just as Anthony was beginning to thaw out. The digital clock on the car's stereo read 8:18 p.m. Anthony gingerly opened the passenger door, taking care to avoid rubbing the snow bank. Squeezing out, he closed the door and followed Ron onto the porch and into the warm, dark house. "I've got some MD 20-20 to warm us up," Ron called as he made his way through the house to the butler's pantry off the kitchen. Anthony opened his coat as he noted the now-familiar scent of the house. He felt the soft rush of air from the iron grate in the floor under the living room windows. "Sit down" was the call from the kitchen. Dropping his coat onto the floor next to him, Anthony sunk into the heavy couch and nodded imperceptibly to Moses, still lost in his anger in the dim room.

Ron returned with two large tumblers of deep-violet liquid. "My wineglasses are dirty." As he was handed his glass, Anthony wondered who had been a guest in this house, dirtying the wineglasses.

This wine was less like apple juice than the Annie Green Springs of his earlier visit. It was still very sweet but much stronger, with a cough syrup finish. With the earlier wine-tasting experience at Ron's his only point of comparison, Anthony noted that this wine seemed more serious.

"Your car is cool," Anthony noted.

"It will probably be shit in the snow," Ron countered, "but I've wanted this car since it came out in fall."

Perhaps because he was nervous, Anthony finished the tall glass of wine in ten minutes while Ron talked about the classes he was starting at the conservatory. "I've got to take these bullshit English and social science classes even though I'm a music major. It's really stupid, because it takes time away from developing my real skills." Anthony had trouble picturing Ron as a student, succumbing to the rules of an institution. "It's things like that that make you realize you can't wait when the important things come along. I should be studying the first chapters of the English lit book tonight, and I'll get to it, but you came to my door, and that's irreplaceable. If I sent you away, I'd never get this time back—this opportunity to ride in my car with you, to talk about things, to share each other. Those other things, like studying, need to get done, but you can't let rules get in the way of happiness when it's standing at your door. That's why you're special, Anthony—you get that. You didn't need to call here tonight; you just showed up. People call me all the time, but I don't answer the phone much. I hate talking on the phone. If I had been gone when you got here tonight, you would have done something else without feeling cheated. But I was here, and now we're having wine and talking, and you were ready for that. You're ready to be connected to the important things that can happen in your life. I wish I had been as together as you when I was your age. Your age is really irrelevant, because you don't seem to be bound by it. You go to school and follow the rules that will get you where you need to go, but then you are open to fill in the time between the rules with the best things. You're a good friend."

Anthony was just beginning to feel the impact of the liquor when Ron popped up from the couch and left the room, returning with the bottle and refilling the empty glass. Anthony drank in the moment as he drank more wine. The house was quiet and placid. It was ordered. The two sat together enjoying the moment—the wine, the conversation, the *adultness* of the time. It was momentous. It was gigantic. To be included in such an event as this night provided. It spoke in deafening volume throughout the silent room.

It was special, because Ron had made it clear that Anthony was special and this time was special. They sat quietly, anticipating something, yet nothing. With their conversation apparently exhausted, Ron again rose, went to the dining room, and dropped the turntable needle onto a record. The somber strings were beautiful, an orchestral piece that would never leave Anthony's memory. Even after other events were buried deep, the sound of the moving symphony would stay. He didn't learn the title that night but cried when he unexpectedly heard it performed years later by Itzhak Perlman and the Detroit Symphony Orchestra.

Ron returned to the sofa and tumbled onto the cushion next to Anthony, his hand landing on Anthony's crotch. "Hey, no tennis ball," he noted with a laugh. "I wonder if I can find it." With that, he began trailing his fingers around Anthony's groin. Anthony closed his eyes, in part because his head was beginning to spin and in part because he didn't want to see what was happening. Truth be told, he had thought this would happen but was completely unprepared for the reality. The sensations and the implications exploded in Anthony's mind. This was wrong. All these jokes about tennis balls and all this "accidental" touching. It had to be wrong. If it wasn't, then everything he'd been taught, been told, was in error.

But it was also clearly within the bounds of his friendship with Ron. Ron had explained it all—no need to be bound by rules, by convention. No need to forgo today's pleasure for tomorrow's promise. They were friends. He was special to Ron. In spite of this justification, Anthony silently recited the prayer he habitually said every week before entering the confessional.

Most merciful God, we confess to you, before the whole company of heaven and one another, that we have sinned in thought, word, and deed, and in what we have failed to do. Forgive us our sins, heal us by your Spirit, and raise us to new life in Christ. Amen.

What was happening was a violation of this weekly prayer. This sin was one of both thought and deed. His action, or inaction, was clearly sinful.

He was scared. He could not stop what was happening. Would not stop. It felt good. In fact, feeling good and evil at the same time had never occurred so completely in him before. This is what Moses had ranted against when he smashed the commandments—the utter rebelling of the people. Could there be any more complete rebellion against the faith instilled in Anthony than to have sex with a church leader? This was a sin against the church—somehow encouraging its respected leader to transgress. Anthony, by his compliance, knew he was encouraging this transgression. But it *felt good.*

Ron's fingers became his entire hand on Anthony's jeans. He could feel the physical reaction in him catching up. The glass of wine left his hand as Ron took it and set it on the end table. At the same time, Ron spoke softly, close to Anthony's face and without humor. "There's that tennis ball. I wonder if it wants to come out to play." The breath was hot. He would have smelled the garlic on Ron's breath, if Anthony had been breathing. As Ron spoke, he unbuttoned the top of the boy's jeans and smoothly opened the zipper. Anthony wondered what he was supposed to be thinking. If he imagined that this was a girl touching him—perhaps Patty Larinski from across the street—would it be less wrong? Pleasure was to be embraced whenever it was found. This time, then, was precious, made so because it was coming at the hands of a leader who said Anthony was a friend, a peer. The hand that filled the church with music, that awed, that counted the beats to the choir whose performance was admired. This was the hand that was on him now. This hand, this man, wanted *him*. He knew he was rejecting two thousand years of Catholic teaching but was content to fall under the weight of two glasses of wine. Jesus fell. Veronica was there to wipe his stain away. People got up after falls. He would as well.

The conflict was chased away in the time it took Ron to slip his hand inside the unzipped pants. As skin touched skin, Anthony's pulse pounded, unsoothed by the moving music. He could not, would not, open his eyes. To do so would be to verify his surroundings, and Anthony could not take the chance that this was happening any differently than he was imagining.

Ron slid off the sofa onto the floor and brought Anthony's jeans from around his waist. He didn't feel himself lift up from the cushion to allow the movement of his clothing, but he must have. As he wondered if this could possibly be happening, he felt the warm, wet softness of Ron's mouth close around him. Only briefly, Anthony opened his eyes. He saw that Ron's hands were over his forearms, holding him down. Anthony had been completely unaware of this until he saw it. He was pinned to the sofa at his sides. Not roughly but with purpose.

Ron's knees were against Anthony's shins. His eyes closed, and he let his head drift back against the cushion. Moses watched judgmentally.

A hundred questions pushed through the music into his mind. Could he go home and be unchanged before his parents? How would he ever be the same? Could he ever live without having this again? Did it make him special? Could his dead sister see him? Did this make him gay? Did he want this? What would happen in choir on Sunday? Was he sinning? Was God interested in this? Was anyone?

Anthony felt himself approaching climax when Ron retreated from his body. Opening his eyes, he saw Ron standing up, quiet and smiling. "I have a tennis ball that wants to play as well. See?" The bulge in Ron's pants was undeniable. "I can do this. I *get* to do this," Anthony told himself. As Ron's pants tumbled to the floor, he stepped forward, and before Anthony could take a breath, he was inside his mouth. Anthony was trying not to choke. His eyes were watering. "Will he think I'm crying?" The music was loud—sweet and gentle, almost sad. But the room seemed wild with energy. This wasn't romantic. Nor was it violent. It was raw. It was frenzied. Ron seemed driven by some internal torment. In the choir loft, he was always striving toward some external measure of perfection in performance. There seemed to be no standard here. Clearly the goal was more important at this point than the method. Yet Anthony wondered if there would be an assessment later. Was there a precise "right" that needed to be attained? If so, Anthony was sure that he wasn't there at this moment. But it seemed to matter little to Ron.

Before he realized what was happening, Anthony climaxed, untouched. The shock caused him to pause. "Keep going!" Ron nearly shouted, heaving back and forth as he began to groan.

Suddenly there was a new taste in Anthony's mouth. He tried to pull away, but Ron had clamped his hands around Anthony's head, holding him in place. Anthony's compliant arms still lay at his sides. Ron's legs were shaking, sending vibrations to the couch. Anthony began to choke as Ron pulled away. As the sweet sound of the orchestra trailed away, Anthony vomited onto the hardwood floor.

Eight

Anthony lay in bed, holding his rosary. His body, his mind, were numb. Light played across the slanted ceiling as cars passed outside. Each of the movements startled him, as if someone were coming for him. He felt trapped by the freedom to which he'd been introduced. Clutching the beads, he didn't pray but had not escaped the habit of taking his rosary into bed with him. In his mind, he reviewed the evening without any sense of order about all that had happened. He'd been bestowed a terrifying honor.

There was a game in the lobby of the neighborhood movie theater in which you could deposit a dime and operate a crane inside the glass case. The goal was to pick up a single treasure from the pile of plush animals and costume jewelry and drop it down the exit chute. Dime after dime was lost as patrons failed to get a good grasp on the item of their desire. This was how Anthony felt. So many thoughts but none within his grasp. In his sociology class, he'd learned that the silence of autistic children was not related to an absence of thought but to the overwhelming myriad of thoughts that couldn't be sorted, filed, processed, and ordered. He knew what that felt like.

Five minutes after it was over, Anthony had left the house with assurances that the cleanup would be easy—not to worry.

Embarrassed, he explained that he wasn't actually sick; he had simply gagged, probably from the wine. Ron didn't seem angry. He didn't seem concerned either. By the time Anthony had sat back up after retching, Ron's pants were fastened, and he was lifting the needle off the record in the next room.

In the immediate quiet, Anthony could again hear and feel the warm air rushing from the nearby vent. He was already hot and thought that perhaps the warm air had provoked his nausea. Ron called, "Are you okay?" Suddenly self-conscious about his nakedness, he didn't answer. He stood, stepping carefully around the vomit, and retrieved his pants from around his ankles. It was when he pulled his underwear and pants up that he realized his thighs were full of his own semen. The feeling of his pants against his sticky legs was immediately uncomfortable but now unavoidable. Anthony had not even realized that he had had an orgasm. Ron disappeared into the kitchen and returned with a roll of paper towels. "The quicker picker-upper!" He chuckled, parroting a popular paper towel commercial as he laid the sheets over the vomit. He didn't apply himself to the cleanup, seeming content at the moment to hide the evidence. "That was great. You are really a good friend," Ron offered.

"Really?" responded Anthony, still looking for a sense of the reality of what had just happened.

Ron smiled broadly. His forehead was sweaty, and he seemed a little out of breath. Garlic permeated the room. "I wouldn't do this with just anybody. I trust you. I knew when I first met you that you were different—even from Lynn and Alan. You really understand a lot for your age."

The weight of the compliment rested on Anthony like Joseph's coat of many colors. "This wasn't random. This man likes me. More than the other kids. More than Alan or Lynn." This realization was a sudden prized possession.

"I could tell you wanted to do this, but I wanted to be sure you could handle it. I was glad to be here for you."

Anthony's mind whirled. "I wanted this?" he thought. Indeed, he had pondered the idea that he might be gay. He had reached out to touch Ron just a few minutes ago—reached out on his own—no one forced him. His view of what had just happened shifted from what Ron had done with him to what Ron had done *for him*. He found himself stammering and finally blurting the most absurd thing. "Thanks."

"Anytime." Ron smiled reassuringly.

Anthony muttered, "I'd better go." Ron was already walking toward the front door. He opened it and stood aside to await the boy's departure.

Anthony walked slowly in the freezing wind without noticing the cold. He did notice that everything seemed different. The moon, the streetlights, the passing salt-covered cars. Everything around him. It wasn't that things looked different to him; it was more that they looked differently *at* him. He repeatedly told himself with incredulity that he had joined the ranks of the *sexually active*. He would go back to school different from when he had last seen his freshmen classmates. He would go to choir rehearsal knowing things that had not even crossed the other members' minds. Anthony, who always felt like the boy who didn't win, who didn't fit in, had just leaped past all those who seemed so superior.

He arrived home minutes before his ten o'clock curfew. No one seemed to notice anything different, except that his mother pronounced him "frozen" as she observed his red cheeks. "If you're going to keep storming away after yelling at me, you may want to storm to the basement for the rest of the winter," she mused. "You cannot just wander the streets in the freezing cold." Anthony quickly explained that the gym at St. V's had been open for the parish basketball league and that he had sat watching the scrimmages for a while. With the story sold, he escaped to his bedroom.

He had lain on his bed for more than a half hour, bereft of organized thought. He stood and pulled the room-darkening shade down—something rare for Anthony. He had always felt comforted by the light trailing into the room through the arched attic window at night. He liked that his room never really got dark, that there was always a foreshadowing of tomorrow, even if it was just the streetlamp. But he felt a need to shut everything out.

Tomorrow was going to be different, and Anthony didn't want to look ahead just yet. He lay on the bed in complete darkness and began pondering more than just the sexual event of the evening. Ron had chosen Anthony as his first passenger in the new Camaro. He had once again treated Anthony like an adult, offering him wine and playing music for him. These were things that friends did. Anthony recited the word *friends* over and over in his mind. "Ron is my friend. He likes me. This secret makes us special. Others won't understand. People cannot know about this because they would make it wrong." It felt so good to be Ron's friend. His best friend. Ron had chosen Anthony to share *lovemaking*. Others might not have seen it that way—there was no kissing, no holding, and no words of love or commitment. Maybe that's what being gay was about. Normal people would have relationships; gay people had sex. No ties. No commitment. Just friendship and sex. Anthony loved him now, more than anyone. Ron was more powerful than any person he knew—more highly praised than his own father and mother, than any teacher, than even Father Francis. And Ron chose him because he was special, because he was worth choosing, over all the other members of the choir. Even before Anthony had known what he really wanted, Ron knew. Omniscient.

But there was a troubling side to his sleepless night that was difficult to push into the darkness. Everything he had been taught said this was wrong. Anthony was not yet fifteen; Ron had just turned twenty-three. Sex before marriage was wrong; sex between boys was wrong. To accept what had happened was to reject everything except the lessons imparted by Ron himself. It meant changing completely, thinking differently, stepping out of his heritage, his family, and his faith. Was this what friend-ship with Ron required? Complete discipleship in a new faith? Anthony pondered his feeling that he had always been more spiritually aware than his siblings, his friends. He had taken that rosary to bed every night for years, praying with the hopeful faith that it would bear fruit. He had even pondered the idea that he was called to the priesthood, that the reason he felt different about girls was that he was indeed different but in a spiritual way. That God himself might be calling him. Was he to reject all this because Ron said his way was better? Near dawn, Anthony dozed fitfully, with all his questions unanswered.

As the morning light negotiated the edges of the room, Anthony summarized. Ron was clearly admired by more than just teenagers. The parents and the priests and nuns loved Ron. Anthony's own mother was captivated. For Anthony to reject what had just happened as wrong would be to put Ron in jeopardy. It would not only ruin Ron; it would ruin Anthony. Ron trusted Anthony. Anthony's mother, the neighborhood, the church trusted Ron. Whether what happened was sinful or not, it was apparently okay with everyone. Ron violated other rules in full view of all—swearing in church, ignoring traditions, even chang-ing aspects of the Mass by altering music. At each turn, the author-ities deferred to him and nodded in assent. Anthony would not test these waters with a contrary story about this powerful man.

Nine

The next morning, Anthony rode with his sister and brother to sing at the eleven o'clock Sunday Mass. Their parents always drove separately, arriving at church just before Mass began. The car windows frosted over immediately as humid breath hit the glacial glass, and Lynn scolded Alan for driving with nothing more than a peek hole through which to see the street.

"It's nine fucking blocks! I'm not waiting for the car to warm up. Get a goddamn grip."

"I can't believe you can talk like that on the way to church!" She began scraping at the inside of the windshield with a Kleenex she grabbed from the box on the car seat.

"Oh, that's just great. It's much easier for me to drive with your fat hands all over the windshield!"

"Eat shit!" came the terse reply. This kind of banter from Anthony's siblings was typical of all car rides. He simply sat in the backseat, appreciative that it was a mere five minutes by car to the church. As the three rushed from the frigid parking lot into St. Veronica's, Anthony made the excuse that he needed to use the bathroom. This assured him that the choir loft would be full when he arrived just five minutes before Mass began.

Ron was preoccupied at the organ console. The section leads were distributing music to the choir members. The sheets were marked according to the voice—soprano, alto, tenor, or bass—and if Anthony, Patty, and Eddie had been accurate at the last rehearsal, the process for Sunday morning would be easy. Even so, getting the right music to the right sections was a chore and at times confusing enough to send Ron into a rage even as the Mass began. As Anthony collected his music and took his place in the tenor section, Ron caught his eye. There was nothing unusual in the look, except that Ron held his gaze for an extra moment, nearly imperceptible. One of the altos lumbered between them, climbing over the boys in the row in front of Anthony. When she had passed, Ron was setting the organ stops for the opening hymn.

Dressing for church in the winter had always been tricky. It could be frigid outside, but the church was always hot. Hot in the summer, since it wasn't air-conditioned. And hotter in the winter, when the heat seemed to have no setting other than "on." The loft was the hottest spot in the church, since all the warm breath of the parishioners below rose like prayers to the upper regions of the building. Ron had opted to forgo choir robes, perhaps in deference to this.

It was during the homily, while Father Francis was pontificating, that Anthony noticed the effect of the sharp winter sun on the glass faces to the left of the sanctuary. There had been incense at the beginning of Mass, and the light trailing through the colored glass was captured in a haze that hung high in the sanctuary. Anthony thought it looked like a movie set. Scanning the windows, he wondered what judgmental Paul thought of him this morning. This bachelor persecutor of the Christians was vibrantly lit, as if he had something to say. After his conversion, Paul had said it was better to stay single, unless you were too consumed with sex to live alone. It was an odd instruction from a saint of the church that seemed to see sex as altogether evil. According to this abrasive founder, a man should marry, basically, only if one required sex. Paul's instruction was clear, and rather demeaning to women. Anthony thought it interesting that this man, who was struck temporarily blind by the light of God at his conversion, would be memorialized in glass that was positioned to stare down the morning sun.

Father Francis droned on about sacrifice and duty as Anthony shifted sideways in his seat to look up at Veronica behind him. She faced north and was therefore never in the line of direct sun. Her colors were always more dappled, her blue robe and the red and gold of her towel soft in the daytime light. Her face was kind. Anthony felt a kinship with Veronica. She was a saint of the church and a contemporary of Jesus, yet she was not in any scriptural account—never mentioned or described. Even her act of wiping the face of Christ was not officially recorded and remained only church lore. He knew how she must have felt to be on the fringe of importance. Her saintly act seemed more born of being in the right place than of anointed ministry. St. Peter had spent three years following Jesus and learning of his ways. Moses had spent decades away from Egypt preparing for his mission. But Veronica was simply nosy enough to stand on the curb and watch the three men being led to their crucifixions. Anthony had once seen a religion book that described Veronica as a "minor saint." So he'd been raised in the parish of a second-rate saint, while the children just one mile south had been reared in the mighty Christ the King Parish.

Anthony wondered what Veronica would think of his last twenty-four hours. He looked into her eyes for a hint of judgment, and there was none. She seemed content. A smooth surface of a slowly moving river. There was activity below the surface, but you couldn't detect it. Certainly she was above the strife and arrogance of the Pauls and Joshuas. Sufficient for sainthood but largely unknown outside of the few parishes

that dutifully took her as their namesake. Paul's great achieve-
ments as the first missionary of the church were made all the
greater by his persecutor past. Mary of Magdala's love of the
Lord was made purer by her harlot history. These were torren-
tial saints, crashing waves of the spiritual with twists and turns
that made them controversial and interesting. Veronica had
neither a spotted past nor a powerful ministry. One originally
unrecorded event made her suitable for stained glass.

The morning light was steady and cool through her eyes.
Perhaps she understood the life of Anthony and sat not so
much in judgment as in forbearance. If any saint cared about
Anthony, it would be Veronica, who lived between the completely unknown and the reverently respected. Whose fame
came from happenstance rather than mission. Who lived on
the fringe. There was no hint of rejection in her beautiful gaze.
He felt acceptance.

Anthony turned forward in the blond wooden seat, sensing
Father coming to the end of his tirade. As he did, Anthony
caught Ron's gaze and found him smiling. Kindly and genuinely. Not deviously. Anthony smiled back, and Ron turned to
open the music for the next piece.

After Mass, Ron passed out purple mimeographed sheets
of paper, still smelling of the volatile organics from which the
ink was made. A choir party was to be held at Ron's home
the next weekend. It was at seven o'clock in the evening, and
each member was to bring a snack or soft drink. The sentence
instructing parents to return at 11:00 p.m. to pick up their children was a clear indication that this was a choir-only party.

On the way home, Anthony's brother announced that a
choir party was no way to spend a Saturday night. Alan had a new
girlfriend with big hair and a loud laugh, and it was clear that
his church choir days were numbered. Lynn, however, planned
to ask to use the family station wagon to take her and Anthony

to the party. Anthony felt grateful to have an older sibling in the choir. If Lynn's plan worked, Anthony's mother would have no reason to get close to the event.

The family partook of their normal Sunday lunch—ham and rolls from Wiersbecki's Bakery on Vine, with potato chips and cold milk. Over the years, as the kids got old enough to navigate the kitchen, Sunday became a day of domestic rest for Annie. She didn't cook, and everyone was to fend for themselves. Ham and rolls became the provided after-church lunch. Dinner was an individual affair—peanut butter sandwiches, fried eggs, or Campbell's soup—whatever one could find was game for dinner. Each family member was to provide and then clean up after his or her own meal. Keith and Annie often went out for dinner without the family on Sunday evenings.

Anthony enjoyed the freedom and often ate at odd times, avoiding the others and pretending that he lived alone. He would slink into the kitchen, quietly make his sandwich, and take it up to his room with a bottle of Fanta Red Cream Soda he'd get from the machine at the Clark gas station on the corner.

Two slices of peanut butter toast next to him on a paper plate, he sat on the edge of his bed, watching darkness fall outside. He looked around the room, sensing the need for his surroundings to reflect the change he was feeling. He'd spent years cutting pictures of the new car models out of the color supplement in the Sunday *Milwaukee Journal.* One wall was nearly completely covered with a collage of the best cars of the past five years. Impala Super Sports. Galaxie 500s. The bulbous AMC Matador from last year. As he perused the wall, he came to a picture of the new Camaro. Fire engine red, not midnight blue. He'd cut it out of the special new-car section last fall. Except for the color, it was identical to Ron's. Taping these pictures up in the room suddenly seemed childish.

In an instant, the words of Father Francis's tirade of earlier that morning came to mind. Something about "putting away childish things." He was quoting Paul saying that when we're children we think and act like children but later we must put away our childish behavior and become grown-ups. Father was, of course, tying the admonition to the behavior of the congregation, probably with regard to meager offerings or attendance. It shocked Anthony to realize that he actually remembered and could apply something from a sermon. He rose from his bed and began tearing the pictures off the wall. He was nearly finished, tearing down perhaps a hundred small pieces of newsprint that had been carefully cut out and taped up on the slanted wall above his dresser when a pang of remorse snuck in. This era was ending. Anthony stood back, looking at the remaining thirty or so pictures. He felt sad and exhilarated at the same time. It was more than the wall that needed to change. He was changing. Needed to continue to change. The pictures had been dreams of what could come. A grown-up world of shiny new cars and the freedom they brought. He'd been a moth in a cocoon of childhood, these pictures a hope for what could be. But now he was out, his wings already spreading, splitting open the dark and protective world. He was in a new place—a gigantic place. Unprotected. Dangerous. Full of allure. He was no longer the child of this household. Everything was different.

The Camaro was among the remaining scraps on the wall. Stepping forward, he tore down what remained of childhood.

He spent the rest of the evening rearranging his furniture—reorienting his room to his new self. He turned the bedspread upside down, revealing the plain navy side while obscuring the logos of baseball teams on the top side. The model cars he'd built went into a bottom dresser drawer. There was nothing to replace these decorations. That would come. It was in sliding his bed to the other side of the room that the vibrations caused a ceramic statue of Jesus to tumble off the glass corner shelf his father had put up seven years earlier. Anthony had received the statue from his godparents, Tony and Carol Wingarten, at his First Communion. They lived in Rockford, Illinois, and Anthony had been named after his godfather, a University of Wisconsin college buddy of his father's. The statue had been blessed by the bishop of Rockford, whose name Anthony could no longer recall. It was presented with much ceremony by the godparents at the lunch after Anthony's First Communion Mass at St. Veronica's. Annie gushed over the statue and had Keith install the shelf the very next week. It had been there since, and from time to time, Annie referred to it as a "special blessing in the house." It lay shattered on the beige tile floor, absolutely destroyed. The symbol of his faith. Often the focus of his prayers as he worked the rosary beads before sleep.

"It is time to put away childish things." Those were the first words in his head when he heard the crash and turned to see the smashed figure. The pictures, the model cars, the statue. They were all icons of his childhood. He was no longer a child. The cocoon had been torn, and he'd gotten out. He was no longer the son, the student, the child. He was Anthony. Ron's friend Anthony. Sexually active Anthony.

Taking the broom from the hall closet, he unceremoniously swept Jesus into a trash bag, thinking how pleased Ron would be with him. It was nearly a year before Annie noticed that the statue was gone.

Ten

The first week of school after the long holiday break began painfully. During a basketball game in gym class, one of the big seniors accidentally poked Anthony in the eye during a scramble for a rebound. As he bent over holding his eye with both hands, he heard one of the other players call him a fag. Gym was the final class of the day, and he never showered, opting instead to head straight for the city bus stop. In later years, he would need to shower in order to go presentably to his part-time job after school. By then, he would be more developed, more experienced, and more comfortable with being naked in front of his peers. But for now, Anthony wondered if the accusation leveled under the basket might be true and if it showed.

That same week, he also blew his algebra midterm. If he were lucky, he would score a D for the semester, avoiding summer school. Central Catholic, like most parochial schools, would not allow a student to return for the next school year with an unresolved failure on the record. Anthony knew that he hadn't studied as he should have for the test, but he also felt entitled to do poorly, as everyone agreed that Miss Kasparic was a lousy teacher. He couldn't rely on luck to get him out of summer school. He approached her after class, asking about working with her to ensure a better second semester.

"What happened to your eye, Mr. Conway?" Her concern was genuine. "It's all bloodshot."

"I got poked in the eye in gym class. Makes it hard to see clearly. But it's okay. My real concern is this class. I can live without basketball, but I really want to understand algebra. I'm not getting it, and I know it's not your teaching. You're a great teacher, but I guess I'm a bad student."

She bought the veiled ploy, assuring him that the semester would work out fine and that she'd be more available to him in the second semester. He returned twice to the topic of her excellent teaching and his poor studentship. As they concluded the discussion, she apologized for not recognizing his interest in algebra and his struggle with the subject. She committed to "getting him through."

Mission accomplished. He'd not studied, not gone to her for assistance during the semester, and continually complained in the halls about her horrible teaching skills. He'd bombed the class. And *she* was apologizing. Years of rosaries prayed had yielded nothing. A few lessons from Ron, and his life was changing. "Recognize that everyone has shit that makes them the lousy people they are," he thought. "Let them off the hook, grab happiness where it is, and don't look to the future."

He didn't mention the grade to his parents, assured he'd see a D on the report card and knowing that, with proper plying, Miss Kasparic would deliver a better grade at year-end. But it would take some attention on his part. He didn't relish in that fact but felt good about his opportunity to control the situation.

The choir didn't practice that week. Ron had granted a break after the heavy holiday schedule. The party on Saturday night would be the only choir event in the first two weeks of January. It was also the only bright spot in an otherwise dismal period for Anthony.

On Saturday, Lynn was pronounced qualified to take the station wagon to the party. She had completed her chores and generally stayed out of the way, avoiding any conflict that would result in the revocation of access to her mother's car. Annie Conway was in the kitchen, feigning stress for having to create three snacks. Although Alan had clearly indicated other plans for the evening, she took pained pleasure in the burden of providing three separate dishes since she had three children in the choir. "Ron is certainly counting on the mothers for the snacks, even with Judy in town to help with the party. If it were up to the kids, there'd be nothing but potato chips!" She beamed. Anthony didn't risk telling her that no self-respecting teenager was going to eat her lime Jell-O torte without parental orders.

As the afternoon sun was beginning its descent behind the naked maple tree outside Anthony's window, he lay on his bed pondering the evening to come. The slanted ceiling of the bedroom started just three feet from the floor. His bed was newly positioned such that his head was just below the ceiling, while he could stand upright at the foot of the bed. It felt to Anthony that the head of his bed was the narrow end of the universe: that everything that existed stretched out from this point. From there, he was looking into the continuum of time and space and focusing on the party.

Should he let it be known that he had been to Ron's house many times—that he and Ron were friends? Perky-breasted Joan would know that Anthony had been there. She might consider herself a friend of Ron's as well. Could there be any- one else from the choir with whom Ron had had sex? Anthony wondered how exactly he should feel about that possibility. Although it seemed unlikely to happen, Anthony felt sure that he would have sex with someone else, given the opportunity. So why not Ron, who most certainly had other opportunities?

If it were true that Anthony was only one of the choir members who had a secret with Ron, he hoped all would keep it secret. He didn't want to know, and he didn't want to see anything that would give cause for suspicion. He'd been called a fag simply for reacting when his eye was poked. He shuddered at the notion that someone would find out that he'd had sex with a man. *A grown-up man.*

He wondered how he wanted Ron to act toward him. He certainly wanted to be special at the party—to be a visibly more important guest. Yet the true nature of what made Anthony special could not be divulged.

Anthony was starting to get nervous about the evening when his mother called him for dinner at half past five. Alan was already gone, and Keith was working the afternoon shift at St. Joseph Hospital, four blocks from the house. He had held his position as a clinical pharmacist there long enough to earn the weekday schedule but often worked on the weekends to cover for less fortunate pharmacists. Keith loved his job and spent a good deal more time there than was required.

After some chit chat about nothing, Annie continued, "I called Ron to see if I should come to help with the party." Anthony and Lynn stared straight across the table at each other in horror. Impending disaster. A bolt of lightning on a crowded golf course—somebody was going to have his or her day ruined. "He'll certainly need help setting up, keeping things moving at the party, and getting it all cleaned up. I doubt that he realizes what a task it is to pull off a big party like this. Thirty kids are coming!" Lynn was visibly holding her breath, but Annie sighed. "But he's sure that he's all set. I doubt that he is, but he said I'll be the first person he'll call if he needs help once the party gets going. Said no one else has even called to offer to help!" She sat back, trying to appear satisfied. She'd been rebuffed but was first on the list of those not needed at the party. It was when she said she'd stay close to the phone for the evening that both of them noticed that she had a pantsuit on and her makeup was done. Lynn exhaled audibly.

"That's really thoughtful of you, Mom," Anthony offered. An experiment. Using someone's shit to make you look better. "Lynn and I will keep a watch on things, and if they get crazy, we'll call you, even if Ron doesn't."

"You two know what it takes to pull off a nice party from watching me. Let me know when Ron's in over his head. He may be a genius in the choir loft, but I doubt he's an enter-tainer!" She laughed and returned to her plate, feeling she'd just *had a moment* with her children. Lynn crossed her eyes and stuck her tongue out at Anthony.

As the dishes were cleared, Anthony and Lynn received instructions for displaying and serving the three dishes they were to take—the family-famous lime Jell-O torte, a meatball-and-sauce creation made possible by the new Rival Crock-Pot Annie had received for Christmas, and a platter of homemade fudge. Annie was certain that no one else had yet mastered Crock-Pot cooking, as the appliance was the newest thing on the market. She had been sure to verify with Ron that the snacks would be set up in an area with accessible electricity, since her Crock-Pot required connection. She beamed with pride while she warned about the dangers of improper transport, display, and serving of the snacks. Clearly the food represented Annie, and she was fully invested in it. Lynn cursed aloud her decision to wear her new white blouse, a gauzy material through which her satin bra was just visible. "If I get *meatballs* on this"—she spat out the word *meatballs* in disgust—"somebody's gonna die!"

"You look really nice," Anthony offered, entering round two of charming the Conway women.

"Don't brownnose me—I'm not as gullible as Mom. Plus, your opinion doesn't matter, you freak." Her voice was only half-hostile. There was some humor there, born of the escape they'd just managed to make from having their mother at the party.

"Fine. But it's not a matter of opinion. You do look nice, and I am just acknowledging it."

"Thanks." The word was spoken cautiously.

The dishes securely packed in the back of the 1968 Chevy Bel Air station wagon, Lynn and Anthony drove away from the house, giggling about the myriad of instructions and warnings they intended to ignore. Lynn even seemed to drive more aggressively, daring one of the valuable snacks to tip or spill.

Although it was only seven ten, they had to park eight houses up the street and carry their parcels through the cold to the door of Ron's apartment. There was no moon, making the street darker and the close-set houses more foreboding. Annie had packaged each dish separately and included a bag of utensils, so both had their hands full. As they ascended the stairs, the cold boards creaked and snapped. Lynn jumped, fearing that the porch was unsafe. Anthony started to tell her that the porch always creaked but caught himself. She looked puzzled at the side-by-side front doors, wondering which one led into the lower-apartment foyer and which opened to a staircase leading to the upper unit. She'd been told that Ron lived downstairs. On closer inspection, the right door was ajar, and voices could be heard inside. Anthony pushed open what he knew to be the correct door, and they stepped inside.

The foyer and living room were not much better lit than on earlier visits. The familiar sounds and smells of the house had hidden themselves, covered by the voices and laughter of the more than twenty teens already there and by the scent of every mother's attempt to attract notice with her signature side dish. It was disorienting. This apartment was nothing like he had come to know, yet it was the same place. The dark drapes, the wood, the furniture. The same but perverted by the presence of people who were there by general invitation only. *People who weren't his real friends.*

He scanned the room, seeing familiar faces of teens—mostly segregated by gender—talking and laughing. Some stood, while a few possessed the limited seating space. Anthony noticed that Carol, perky Joan's older sister, occupied the space on the sofa where Anthony and Ron had had sex. He wondered if there was evidence there that the trained eye might see. Rock music blared, something by Kansas or Uriah Heep. Alan would have known which band and which album were playing. It was loud but not deafening—out of place. Anthony had seen no evidence of Ron's interest in anything other than classical music, and he wondered if the rock albums had been brought by some of the choir members.

Ron was not in the front rooms. There were more teens in the dim dining room, and it appeared that the food was in the kitchen. Anthony followed Lynn through the crowd as they threaded their way to the kitchen to unload their parcels. Lynn turned to her brother as they made their way. "There's a piano in the dining room. Mother would die!" Their eyes met, and Lynn giggled. "Seems like everything's under control here. I don't think we'll need to call her." Anthony nodded his assent as he maneuvered his parcels between the piano and the people.

The Formica table was already loaded with snacks, obviously prepared by doting mothers. While each mother may have mused about Ron arranging her signature dish in a place of prominence among the offerings, it was clear that no sense of order reigned at this buffet. Lynn started pushing dishes together as Anthony set the Crock-Pot near the back of the table, close to the wall socket beneath. He bent down and plugged the cord into the same outlet that had been used by Ron for his electric fry pan tomato soup.

There were three plates of fudge already on the table but nothing resembling the lime torte and no other Crock-Pot. Paper plates flanked the corner of the table but no napkins. Instead, a roll of paper towels lay on the chair next to the table. Ron had apparently forgotten to buy napkins and had made a last-minute substitution. The sight of the paper-towel roll, perhaps the same roll from a week ago, made Anthony feel slightly aroused. He began overlaying his reality of the house onto this night. The snacks were innocently displayed on the same table where Anthony began to discover the reality of what people and relationships were all about. Eddie was telling a dirty story in the same spot in the dining room where he'd lain on the floor to sing, while Jeannie and Fran were sitting at the piano bench where Ron had gotten erect. Someone was probably standing where Ron had led him through the darkened house, touching him for the first time. A group of choir mates were near the couch where it had actually happened. This was the same house, the same space, where his life had changed. Yet the change was invisible to the people who stood and sat in the identical places. They were shrouded from view by the veil of time that separated them. The people here tonight were not *attached to this place*, were not *attached to Ron*, as he was. They couldn't imagine the reality of this place.

After a few minutes of jostling, the food setup was complete. As Anthony surveyed the room, he noted that Ron was not in the kitchen either.

The rear bedroom door, visible off the kitchen, opened. Out of the darkened room stepped one of the older boys from the choir, blinking his eyes sheepishly as he closed the door behind him. Just as Anthony's mind began to race through the possibilities, he heard Ron's voice from the other room. He didn't make out the words, but the dutiful laugh of a few teens followed whatever Ron had said. Anthony turned to leave the kitchen in search of the voice as a somewhat disheveled soprano exited the bedroom from which the boy had just come. While this seemed interesting to the rest of the kitchen occupants, Anthony moved back into the dining room. Ron was standing in the living room, head back, taking a long draft from a bottle of Pabst Blue Ribbon beer. He looked so at ease, so playful. Mother always appeared so politely wound up when she entertained. Everything was always perfect, but her pleasure in the event was simply a role. Under her smiles and mock enjoyment was the fear that something would go wrong. But here, nothing could go wrong, since Ron hadn't set expectations. Once he admitted the first guests, he was simply a fellow reveler at the party. Such a different approach to the same kind of event.

Other choir members were taking beer from a case sitting on the sofa behind Ron. "Hey, Anthony's here! Judy stood me up, the bitch. But Anthony's here!" Ron bellowed. "Come have a beer!" Anthony felt both pride and discomfort at the attention and at the linking of Judy with Anthony. She was his girlfriend, but Anthony did not want to be put in that category, at least not publicly.

The thought that Ron would betray their secret had not entered his mind until this moment. The disaster of such an indiscretion would be life ending. Ron appeared drunk, swaying a little as he leaned on the breakfront between the dining and living rooms. Walking in behind Ron were two of the older boys, each holding two more cases of Pabst. For the briefest of moments, Anthony wished his mother were there. He felt vulnerable. Cornered. Controlled. Also vulnerable was Moses, as Ron's careless lean against the perch on which Moses resided was unsteady. "Give my pal Anthony a beer!" Ron ordered. He was handed an opened bottle.

Ron stepped forward and clinked his bottleneck with Anthony's. "To tennis!" he bellowed. Anthony laughed uncomfortably, noticing that the others around didn't seem to perceive any insinuation in the toast. Anthony drank from the bottle, expecting that he would taste the smell he savored on his walks through Miller Valley. The beer, however, tasted nothing like the scent—it was bitter and sharp. Anthony swallowed quickly, hoping not to gag for the second time in this room. With a gleam in his eye, Ron smiled at Anthony and then turned and put his arm around Carol, who had left the couch to come near him, sporting a tight-knit sweater that accentuated her breasts. "Where's Joan? My girlfriend, Judy, couldn't come down this weekend. Don't tell me Joan stood me up too!"

Carol responded, "I told you—she's got strep throat." With that, Carol moved out from under Ron's arm and across the room. She seemed annoyed. Ron didn't appear to notice. He turned and spotted Lynn. With two steps, he was beside her, his arm around her. Unlike Carol, Anthony's sister made no move to escape the attention. She smiled, clearly enjoying the spotlight. Carol looked suddenly jealous. Lynn's smile included some confusion as Ron's hand trailed down her back and over the seat of her jeans. But even as his hand rested inappropriately on the seventeen-year-old, his attention turned toward the kitchen. "I need some food!" he announced as he left Lynn's side and headed toward the light. "Come with me," he said as he placed his hand on Anthony's shoulder to steady himself. Lynn could be heard laughing with her friends near the beer as he followed Ron to the kitchen. Once there, Ron began inspecting the table of food. "Who made this green shit?" He laughed.

Anthony replied, "My mother—it's pretty good." Even as the words escaped his mouth, he realized he was defending his mother and the very dish he and Lynn had laughed about earlier. He pictured her, sitting uncomfortably on the couch awaiting a call informing her that she was needed. Ready to step into the light of Ron's attention.

"Hey, what's this?" Ron asked, lifting the lid of the Crock-Pot. "Cool! Gimme a plate." Anthony handed Ron a paper plate just in time for the scoop of meatballs to find a home. Ron picked up a plastic fork from the pile supplied by Anthony's mother. "These are great!" Ron said too loudly through this mouth full of beer and meatballs. Anthony set his beer down on the stove, hoping the abandonment would go unnoticed.

"Because Kevin's a fag!" Anthony heard someone shout over the music. In the doorway to the kitchen came Eddie, choir tough guy. Looking more like a football center than a youth choir bass, Eddie was apparently making fun of Kevin, a younger and smaller boy in the dining room.

While Anthony hoped to ignore Eddie, Ron immediately asked, "Why's Kevin a fag?"

"Hey, you join football to smash guys and get girls, and you join a choir either because you *love to sing* or because you love to get girls." Eddie's voice had gone into a feminine range on *love to sing.* "Fags love to sing, and Kevin ain't never had a girlfriend—wouldn't know what to do with one!" Eddie was into his second beer and loud. The kids around him were looking a little uncomfortable.

But Ron pressed on. "I like music and girls, and I could play football too!" Ron said with an increased volume.

"Oh yeah—you're a tough guy" came Eddie's sarcastic reply.

With that, Ron strode across the kitchen to the refrigerator and shouted, "Does this look like a fag?" He began kicking the refrigerator door, stepping back to get his leg high and planting the sole of his shoe firmly in the center of the old white Kelvinator. The first few incursions made a dent that sprang back when the foot was removed. By the fifth or sixth kick, it was clear that a dent had been permanently placed in the refrigerator door. A few teens were laughing at the spectacle, but most looked confused by the development—the only grown man in the house kicking in a refrigerator door in a drunken exercise to show his fitness for football.

When Ron stopped and looked over, Eddie was looking on, amused. "Yeah, you're a tough guy." Eddie turned and moved back into the dining room. "Beer time!"

With the excitement over, the kitchen emptied out. Lime Jell-O torte was no match for Pabst Blue Ribbon beer. Ron took Anthony by the shoulder. "I need to lie down," he sputtered as he walked toward the bedroom door, girded by the shoulder he leaned on. Anthony felt honored to be the friend Ron needed to assist him but was still a little scared that disaster was nearby.

"I hope you don't get in trouble for denting the refrigerator," Anthony spoke as they made their way into the darkened bedroom.

"Fuck you!" came the reply. "I don't believe in getting in trouble." Ron seemed bothered rather than angry. With his free hand, he swung the bedroom door closed behind them, while his other hand dropped from Anthony's shoulder to his waist. Latching onto Anthony's belt, Ron tumbled onto the bed. Anthony fell with him, coming to rest on top of Ron. The room was pitch-black. "I see what you want," Ron said too loudly as his hand slid inside the front of Anthony's pants. He fumbled to get into the boy's underpants as Anthony tried to slide away. Ron bristled, "Oh, no you don't. You started this; now you've got me going. You're going to have to finish it. Hurry up before people come looking for their coats." It wasn't until this moment that Anthony realized that he was lying not just on the bed but on top of the thirty or more jackets that had been piled there. His fear that Ron might betray him with a story about their relationship quickly turned into panic that they might be caught in the act. Ron continued to fumble with the clothing as he began to mutter. Anthony slid off Ron to his side and realized that he now lay with his right hand against the man's crotch. He could feel the soft erection through Ron's pants. Ron wasn't rock hard, as he'd been in the past. He had no time to sort out his panic and excitement.

"Let me go," Anthony pleaded softly.

He heard Carol in the kitchen. "Where are all the coats?"

"She's coming!" Anthony cried as he pulled away.

"I'll let you go if you promise to stay until everyone else is gone," Ron bargained. Anthony barked out his panicked agreement, and Ron released him. Anthony flipped the wall switch to light the ceiling fixture, and Carol burst through the door. Ron said slyly, "I knew you wanted me."

"What?" she asked, looking suspiciously at Anthony.

"Nothing. I think he's drunk."

Ron lay on his back, squinting in the bright light. As Anthony brushed past Carol, he heard Ron say, "Nobody wants me, nobody likes me," to which he heard Carol raise a sympathetic protest.

Anthony was in the living room near his sister fifteen minutes later when Carol came through, coat over her arm, looking more than slightly nonplussed. She moved quickly through the crowd and out the front door. "What's wrong with her?" Lynn said as she leaned toward Anthony.

"No idea" was his terse response.

By ten o'clock, Anthony was getting worried about the commitment he had made to Ron. The idea of another encounter with Ron once everyone was gone was intimidating because of Ron's current condition. But the party was to last until eleven, and Anthony needed to ride home with his sister. He had no idea how he could pull off what he had promised. If he called home to say that he was staying behind to help clean up, his mother would surely come to the apartment. Ron had rejoined the party and was drinking heavily. Many of the underage teens were drunk as well. The group started to thin, and at quarter to eleven, Lynn began gathering up the family dishes from the kitchen. Ron was slumped on the couch discussing religion with three of the choir members, stringing together completely unrelated thoughts in sentences spoken with confidence. One of the tails of his shirt was out, and his shoes were off. There was a hole in his black sock, the tip of his second toe visible. When Lynn announced that she and Anthony were leaving, Ron looked confused. "Anthony can't leave! He's my best friend."

Lynn responded, "If I don't get home by eleven with Anthony and this Crock-Pot, my mother will be over here by eleven ten."

"Wait!" Ron shouted, and he jumped from the couch. Anthony panicked at what might come next. Ron strode over with his hand outstretched. Confused, Anthony took the hand and received a hearty handshake. "We need more basses for 'Ecce Homo' at Easter, so behold the man!" While Anthony would be pleased later to have achieved "bass status," he was frightened by accusation of Ron's homo reference in referring to anything having to do with him. There was a nervous laugh, during which he noticed a chilling gleam in Ron's eye.

Lynn prattled all the way home about Ron's attention to her—that she hadn't previously thought that Ron even knew her name, that he had put his arm around her three times during the evening, and that he had asked her opinion about the idea of a choir trip. On and on and on. Anthony felt robbed of his place of honor by the need for secrecy.

Annie was up and dressed when they arrived home. While it might be assumed that she was playing the protective mother while her children were out in the world, she was actually awaiting the arrival of information. Lynn talked about Ron—this funny thing he said, that question he asked her, and the piano in the dining room. But Anthony perceived that his mother's interest was self-focused. Waiting for Lynn to pause for breath, he congratulated his mother on the success of the food—hers was clearly the best, and Ron really liked the meatballs. Annie beamed. Lynn rolled her eyes. Anthony found it curious that she never asked if he had enjoyed the party. Making his way up the kitchen staircase, he observed that he was just one of three Conways now under the spell of Ron Wilcox.

Eleven

In the week following the party, Anthony was amazed that there were no repercussions. No parents inquired as to anything that happened—no questions about underage drinking, about Ron's anti-God ranting to choir members, or about inappropriate behavior of any kind. Ron's antics, generally a parent's nightmare, were ignored. Instead, the fact that he provided social opportunities for their children allowed him to emerge more respected than ever. The choir resumed rehearsals, the church leaders beamed, the parents swooned, and the teens were continually educated by their leader.

Anthony began a pattern of sex with Ron that would last throughout his high school years. He would arrive unannounced at Ron's house a few times each month, looking for Ron's attention, knowing the price of being a friend. Ron was often there. When he was, the two would listen to music, discuss Ron's philosophies, and have sex. This became the center of Anthony's life, his most treasured relationship. Ron never kissed or held Anthony. He never asked Anthony's thoughts on a topic or showed an interest in the other major aspects of his life, like school or family. Yet Anthony felt privilege at his inclusion in Ron's life. He never considered its impact on his own psyche and never considered telling anyone. Ron continued to train Anthony in his philosophies of life, love, and faith. Anthony never felt either physically or psychologically threatened. But it created a secret aspect in life that separated him from everything else—his family, schoolmates, and friends. It put him on the fringe, but by choice. And his awe at Ron's ability to lead the church while exhibiting such overtly evil behavior never ebbed.

As the winter of 1973 wore on, Ron took Anthony to the church one evening. It was late—perhaps ten o'clock. Anthony's weekend curfew had been extended to eleven, and he had been diligent in being home by that time so as not to forfeit the privilege. They were in the loft, sorting music.

"Let's have sex in someone's seat! Whose seat?" Ron asked Anthony.

Anthony considered the choices. Eddie was annoying and so butch. It might be fun to know that Eddie was sitting in a seat where they'd done it. "Wouldn't Eddie's head explode if he knew we had sex in his seat?" Anthony pointed toward a chair in the second row of the bass section. "Or in Joan's seat? I could stick some music under my shirt, and you could pretend I have big boobs!"

"I don't want to have sex somewhere you think is funny, Anthony. Choose a place that means something."

Anthony felt chastised. But the idea that Ron wanted a place that was special touched him. He chose a seat far to the side of the loft rather than a seat where another member usually sat. Ron seemed puzzled but approved. It was here, when seated to one side in the chair with his pants around his ankles, that Anthony could lie back and watch the face of Veronica. As Ron brought him to orgasm, Anthony stared into the eyes of the saint, half in rebellion and half with the hope of finding acceptance. At the moment of ejaculation, a car rounded the corner outside with squealing tires, and its headlights emblazoned the scourged face of Jesus on the towel Veronica held. "Who will wipe this sin from my brow?" thought Anthony as he wondered whether the location of his orgasm was more sinful than the cause. Even as his pulses began to wane, Anthony found himself silently reciting the prayer to St. Michael the Archangel.

> *Saint Michael the Archangel, defend us in our hour*
> *of conflict. Be our safeguard against the wickedness*
> *and snares of the Devil. May God restrain Him, we*
> *humbly pray, and do Thou, O Prince of the Heavenly*
> *Host, by the power of God, cast Satan into Hell,*
> *and with him all the other evil spirits, who wander*
> *through the world, for the ruin of souls. Amen.*

Ron lay on the floor in the choir loft, pants down. Anthony obliged. Ron seemed thrilled by Anthony's willingness to have sex in the church. Almost wild when touched, he was finished in a matter of seconds. It was the first time that Anthony felt any sense of power with Ron.

Later that week, Anthony was again at the church on a week-night with Ron. There were some forms to copy, and the two went into the rectory to use the photocopy machine. Father Martin was there. A young priest on his first assignment after ordination, he seemed pleased to see them and offered a visit and snack when the copying was done. The ten-thousand-square-foot rectory was a maze of hallways with a residence wing and office suite. It housed three priests and a seminarian, plus a daytime office staff. The copying was completed in less than five minutes, and as Ron led Anthony back through the laby-rinth, they stepped into a darkened, unused bedroom. Without a word, they had sex—quickly and nearly silently. Again, Ron was nearly wild at the danger involved in having sex at this loca-tion, writhing when touched. The deed done, they went into the parlor with Father Martin and enjoyed sodas and Fritos.

Anthony had settled into the sexual component of his relationship with Ron, ignoring any thoughts of impropriety or danger. The intimacy the two shared was never expressed, never even implied. But Anthony was sure it was there. He enjoyed the few occasions when they talked, really talked, as much as the more frequent sexual episodes. Ron would pontificate angrily about God, relationships, family, and the church. On rare occasions, once spent from his railings, he would provide hints as to the genesis of these philosophies. Ron's now-dead father was a difficult man who drank and had been "rough" with the family. He never elaborated on the term *rough*, but it seemed apparent that Ron, his much older sister, and his mother had all been hit by the man at times. Ron's comments also betrayed high school years spent in unpopularity. He never spoke with any pleasure about his youth.

As Anthony became more connected to Ron, his rebellion toward his parents—more Annie than Keith—heightened. Even Anthony failed to understand why his resentment toward his mother was accelerating. It was out of step in relation to anything she had done to him. His fear that he was gay was more and more expressed as rebellion against the world. Ron validated the evidence that he was gay, and Annie encouraged Anthony's friendship with Ron at every turn. Yet Anthony knew she would reject a son with such a defect. He dated girls—even had a girlfriend—but found the relationships lacking. He longed to be convinced that his life was not chaos. That his family, his friends, his girlfriend were sufficient to the task of making him whole. But they all paled in comparison to the power that was Ron. Efforts by others to express love for him went unrequited. Anthony clung to all that he'd learned from Ron. He was a parasite, drawing life from the host. If he was ultimately gay, then in due course he would be rejected, judged unqualified to ever feel intimacy and love. He had to become Ron. To protect himself.

Spring came, the frozen infantry on the Lake Michigan shore retreated, and the choir prepared for the trip to Chicago. Easter services went well. The three-hour Easter Vigil at any Catholic church features a long and onerous Litany of the Saints, a sung prayer of interminable duration. The litany is the oldest in use in the church, tracing its heritage to Pope Gregory the Great. Led by a cantor and sung in Gregorian chant, it begins with a series of pleadings for mercy. The leader sings the supplication, and the congregation responds, all in a monotone chant. "Lord have mercy. Lord have mercy. Christ have mercy. Christ have mercy. Lord have mercy. Lord have mercy." After this introduction, the cantor begins singing saints' names, to which the congregation sings "Pray for us." Over sixty names are sung, one at a time. They range from Mary, the Mother of God, to each apostle, to the various martyrs and saints. James and John, roommates in their window at St. Veronica's, are granted separate lines in the litany. While the names of such unheard-of saints as Ambrose, Cosmos, and Thaddeus are chanted, St. Veronica is noticeably missing from the official litany. Each parish is allowed to add its patron saint to the fray, and St. V's dutifully recognized its namesake at the Easter Vigil Mass. She was, however, absent from the official text in the missal. The litany continues with prayers for deliverance from such horrors as sudden death, scourge of earthquake, and the spirit of fornication, each responded to by the congregation with "O Lord, deliver us." The entire fifteen-minute prayer is sung in alternating cantor and response. Monotone. Slow. Boring. Ron, completely unwilling to have any music in his presence that neither met its potential nor moved its listener, had half the choir lead the cantor parts in two-part harmony, with the balance of the group leading the congregational response in three-part harmony. Further, he had the cantor section begin each succeeding chant on the final note of the congregational response. Thus, when the congregation—supported in three-part harmony by the basses and altos of the choir—sang the last word in the "Pray for us" response, the choir's sopranos and tenors sang the name of the next saint. The result was a fast-tempo, melodious Litany of the Saints that surprised the packed church. It was beautiful. The ancient prayer became a musical number. Once again, Ron broke the rules, but the accolades poured in after the Mass.

Just after the Easter triumph, Ron announced that the trip required a planning committee. By now, the choir had grown to nearly seventy-five teens, ranging in age from thirteen to twenty. Alan still belonged to the choir, as did Lynn. The trip logistics were to be managed by a group of the choir members, with some parental oversight. This was the opportunity Annie Conway was awaiting, and she was the first parent to volunteer.

The St. Veronica Youth Choir became a Conway family obsession. The organizational meetings were at the Conway house, as were the choir-uniform sewing groups. Each girl wore a green-and-white-checkered floor-length jumper with a white blouse, while each boy wore black dress pants and a light-green shirt with a clip-on bow tie made from the same material as the girls' dresses. They were fairly hideous: a "Marcia and Greg Brady" attempt at modern professionalism. The planning committee became a permanent group, and there were meetings to paint banners, discuss upcoming concerts, plan choir potluck parties, and coordinate holiday events. Through this process, Annie became the "choir mom," listening to girls cry about their boyfriends, advising teens on succeeding with parents and at school, and negotiating truces between warring factions of the choir. The choir was Annie's prize possession.

Anthony felt more and more on the fringe of his own family. He was not the high school football player and college science major that Alan was. He was not the pom-pom girl with suitors and academic accolades that Lynn was. And apparently, he was not as interesting as the other choir members who began regularly appearing around the table at mealtimes. Annie *listened* to them. At times, Anthony wanted someone with whom he could discuss his rising fear that he was gay, someone who would listen to his stories of sex with Ron and tell him it was okay. Annie wasn't going to be that person; she existed for other choir teens. Keith became more distant from the family in general, spending more time at work. He didn't dislike the choir but was not interested in spending his evenings and weekends in a basement full of singing teenagers. The house became raucous and full of energy, and Anthony felt superfluous in the family equation. Statistically speaking, he was an outlier, his only source of guidance Ron Wilcox.

Ron was there—more frequently now—for family dinners. Anthony knew that he had something with him that no one else around the table could claim. Lynn would wear a tight sweater to dinner on the nights he was coming. Annie would begin cooking an hour earlier, making everything just right. Then she'd prattle on through the dinner, talking with excitement about every detail of the upcoming trip, the new uniforms, and the events she was planning. Lynn counted on her beauty and charm to attract Ron. Annie counted on her ability to do his bidding in choir administration. But it was Anthony who had been chosen to share the secret. Anthony was convinced that both of the women in the family would sleep with Ron if they had the chance. But he'd *been chosen.* He *was special.* No one else saw him that way. Ignored by his father. Henpecked by his mother. Categorized as completely average at school. If only they all knew. In the end, Anthony became more withdrawn from the family and more and more dependent on the crumbs of acceptance that fell from Ron's table.

Twelve

All focus was on the trip to Chicago, which was planned for the first weekend in June. Choir members would need to leave school by noon to board one of two Trailways Luxury Liner buses at two o'clock. Sixty-five teens were making the trip, with Ron and five other adults, including Annie Conway and Ron's girlfriend, Judy. Keith Conway was staying home, as was Alan. Anthony and his sister boarded the bus after stowing their duffels and sleeping bags. The next two nights would be spent on gym floors as the choir toured the Windy City, singing three concerts and three services in five different locations.

Annie beamed as she boarded the bus Anthony was on, clutching a clipboard full of permission slips in one hand and the time schedule for the day in the other. Asking a choir member to vacate his seat near the front, she sat down next to Ron and pronounced the choir ready for departure. As the buses lumbered out of the St. Veronica's parking lot, Anthony wondered if his mother even knew which bus he was on.

The trip south on Interstate 94 was loud, filled with laughter and shouts between rows. Two hours later, the group disembarked on Cermak Road in Chicago's Chinatown area, south of the Loop. The teens formed small groups and were released for an hour of free time before they were to meet at the Three Happiness Restaurant, a longtime fixture in Chinatown. After dinner, the buses took the choir to the historic St. Adalbert's Polish Catholic Church in the Lower West Side, only five minutes from the restaurant. Built in 1914, the massive white stone church had twin towers on each of the street-facing corners. While this parish was once home to over four thousand families, there were barely six hundred on the roll by 1970. The church was significantly larger than St. Veronica's and was made entirely of stone and marble. While its windows couldn't compare with St. V's, the interior was cavernous, and the acoustics were far superior. The choir was to present a concert at seven thirty that evening. About two hundred of the parish faithful had gathered by that time, and for the first time, Anthony felt a sense of responsibility on behalf of the choir. These people had given their Friday evening to listen to this upstart choir from the city to the north.

The concert went well, and Ron seemed pleased as the elderly women greeted his descent from the loft with handshakes and smiles. The buses released for the evening, the choir settled into St. Adalbert's gymnasium for the night. One parent tried to enforce a policy of separating girls and boys for the night on the gym floor, but the group was too chaotic to control. The scene was a joyful refugee camp, with teens laughing and staking their territory on the floor, reserving spots for friends and using canvas bags and suitcases to construct boundaries. Pizza was delivered at eleven o'clock, after which the teens were to settle in for the evening. As is the typical custom of young people, the conversations and laugher went through the night. The morning brought a frenzy of girls blowing bathroom fuses with curling irons and hair dryers. The parent chaperones were only beginning to realize the gravity of their situation—the choir seemed to experience no ill effects from the sleepless night on the gym floor. This could be a long weekend for the parents, who seemed bleary-eyed and stressed.

All except Annie. She beamed as she organized the forty girls who needed makeup and hair attention, at one point shooing the boys from their bathroom to allow some girls to use the electrical outlets and mirrors. She counted the kids on the bus, laughing and teasing, and pronounced the choir fit for its next destination. Donuts were distributed as they made their way to Michigan Avenue for a few hours of loitering, followed by an early-afternoon visit to the Adler Planetarium. What could have been a memorable journey through the galaxy became a source of jokes for years to come as two of the adults snored their way through the presentation.

In the late afternoon, the choir gathered at Holy Name Cathedral on North State Street, just off the Magnificent Mile—the Michigan Avenue shopping district. The teens set about changing into their uniforms and preparing for the five o'clock liturgy. Ron went immediately to the choir loft to begin setting stops on the massive pipe organ. Unlike the detailed portraits in the St. Veronica's windows, those in the cathedral were abstract, dominated by deep blues and reds near the rear of the church and progressing to whites and golds around the altar. The effect was to focus the brightest natural light at the front of the church. With about five hundred in attendance, the choir sang at Mass, performing its most classical of pieces. Following the service, they moved from the loft to the altar steps for a short concert. The cathedral had advertised the concert, and nearly three hundred attended. It was here that the choir first performed the African Mass Missa Luba, accompanied only by drums and native African percussion. Sung in Latin, the choir moved through the Kyrie, Sanctus, and Agnus Dei. One of the best tenors sang the solo lines, and the audience was moved from fear at the sight of the drums to complete enjoyment of the music. The choir received its first standing ovation.

Ron was giddy with pleasure after the concert as the choir moved from the sanctuary to the education wing, where the gym had been prepared for the choir sleepover. The cathedral staff had prepared soup and sandwiches, and Cardinal Cody himself joined the choir for the dinner, congratulating Ron and praying a blessing over the teens.

The choir settled down for the evening, a bit more subdued than the night before, as even the teens began to tire. By one o'clock, when Anthony made his way over the sleeping bodies and into the long hallway to the bathroom, the building was nearly silent. To his surprise, he found Ron in the dimly lit bathroom, washing his face and studying a dry patch of skin on his cheek. Most of the lights in the large bathroom were off, and Ron was standing beneath the one light that apparently remained on at all times. There were no windows, and the white ceramic tile that covered the floors and walls made the room resonant and alive to sound. "Coming to see me?" Ron quipped as Anthony stepped to one of the dozen urinals and opened his jeans.

"Coming to piss. What are you doing?" Anthony replied.

"Can't sleep. You know how music makes me horny. I've been sitting around thinking about how I could get next to you on the gym floor. Now here you are."

As Anthony finished urinating and stepped away from the wall, Ron stepped between him and the sinks. Always taught to wash his hands after using the bathroom, Anthony moved around Ron and turned on the water on one of the six sinks mounted in a row under the mirrors. Ron stepped behind Anthony and reached around him. "You look warm. Perhaps you need some fresh air." As he spoke, he was unfastening Anthony's pants. Scared and excited, Anthony was being led toward the end stall. At least there would be a measure of safety there. He could feel Ron's erection against his backside as they slid into the nearly dark stall. Ron's hands were already on Anthony's exposed penis as Anthony turned to fasten the swinging door behind them. As he turned, he noticed the message scratched into the melon-green enamel on the metal stall partition. *What are you doing, fag?*

From outside the bathroom, the cheerful voice of Annie Conway boomed. "Hey, you boys, quit your foolin' around and get back to your sleeping bags." Her tone was almost cute. Anthony pulled away from Ron and began fastening his pants as Annie called, "Don't make me come in there! I have two sons and no fear of the boys' bathroom!" It was clear that she was not leaving and might momentarily be inside the room.

In his best Eddie Haskell voice, Ron called, "Coming, Mrs. Conway," and laughed aloud. He buckled his belt, left the stall, and went out into the hall seemingly recovered from being nearly caught with Annie's son. Anthony could hear his mother apologizing to Ron for assuming the voices from the bathroom to be from boys misbehaving. "Your son is the only one left in there, and I think he'll be done in a minute," Ron said. Anthony was panting as he stood at the sink under the single light, measuring the gravity of the situation by the look on the face in the mirror.

Collecting himself, he hoped to face his mother with as much ease as Ron had. But there was no one in the hall. Annie had followed Ron back to the gym, apparently unconcerned about her son or what he might have been doing in the bathroom. Anthony slumped to the floor against the hallway wall and buried his face in his hands. He was sure he hadn't wanted to be caught. Yet he had felt somewhat valued to think that she had been checking on what was going on, even though she didn't know it was Anthony in the bathroom. Considering now that his mother had followed Ron back to the gym—knowing Anthony was still in the bathroom—he was devastated. He longed to be protected by his mother. But she seemed fully under the spell of the person from whom Anthony needed to be protected.

Returning unnoticed to his sleeping bag, Anthony felt a sense of satisfaction knowing that Ron had been left "unfinished" in the bathroom. He slept well for the remainder of the night.

In the morning, the choir boarded the bus for Oak Park. Ron had somehow arranged for the choir to perform at the early-morning service at Unity Temple, a Unitarian church designed by Frank Lloyd Wright. The historic building, completed in 1908, was on the National Register of Historic Places. The main worship space, called the Temple, was square, with two shallow balconies on each of three walls. It was small, seating about four hundred, mostly in the balconies. The building was a masterpiece in the classic Frank Lloyd Wright style. Wright was noted as a Unitarian himself by the minister who welcomed the choir into the building.

It had been arranged that the choir would occupy the main floor, with all parishioners in the balconies. As they gathered in one of the meeting rooms before the service, Ron distributed the music for the African Missa Luba Mass, explaining that the minister was planning to compare and contrast the Unitarian service with the Catholic Mass and that the choir would sing as designated during the presentation. Ron also announced that Anthony would sing the solo parts of the music, as the regular tenor soloist was not feeling well. Anthony was shocked, honored, and excited. The service was fascinating—the first non-Catholic service Anthony had ever attended. His solos went well, and his mother seemed proud of him. It seemed on first impression to be a Christian faith, as its core, but the service was more about a celebration of life than about the instructions or judgment of God. In the years after that Sunday, Annie would describe the simplistic beauty of the historic Unity Temple to friends, always making sure to mention that her son soloed there. Anthony never forgot that day.

Immediately after the service, the choir sang at the late-morning Mass at a neighboring Catholic church and then finished with an early-afternoon concert at a large retirement community north of the city. They returned home around dinnertime, and the parking lot at St. Veronica's was hectic with parents collecting their teens. As Anthony stepped from the bus, Ron was talking with Keith Conway, who was there to meet his wife and two children. Annie was at Keith's side as Ron winked at Anthony and called, "You owe me." Annie immediately began explaining Anthony's solo to her husband, assuming Ron's joke was indicating that the solo had been a favor for which Anthony owed the director. But Anthony knew full well what was meant.

Thirteen

Sophomore year of high school was clumsy. Still shorter than most boys and many of the girls, Anthony remained largely invisible. He had some friends but still occupied the dead zone between the nerds and the cool. Two months into the school year, David, a popular, handsome, somewhat effeminate senior, came out, telling his friends that he was gay. The news was water breaching a dam, crashing downstream with amazing speed. By midweek it was the talk of the school. David, however, seemed confident, unshaken by the strong reaction. He endured some name-calling from boys, but the girls seemed to swoon over him, a safe potential playmate. In the locker room after Thursday's gym class, two boys accused David of staring at them in the showers. As thirty other boys stood back, they beat his head against a gray metal locker and then threw the fully clothed youth into the showers, nose bleeding and eye swelling. By Monday, the news was that David had decided to transfer to another school. Later, the truth came out that Father Oakley, Central Catholic's principal, had expelled the youth for violating church law with his lifestyle. *Lifestyle.* The word burned again in Anthony's mind. Straight people had lives; gay people had lifestyles.

A few weeks later, the evening before Thanksgiving, Anthony walked to Ron's carrying a new album by Pink Floyd, now his favorite rock band. Ron answered the door, voice hoarse, hair disheveled. He'd shown signs of a cold at Mass on the previous Sunday, and it had obviously overtaken him. "Hey" was the only greeting he could muster. Stepping aside, Anthony passed through the door and into the typically darkened house.

Glad to find Ron home in any condition, Anthony dropped his coat on the chair in the living room and went to the record changer in the dining room. "I got the new *The Dark Side of the Moon* album. Pink Floyd, ya know?" Ron grunted his assent as he dropped onto the couch. They had become comfortable spending time together. It spoke to the relationship that had evolved. Anthony knew his way around the house, Ron having no need to act as host. He loved that he needed no tending to negotiate his way through time spent at Ron's. Walking to the dining room, Anthony slid the shiny record out, started the stereo, and placed the needle on the last track on the album.

"This album has some kind of secret music. They were talking about it at school. At the very end of one of the songs, if I turn it up real loud, you can hear another song playing. Some other music." The music started, and they listened.

Anthony was excited to share the secret of the music with Ron. He sat on the couch next to him, and they listened quietly. He loved that Ron would let him barge in, drop a record on the player, and guide him through a song. Anthony belonged there with Ron.

As the two-minute song wound toward its conclusion, Anthony went back to the stereo and began increasing the volume.

The last line of the song was spoken as the music trailed away. Turning the volume up to its maximum, a faint echo of music could be heard. Ron leaned forward. As he got his bearing on the soft undertow, it was gone. "Play that last part again," he ordered. Before they were done, Anthony had played the last ten seconds of the album perhaps eight times. He'd shared with Ron the various theories—it was something classical, it was a Beatles tune, it was sound captured by accident from a neighboring recording studio. A burnout at school had said that part of the music sounded like a Jethro Tull song.

Ron blew his nose and showed signs of tiring of the topic. "I feel like shit. Tell me something to make me feel better."

Anthony thought for a moment. "I don't really know anything cheerful. Everything's so fucked up all the time. A guy at school told everyone he was gay, and some guys beat him up. Then he got kicked out of school."

Ron was quiet. When he finally spoke, his volume was startling. "Stupid ass! The kid's in a fuckin' *Catholic* school. You can't tell people who you are—no matter what that is. Everyone is unacceptable to the church! Besides, why would you tell someone you were gay? It's all so unnecessary. Labels. Categories. All such bullshit."

They sat in silence for a while. Anthony went back to the stereo and started the album at its beginning. Ron spoke again. More quietly. Subdued. "What do you think, Anthony? Are you gay?"

They sat in silence through the second song, entitled "Breathe." Ron seemed content to wait, but Anthony knew there was no escape. "I'm not really thinking about labels. I am me. Who I have sex with is just a part of me. It doesn't define me."

"You're right about that. But even if you ever feel differently, don't ever tell anyone you're gay." Ron's voice betrayed concern rather than instruction.

Anthony asked no more questions, and they discussed it no further. After two hours, Anthony left for home. Ron was clearly not feeling well, dozing on and off while the music played. This was one of the few sexless times they'd spent alone with each other in the past year, and Anthony felt good to have shared time with his ailing friend.

The winter passed quietly. Anthony and Ron continued to spend time together. A relationship based on love and trust grew on Anthony's side. He told no one of his feelings. Annie continued to expand her integral role in the choir, hosting planning sessions, distributing advice on all sorts of issues to a wide array of choir members, and generally making the choir her hobby.

One chilly spring evening, Lynn announced that she was taking the car to go for pizza after a rehearsal—a girls' night out with the rest of her section. Alan, whose attendance in the choir had grown inconsistent, grumbled but agreed to walk home. As he and Anthony walked, Alan took a small plastic bag of marijuana out of his flak jacket and rolled a joint. The speed with which he completed the task and lit the joint indicated that this clearly wasn't his first time. They exchanged no words, and after a few drags, Alan silently offered the joint to Anthony. Pausing only briefly, he took the joint to his lips and inhaled only slightly. Alan seemed impressed that his little brother didn't choke. "Cool," he quietly spoke as he took the joint back and sucked on it deeply. Without discussion, they turned away from their route home, walking a two-mile circuitous route to the house, during which they shared two joints. They never spoke of the experience, but it was clear that Alan had included his brother in confidence, and the challenge was met. A month later, Alan moved in to his own apartment. The brothers rarely ever fought again, although they never really became close.

Fourteen

As Anthony entered his third year in high school, his luck began to change. Most importantly, he grew. Five foot four the previous Christmas, Anthony was nearly five ten when the school year began in 1974. He grew two more inches during that year and developed physically in other ways. His voice deepened, and by the end of the school year, he was shaving, though only once a week. He became more outgoing and made more friends at school. He began writing for the school newspaper, the *Central Catholic Standard*. He briefly dated the editorial writer, Kristine.

Kristine was a serious student who seemed popular with other serious students. She was not ugly, but she didn't really try to be beautiful. It was as if she didn't want to be noticed. But in conversation she was quite funny, and she seemed to really enjoy Anthony's company. Their dates consisted of meeting at the football games on Friday night, then heading to the school's drive-in burger hangout afterward. While Kristine seemed quiet and reserved to those who might observe her in the hallway at school, she was actually adventurous. When Anthony suggested that they go for a walk in the dark park across from the drive-in, she was eager. Stopping on the nearly pitch-black path to talk, it was Kristine who kissed Anthony. A real, adult kiss, with the requisite trading of tongues. Following what he heard from bragging boys at school, Anthony returned the kisses, then brought his hand up Kristine's back and around to her right breast. Awaiting rejection of his brazen move, he received no acknowledgement of the act whatsoever. This happened twice, on two consecutive Friday nights. Anthony made no other moves on her, and the third week's opportunity was cancelled by a cold fall rainstorm. Before the next week of football, Anthony sat with Kristine in the newspaper office at school and told her of his desire to end the relationship.

"I've got a lot of shit going on at home right now" he offered. "I can't really go into it, but I may have to move. Things are bad. It's best that I don't make any commitments right now." None of that was true, but it did have the desired result. Kristine was supportive, offered her continued friendship, and didn't seem broken hearted. She didn't press him further, and Anthony was relieved. He had concluded that he did not want any sort of commitment to Kristine, but didn't really want to hurt her either. It all worked out smoothly.

Just after Christmas, he auditioned for the spring musical and landed the small part of Harry the Horse in *Guys and Dolls*. For the first time, Anthony found activities outside the choir. He went to the football and basketball games and the dances. As with all teenage boys, the most significant thing that could happen, once you had pubic hair, was to get your driver's license. Anthony took the required classes and passed on his first try.

Ron remained a central force in Anthony's life. They had a relationship with facets. There was Anthony the choir member and Ron the director. But for Anthony, there was also Anthony and Ron the friends. The buddies. People saw that—he was sure of it. People knew that the two *hung out*. Annie Conway likely wished it had been Lynn—perhaps dreamed of such a connection bringing Ron permanently into the family, her son insufficient for that task. And there were Anthony and Ron the musicians. Anthony knew what music the choir would learn next and could tell people which pieces would be really hard—which ones had a dissonant countermelody or a particularly high soprano line. And there were Anthony and Ron the lovers. That secret was held almost as closely as the experience itself. What others would find worthless as coal was held tightly enough by Ron to become diamonds for Anthony. Ron was Anthony's private accomplishment—something wrong yet right. Secret deeds in a public forum. A breaking of the biggest of rules in the area where his upbringing pushed him to conform—his parents' religion.

It was in his junior year that Anthony, with broadened his horizons, landed a part-time job after-school at Midwest Electronics, a small shop that sold and repaired ham radio equipment and CB radios. The owner was an elderly man who lived behind the shop and left the daily business to the four or five high schoolers he hired. Often, when the owner was in his apartment, Anthony would head to the basement storeroom with another employee to smoke pot. Returning to the sales floor high, the transgression seemed to escape the notice of not only the owner but of the mostly nerdy customers who came in for supplies.

Anthony still made time for Ron, even as other activities squeezed in. Ron continued to want sex with Anthony whenever the opportunity was there. Anthony would appear at Ron's house more frequently on weeknights than on the weekends, which were prime time for being with school friends. In psychoanalysis years later, Anthony spent many sessions pondering why he continued to make himself available to Ron. It was this fact that became most complicated as Anthony considered the impact Ron had on his life. It was difficult to hold Ron responsible, to say that Ron did anything wrong, since it was always Anthony who appeared at Ron's door. Ron rarely called Anthony, rarely asked about his life or activities, and shared no emotion with Anthony. Yet he was always pleased to see Anthony, and the sexual relationship seemed to come easy to both of them.

Ron's apartment became comfortable for Anthony. He often brought over records from his growing classical collection and played them. He was developing his own taste—Richard Strauss's *Der Rosenkavalier*, Corelli's concertos, and the choral sounds of the boys' choirs of Europe. He would help himself to soda when Ron's dented refrigerator had some to offer or bring cartons of Fanta Red Cream Soda to Ron's and leave them there for his next visit. Ron also usually offered cheap wine to Anthony and something new—a chemical to be inhaled, called poppers.

They began having sex in the bedroom rather than in the living room. There was still no intimacy, no holding or kissing. Anthony liked the idea of holding and kissing someone but had been taught by Ron's example that men didn't do that. He had enjoyed kissing Kristine but was afraid of any real intimacy. If truthful, Anthony would have regarded Ron as his most intimate relationship, based mostly on the idea that sex in a bed was more "official" and therefore intimate. He had not yet had intercourse with a girl. He wanted to but didn't find himself really looking for an opportunity. The girls he dated were probably not ready to take that step, and Anthony had not pushed Kristine beyond giving him periodic access to her breasts. His friends began talking about their sexual exploits—stories more fabrication than fact. Anthony, of course, could not share his best stories. No one seemed to suspect the truth.

Near the end of his junior year, he began missing choir practices. There was a subconscious longing in him for some measure of power in the unbalanced relationship with Ron, and a missed rehearsal was all he could muster. He waited for Ron to ask about him, to call or ask Annie to intervene. Should she ask, Anthony would provide no reason for his sudden disinterest in the choir. He longed to have the opportunity to tell his mother what had been happening for the past two years, although he would never betray the secret. He played the scenario out in his mind nearly every day. His mother and father would come to him and express their observation that something was wrong with Anthony. Tell him they loved him. They would *reveal their worry*. The three would talk, but Anthony would not release the core of the abscess in his heart. When it was over, he could at least then say that his parents showed concern about what was happening in his life.

Annie, however, didn't ask. She scolded. According to Annie, Anthony had made a commitment to the choir and needed to honor it. The choir had brought the family closer to one another and closer to God. Ron had been a great influence on Anthony's life, as evidenced by the classical records he played upstairs in his bedroom and by his interest in singing. He had Ron to thank for his expanded self-confidence in school and the new friends he made by being involved in the school play. It was clear that Annie believed Ron to be the source of any success Anthony was enjoying. She was not about to allow the teen to back away from the opportunity to continue growing in the shadow of the hero Ron.

In the end, after a rebellion of a mere three weeks, Anthony rejoined the choir, knowing that a connection to Ron was his only hope of being worthy enough to enter the center of something important. Ron seemed pleased. Anthony became more withdrawn from the family. He began smoking marijuana regularly and occasionally popping pills—some kind of mild speed called white cross. His performance in school, although not stellar, was decent. He was modestly popular, involved in extracurricular activities, and a soloist in the choir. Yet he was having gay sex with a much older authority figure, taking drugs, and hating God and his parents. It was during this time that Anthony caught a glimpse of what he could be. He was breaking rules and succeeding. He could see himself becoming Ron. The realization was startling and unleashed a period of reckless behavior that would last well into Anthony's twenties.

Just before his seventeenth birthday, with fake ID in hand, Anthony began frequenting the Depot, a large gay dance bar in the ugly warehouse district just south of downtown. He would accept drinks from older men and often have sex in their cars or, if they lived near the bar, at their apartments. He met Tom, a thirty-two-year-old architect, and went back to his apartment the first night, coming home well past curfew. The following week, he basked in the standing ovation the cast of the school play received. When he walked out for the curtain call and the applause rose, he felt like the child he was, receiving unfiltered approval from the hundreds of parents and teachers in the audience.

Anthony went to Ron's hometown with him for a weekend, staying at Ron's mother's house. As he prepared to leave for the weekend, Annie reminded him that he would be nearly two hours away and couldn't call to come home if he didn't want to spend the night. Annie's counsel was a reminder that when he was young, Anthony had failed numerous times to stay the night at a friend's house. He would leave home with the best of intentions but become sick to his stomach as bedtime approached, ending the night in tearful embarrassment, awaiting his father to take him back home. Anthony was bewildered that his mother's alarm lay in reminding him that he might still be the fearful child of the past. She had no concerns about why a man in his midtwenties would want to spend a weekend with her teenage son. But Anthony would break the rules of old.

He would not come home. He would instead have sex with the role model who had taught him that there were no rules. Twice that weekend, the two found themselves in Ron's childhood bed, while Mrs. Wilcox slept peacefully down the hall.

The only evidence of the old Anthony—the shy, clumsy, tortured Anthony—was revealed in the infrequent moments when he would stop at St. Veronica's and sit quietly in the church. He was running so fast, avoiding self-reflection. School and its activities, the choir, a part-time job, friends and dating, drugs. He stayed incredibly occupied, with no time for thoughts. During the brief visits to the empty church, the body, mind, and spirit would reunite. Sitting in the same pew as always, he would contemplate the glass saints, knowing that they truly knew what was going on in his life. He rarely saw the elderly woman who used to share this quiet space. He had seen her name on the prayer list in the bulletin and assumed her cramming time was done—the final exam scheduled.

Since the loft staircase was locked during the week, Anthony couldn't get close enough to Veronica to fully discern what she thought of him during these quiet visits. He would turn in the pew and gaze up at her, feeling it appropriate that he could not come close to her. Perhaps even her patience with Anthony was wearing thin. He never pondered the Christ of the rose window at the front of the church. Anthony had become a reflection of Ron—God was fucked up and should be regarded only from a distance. The saints—these were people devoted to this God, regardless of his condition. Saints like acrimonious Paul should be ignored. But others, like Veronica, could be the true inspiration to a lost life because her faith and actions were born of genuine love. Then again, Anthony was convinced that there was no genuine love.

Late in his junior year, the choir recorded an album. Anthony had a solo, his baritone voice now nicely developed.

The choir enjoyed a citywide reputation and was asked to sing at the service of ordination for the new priests at St. Francis Seminary. It was in suburban Milwaukee and was among the oldest of Roman Catholic seminaries in the United States. The Mass was one of the highest services of the year, celebrated by the archbishop himself. Singing at the solemn event was a first for any youth choir, the venerable concert choir of St. John the Divine Cathedral displaced to make room. The service was long and filled with mystical symbolism. The choir sang the best of its classical pieces, accompanied by the huge pipe organ, plus brass and timpani. The crowd was awed, clapping for nearly thirty seconds after the choir finished its postlude—a piece by Randall Thompson entitled "The Last Words of David." The words of the song were appropriate for the climax of an ordination service, speaking to the idea that rulers must be just, fearing God.

The piece was majestic, with huge runs on the organ and thrilling crescendos by the choir. The great *amen* at the end of the piece rose and fell with power and intensity. The song was fitting. It seemed to speak of the awesome power and responsibility granted to the new priests—those who would now *rule over man* and who *must be just.* Anthony couldn't help but think, as he sang, that the song could be a tribute to Ron. Ron ruled over the congregation of St. Veronica's justly, as he defined justice. He had no fear of God or of his priests. Rather, Anthony believed, perhaps it was God who feared Ron. After all, it was Ron who rose like the morning sun to rule the kingdom of St. V's. Even this song was a "fuck you" to the church, to God, and to all those who believed Ron was as advertised—a spiritual leader of a vibrant Catholic youth choir.

Fifteen

Anthony's senior year was unlike any year before. He had the lead in Central Catholic's production of *Brigadoon*, was elected to the prom court, began a real relationship with a pretty pom pom girl named Claire, was editor in chief of the school paper, and bought his first car—a 1968 Plymouth Fury. He had sex with the first male of his age group—a boy named John, a junior from the high school concert choir. He turned eighteen and was able to drink legally in Wisconsin. As the year went on, a pattern emerged of picking up older men for sex on Friday nights at the Depot and then spending Saturday nights with Claire. While sex was nearly guaranteed every Friday night, his physical relationship with Claire was more tentative. Anthony liked the idea of sex with her but was never comfortable mentally with the whole process. It seemed clumsy and manufactured, and therefore didn't go very far. Picking up older men, on the other hand, provided lessons that Ron had never taught—how to kiss a man, dance, flirt, and, in the end, have better sexual technique. Yet any emotion in these one-night stands was clearly contrived for the moment.

Anthony had met Claire just after the school year began. She had been in the high school since the ninth grade, but Anthony had never talked to her. She was in the concert choir and landed a chorus part in the school play. Anthony asked her out because it seemed appropriate. She was attractive, with long blond hair and a cute figure. She was permanently cheerful, like all of the members of her pom-pom squad. The relationship grew quickly, as high school loves do. Claire seemed to truly care for Anthony, but he couldn't figure out why. He cherished talking with her and had perhaps the most interesting and meaningful conversations of his life with her, on topics ranging from God to lunchroom choices. The debate that characterized many of their conversations was satisfying to Anthony. Anthony's ideas were, of course, Ron's ideas. Claire didn't know that. But she was the first person who truly considered the ideas objectively, neither repulsed by their absurdity nor awed by the author. He shared his philosophies about God, relationships, and love. Claire listened, considered, and debated with Anthony. The mental and emotional connection was unlike anything he had experienced before. But even on good days, it was so uncomfortable to touch her.

Some of their favorite activities were kite flying and going on picnics. Just after they began dating, they planned a Saturday afternoon picnic at Lake Park, high on a bluff overlooking Lake Michigan, just north of downtown. It was one of the last warm days of fall in 1975. Always breezy near the lake, it was a simple task to put a kite high into the air and then tie the line to a tree while the picnic dinner was eaten. Claire had made Rice Krispies Treats, while Anthony had brought a portable grill, hot dogs, chips, and soda. Just after dinner the sun fell, the breeze began to die, and Claire reeled in the store-bought red kite with its homemade rag tail. Anthony took the cooled grill and kite back to the car and returned to find Claire sitting wrapped in the picnic blanket under a crab apple tree just feet from the bluff overlooking the water. Neither had brought a jacket, and with the sun down, the temperature had dropped from the midsixties into the fifties in less than an hour. Anthony joined her, and she wrapped the blanket around the two of them as they stared out at the endless lake, shimmering in the waning light.

"Do you, deep inside, actually believe in God?" Claire asked. "You say you don't. But you also say that God, if He exists, is all screwed up, and you talk as if you're really angry at Him. If He doesn't exist, who are you mad at?"

Anthony thought for a long time. Claire was the only person Anthony knew who would always wait, unperturbed. "I think that I prefer not to believe in God, because then I don't have to make sense of anything. But I am afraid of not believing."

"What are you afraid of?"

"I am afraid to be wrong. I'm afraid of rejecting what I was taught—that God is the only real constant in life and the only hope for eternity."

"And what is it about believing that makes you afraid?"

Another long pause. "I guess it's that if there is a God, I am angry that He lets people get so screwed up."

"Are you screwed up, Anthony?"

"You know that I am. You know better than anyone."

"Then I must be screwed up, because I love you." She kissed him on the cheek, and Anthony felt like crying. Claire continued, the darkness obscuring Anthony's emotion. "Have you ever thought that perhaps God exists but not the way religion class says He exists? I think that God is right here for me, but I don't find Him through written prayers or Sunday masses. I find Him inside, not outside. For me, He's not far away, like someone you have to look for. I am part of God, and He is part of me—when I make myself better, I make God better. We're in this life together. He provides for me, and I provide for Him."

Anthony had no response, and Claire seemed to need none. They sat quietly, wrapped in the blanket and by the closing darkness. Anthony realized, as he felt Claire's arm around his waist, that this was what was missing in gay relationships. He felt completely enveloped by Claire, safe and secure. She was close to him both physically and emotionally. He wasn't sure he agreed with her spiritual insights, but it was okay. He laid his head on her shoulder, and they gently rocked side to side as the surface of the lake below faded from blue to indigo to black. It was well past eight o'clock and pitch-black in the park. Claire kissed Anthony, on the cheek first and then deeply on the lips. Her free arm came around his neck, and she whispered, "I want you." Claire held Anthony as he fumbled with their clothing, and they made love for the first time. It felt good physically, and Anthony truly felt love for Claire. They held each other a long time after they were done. Then, as they gathered up the blanket, Anthony turned to Claire in the dark. "Will you always love me, or will you grow tired of me?"

"I don't know the future, Anthony, but even if we're not together someday, I will always love the you that I have in my life today."

He knew that he should treasure everything about Claire, and he tried to. She was wonderful. Loving, fun, and interesting. He'd just had sex with her for the first time—her first time ever and his first time with a girl. It was incredibly special. But something was missing. Anthony felt a trap closing on him. He couldn't explain it, but he could feel it.

During his final year of high school, Anthony had become openly hostile toward his mother. While she became an important part of the choir community, a revered and trusted adult for many of the teens, Anthony berated and abused her continually. He was smoking marijuana two or three times each week and hardly hid it from his parents. Yet they said nothing. Years later, Lynn would tell him that they simply didn't know what to do, but Anthony would never escape the feeling that his parents stood by as his life spun out of control.

Anthony was becoming Ron. He took drugs and stayed out late but pulled all As and Bs at school. His prerequisites covered, his last semester was filled with classes like art appreciation and varsity choir, making good grades an easy goal. He was popular with both the burnouts and the brains. Through his relationship with pom-pom girl Claire, he gained acceptance with the jocks. He used his position as editor of the *Standard* to investigate administration politics and to criticize the monthly school liturgies. But he did it with intelligent, respectful articles. On each occasion when he was called to the principal's office, he made it very clear that to squelch his articles would be to undermine the very education the school had provided him. He found himself encouraging the principal to step up and discuss the issues rather than shrink from them to an authoritarian position. At times, he could actually see some fear of him in the principal's eyes. In the end, Anthony's ability to debate on a mature, collaborative level won over those in authority who hated what he had to say. Anthony became a fine manipulator—his stated position admirable but his secret agenda evil. He invited school leaders to enter into open debate in the school paper—producing point-counterpoint articles about the existence of God and the quality of the academic programs. The whole school talked about whatever Anthony wanted them to talk about. There were times that he didn't even hold to the positions he put forward in the paper. He simply basked in the power he felt in shaping discussions and perceptions. He broke the rules and was liked by all. Claire was the one anomaly in his life, because the relationship seemed genuine. He wondered if Claire was to him what Judy, whom Ron was still dating, was to Ron—the sane bulwark against the world's storm.

With all his success, Anthony could not escape the feeling of being a fraud, the feeling that if anyone knew the truth, they would reject him. All his accomplishments—the standing ovations at the performances of *Brigadoon*, the Wisconsin High School Press Awards won by the school paper, and the recognition by fellow students—all of it, in Anthony's mind, was based on lies. They were based on the Anthony created by Ron, not the Anthony that really existed. He could revel in the recognition but never in the reality.

With the release of the choir's record and the achievement at the ordination ceremony, Ron was not to be denied. He convinced the parish to spend $110,000 to upgrade the pipe organ and install a sound system in the loft. He added a Moog synthesizer to the music of the choir, blending the eerie new sounds of the electronic instrument with the centuries-old tones of the organ. The choir was at its peak with eighty-six members. More trips were scheduled—Minneapolis, St. Louis, and a spring-break trip to Orlando that mixed the business of the choir with the pleasure of Disney.

The business of the choir—the extra rehearsals, the trips, the activities—offered Annie Conway a mission in life. She was involved weekly. With the exception of the Thursday evening rehearsals, she was there for everything. Ron encouraged her—perhaps enjoying Annie's worship of him while violating her son.

Although never spoken about, it was clear that Ron recognized the growing power that Anthony had in the relationship. Anthony's recklessness with drugs and confrontations with his parents clearly gave Ron reason to fear that he might be betrayed by the dysfunctional youth he had helped to create. Ron would occasionally go to the Depot with Anthony on Friday nights, although he was uncomfortable with the risk of being seen at a gay bar. To make matters worse for Ron,

Anthony seemed to know many people there and took great pleasure in introducing Ron to these new friends.

By spring, as graduation approached, Anthony began to feel a sense of equality in the relationship. But Ron quickly turned the tables. At a choir rehearsal, Ron distributed a piece of music for which a bass soloist was required. He explained that he was searching at the Conservatory of Music for a guest soloist, as there was not a strong enough soloist among the basses in the choir. Then, looking directly at Anthony, Ron thanked those who had soloed in the past and explained that this piece was beyond their capabilities. Later, in a private conversation, Ron expounded on that point, telling Anthony that he would never put him into a position of possible embarrassment by asking of him more than he was capable of producing. The circle was reestablished, with Ron in the center. Anthony was still there but would never occupy the center. He was there at Ron's bidding. Of that he could be sure. It was no different than grade school, where being bullied and abused was sometimes the price necessary to remain close to the powerful ones. He would never—could never—be truly successful, truly admired, or truly loved.

At the end of the following week's rehearsal, Ron announced his engagement to Judy. She was moving to Milwaukee, having finished nursing school upstate, and they would be married the following winter. Annie was ecstatic at the engagement and offered to have Judy stay at the Conway house until she had a job in the city and could get her own place. Ron accepted on Judy's behalf, and just after Anthony's high school graduation, Judy arrived with bags in tow to share Lynn's bedroom. Ron began coming to the house more frequently, and Anthony could only watch as Ron and Judy began double-dating with Lynn and her boyfriend du jour on Friday nights. Anthony felt minimized. Again.

Worst of all, only a month after Judy's arrival, Ron announced that he was leaving St. Veronica's for a position in San Francisco. He had been offered a full-time position as organist and choir-master at the new Cathedral of St. Mary, a spectacular modern building of architectural significance. He had also received a scholarship to complete his study of music at San Francisco State University's School of Music and Dance. He was to leave in August, and Judy would move in to Ron's Forty-Seventh Street apartment for six months to plan the wedding. Ron would return to Wisconsin for the nuptials, which were to take place in the church of their youth in Ron's hometown. Then the couple would take up permanent residence in San Francisco.

In the weeks leading up to Ron's departure, the choir made plans for a send-off party, a new choir director was sought, and Ron spent little time with Anthony. Most of his time was spent with Judy and with Lynn, who had grown close to Ron. Lynn was now between boyfriends, and Judy had started a nursing job working second shift at St. Albert Hospital on the south side of Milwaukee. Ron and Lynn often spent evenings together, talking about the wedding and impending move to California.

A week before Ron's departure, Anthony was at Ron's apartment. Receiving instruction to do so, he was undressed and in Ron's bed, awaiting the arrival of his lover, who was in the dining room putting music on the stereo. Anthony believed that this would be their last session of sex and was nearly overcome with emotion when he heard the strings of the same memorable piece that Ron played on the night they first had sex. Could Ron have remembered the significance of this music, or was it a coincidence? Was this the music he played whenever a sexual milestone—a beginning or end of a relationship—took place? Anthony didn't ask, and Ron didn't comment. The sex was not special, following the same pattern of the past four years. Afterward they dressed and sat in the kitchen eating Oreo cookies with glasses of water. Ron nearly always kept Oreos in the house but never graced his dented refrigerator with the requisite carton of milk to complete the snack.

As Ron talked about his packing and the route he planned to take in his drive to California, he cursed the short supply of storage in his Camaro. "I might buy a conversion van when I get there," he mused. "Everyone who lives near the beach has one. They're good for partying. I can tell you the Camaro is not a good place to have sex; I thought I would break your sister's hip this summer!" Ron chuckled and looked sheepishly at Anthony. Trying not to react, Anthony concentrated on the task of twisting the two halves of the cookie apart. Was this Ron's final blow? While the engagement had clearly placed Judy at the center of Ron's life, it now appeared that Anthony was joined in the periphery by his own sister, another conquest of Ron's. "Don't say anything to her," Ron pleaded. "But she'd been after me for a long time, and I figured I owed it to her."

They finished the cookies in silence, after which Anthony said good-bye, explaining that he had to work on the night of the bon voyage party. He drove down to the lakefront, sitting near the art museum and watching the waves until dark. The relief he felt that this aspect of his life was coming to an end was matched only by the grief he felt at the loss. He spent the last few weeks of the summer alone, going to his part-time job but staying away from the bars, his friends, and Claire. He knew he was hurting her but also knew that he would not pursue a committed relationship with her.

Sixteen

Anthony began his freshman year at St. Norbert College on the shore of the Fox River in De Pere, Wisconsin, five miles from Green Bay. Claire stayed in Milwaukee, working full-time for a few months and planning to start at St. Norbert in the winter semester. Anthony's major was to be music education, and his first task was to audition for Sweet Harmony, the college madrigal group. He had been told how unusual it was for freshmen to make the cut but was nevertheless devastated when he received the news. After a week of mourning, he settled into a fifteen-credit-hour schedule that featured only three credits relating to music. Freshmen were historically assigned to two specific dormitory buildings on the north side of the campus near the river. However, an overly full new class resulted in Anthony's placement in the upperclassman Mary Minahan McCormick Hall, near the Shrine of St. Mary. He was assigned to a two-room suite with an adjoining bathroom. Four men shared the suite, laid out so that two occupants would share each room, with the group sharing the bathroom. This arrangement was thought to be an upgrade, since the freshman dorms featured a single, locker room–style bathroom on each floor. However, for Anthony, it meant he was once again on the fringe of acceptance—the only freshman among the sophomores and juniors at MMM. The five-story building was coed, with men on the first, third, and fifth floors and women sandwiched between them.

Only two days into the semester, Anthony's three room-mates proclaimed that they would stack the beds into two sets of bunks in the rear-facing room in order to create a party room in the front. In less than two hours, the feat was accom-plished, and that night, the first party was held. This began a semester of nearly continuous parties, and Anthony would have flunked out of school had it not been for his newfound relationship with a quiet, openly gay student down the hall. Frankie Bohne was a junior from New York and a member of Sweet Harmony. As luck or roommate preference would have it, Frankie did not share his half of the dorm suite with a roommate His two roommates, both straight, occupied the other half of the suite. Frankie and Anthony spent long hours, and often whole nights, studying, talking, and sleeping together.

In spite of the gender similarity, having sex with Frankie was nothing like the times with Ron. It was really much more like his limited experience with Claire. Frankie was romantic, kissing him tenderly and holding him when they lay together in bed. All of the sexual interactions with Ron had involved some oral sex followed by masturbation. Other than the very first encounter where Ron had ejaculated unexpectedly into Anthony's mouth, the subsequent sex had always ended with Ron masturbating Anthony and then demanding the same in return. But with Frankie, there were real elements of a relation-ship. A few weeks into the semester, Frankie asked Anthony to have intercourse with him. Producing a tube of K-Y Jelly from the drawer of his nightstand, Frankie kissed Anthony on the cheek and simply said, "Make love to me." The two spent the entire night together in the narrow dorm-room bed for the first time.

Anthony wasn't sure he was comfortable with a romantic sexual experience with a man. And he found himself afraid of the implication of feeling emotionally attached to Frankie—to anyone, really. But it was clear by October that Frankie was falling in love with Anthony.

Frankie's roommates were friendly and tolerant—both serious students who cared little about sexual preference, as long as it was expressed quietly. It was a stark contrast to Anthony's three roommates. As it became known that Frankie and Anthony were a couple, Anthony's roommates became politely distant.

This was Anthony's first experience of "being out," and he was shaken by it, feeling unprepared as he had not made any formal decision that he was actually gay. All evidence to the contrary, he still considered himself straight, although he couldn't exactly explain why. He continued to talk with Claire regularly and planned to see her every two or three weeks when he returned to Milwaukee. He never spoke of her at college—she didn't belong in this world. And he never spoke of Frankie at home. The conversations with Claire were still deep, and it was clear that she loved Anthony. He enjoyed spending time talking with her but felt uncomfortable—on the edge of being exposed. Just before Thanksgiving, on a weekend filled with snow flurries and biting winds, they sat parked at the lakefront in the rusted Plymouth. Anthony wondered when the lake would begin to freeze, creating the frozen centurions on the shore to watch over winter. "Penny for your thoughts," Claire said as she moved to the middle of the car and laid her head on Anthony's shoulder.

"I feel fractured," Anthony said after an atypically long pause. While someone else might have laughed at the statement, or would have begun asking questions, Claire sat quietly, awaiting more. "There is this huge chasm between here and school. There is a reality there and another one here.

And they don't match." Claire waited for more. "Going away to school was an opportunity to recreate myself, to escape all my shit here and be new. But the problem is that I went along with me to school. I'm setting up the same mess there that I've had here." He made that statement without thinking that she would probably want him to define "the same mess," and his anxiety rose as he waited for the question.

But Claire was the only person to ever come into Anthony's life who seemed to accept emotions over facts. She didn't need the details, because they were—well, just details. She was more interested in what was happening inside than how it was evidenced outside. "Anthony, can I help you?"

"No."

"Why?"

"Because some things just are. They're not contrived, they're not created, and they're not escapable. They just are. This is who I am. It's not who I've become. I've been who I am all along. I was reading about famous sculptors in my art appreciation class, and one of them—I don't remember which one—said that the beautiful statue is in the block of marble all along, that the sculptor doesn't create it so much as to chisel away all that is superfluous in order to release what was there from the beginning. I think that's what's happening with me— everything that's happened—my fucked-up mother, my sister dying, all the shit of high school, and now college. It's all just chipping away to reveal who I've always been. I'm not so much changing as recognizing who and what I am. And I'm broken. I'm ugly inside. Defective. Coming back to Milwaukee for weekends is like trying to put pieces of marble back on the block to obscure what's been uncovered. It's uncomfortable being here, because once the piece falls off the statue, it doesn't fit back on. The fracture between what's supposed to remain and what's been carved away can't be mended."

Claire sat quietly, a tear rolling down her cheek. "I don't completely understand, but I don't need to. You don't have to be alone, Anthony."

"I am alone," Anthony replied and started the car. They spent the rest of the afternoon together but remained quiet. Anthony dropped Claire off before eight and headed down to the Depot. He sat at the bar drinking Coke, considering how sad the bar and its patrons looked through sober eyes. He didn't know the Saturday-night crowd, talked to no one, and left before closing time, stopping at home to leave a note and going back to De Pere, arriving as the first light was appearing in the eastern sky.

Anthony knew that he loved Claire. However, it was clear that the relationship was failing. Claire often said that there was a part of Anthony that was unavailable—to her or to anyone. In December, she broke the news that she was leaving right after Christmas for Mt. Pleasant, Michigan. She had been accepted at Central Michigan University. Anthony felt anguish at the thought of losing Claire yet realized that she could not become a permanent part of his life. After all, he reminded himself, no one can really commit to anyone. The five-year-old philosophy, sunk deep into his psyche, was producing fruit. After hearing of Claire's planned departure for Michigan, Anthony did not contact her again. She never visited St. Norbert, never met Frankie, and never knew the man Anthony was becoming at college.

In the unusually snowy February of 1977, Ron and Judy had their wedding in Oshkosh. It was a small wedding party, with only two couples at the altar with Ron and Judy. Ron's cousin was his best man and a childhood friend his other grooms- man. The wedding was attended by 250 friends and family, and the choir of St. Veronica's made the trip upstate to sing. St. Mary's was a beautiful church, nearly one hundred years old. It featured a huge and historic pipe organ, the instrument on which Ron had learned to play. No longer in the choir, Anthony sat with his parents. His sister Lynn still sang with the choir, now the oldest member and well beyond the stated maximum age. Under the new director, the choir still sounded wonderful. Annie remarked that it was the most awe-inspiring wedding she had witnessed, that "everything that choir does just turns out perfectly!"

The reception was typical of a small-town blue-collar affair. Free beer, a polka band, and a buffet of chicken, ham, and spaghetti. Anthony, not a fan of beer and not financially successful enough to enjoy the optional cash bar, was fairly sober as the night wore on and the locals got drunk. His dad had bought him two gin and tonics, but these were spaced sufficiently to ensure that the buzz was only mild. Ron, fairly drunk, was leaning noticeably at the wedding party waltz. Anthony longed to drive back to school and find Frankie. He would probably be sitting at Rosco's, the lone gay bar in Green Bay, visiting with friends. Anthony had been invited to bring a guest to the wedding, but he had come alone. He was done with Claire and not ready to bring Frankie into his world. Heading to the bathroom, he met Ron heading in the same direction. Standing side by side at the two ice-filled urinals, Ron leaned over to look at Anthony's penis. "Remember the last time we met in the bathroom? You didn't finish me. You still owe me!" With that, he reached down and took hold of Anthony's flaccid organ. The danger and the wrongness of what could happen if they were caught on this day of all days took hold of Anthony. He grabbed Ron, who was almost finished urinating, and pushed him into the stall. Try as Ron might over the next several minutes, however, it was clear that his state of inebriation would overshadow his sexual response. Anthony took Ron's face in his hands and said, "I still owe you, and someday I'll pay." Anthony was shaking as he left the men's room. Locating Judy, he hugged her and wished her luck in California. He said good-bye to his parents and found his car in the gravel parking lot.

It was not that Anthony felt nothing driving back to the college. Rather, it was that he felt everything. Happiness that Ron would now be gone for good. Sadness at the same. Encouragement at the fact that if Ron could have sex with boys and then marry, perhaps Anthony could as well. Cheated to think that perhaps the relationship with Ron was not first love but was, instead, something else. Something uglier. Jealous that Judy, in the end, got to share life with Ron just when Anthony was old enough to make that commitment. Confused by the events of the night and what they meant for the growing relationship he shared with Frankie. Anger that Ron would, even on his own wedding night, want to break the rules so significantly. Exhilaration that Anthony had so intentionally broken those same rules with Ron.

Two days into the next week, Frankie and Anthony sat on barstools at Rosco's early in the evening when the bar was nearly empty. Frankie was horrified to hear that his boyfriend had been willing to have sex with a groom at his wedding. It was not that Frankie felt he had been cheated on; it was that he realized for the first time the complete lack of all moral boundaries in Anthony. "I don't understand you. How could you have sex with this Ron guy on his own wedding day? You knew the bride, right? I don't understand." Frankie held his glass of beer, rotating it as he edged the white foam to the rim of the glass and then stopping to watch it slide back down to the amber brew. The tavern was dark, although it was still bright outside. Most of the interior was lit by two neon beer signs hanging on either side of the bar. The dim green lights mounted under the inside lip of the bar gave the bartender a ghoulish glow as he stocked the well with liquor in anticipation of another busy night. There were only two other people in the building, one at the opposite end of the bar trying hard to eavesdrop and another in a booth immersed in his copy of *Jonathan Livingston Seagull.*

Frankie hadn't really looked Anthony in the eye since the weekend, even though they'd had sex on Sunday morning. "Whose idea was it? I know you said that Ron was really drunk, but what was your excuse for being part of it—for helping him cheat on a bride on her wedding day?" Frankie wasn't waiting for answers as he fired off questions with incredulity. "Didn't you have any respect for the commitment they'd just made, even if this asshole Ron didn't?"

"You don't understand," Anthony said with an air of finality.

"Help me, then," Frankie pleaded. He wasn't so much mad as dismayed.

"There is no such thing as real commitment. No one can say they really commit to anyone. Parents can only provide so much love because of their own shit. It's the same with lovers. The only key to survival is to become independent emotionally. Connection is what creates complications, pain. It doesn't matter if it's parents, friends, lovers, spouses, or even God—connection is pain. The universe can only make sense if there is no God, because then there's no one to blame. If God does exist, He's defective. We get so caught up in 'what's supposed to be' that we fuck everything up. Frankie, you need to grab happiness where it can be found. There is no happiness in the future; there's only what can be found today. People go about the day, saddled with wrongs and rights and definitions of what 'should be.' That kind of thinking doesn't ultimately bring any happiness or peace. There is no ultimate happiness, no peace to be gained. Sit back and grab the bits of it that are around you all the time."

As the words left Anthony's mouth, he could hear Ron's voice in his head. He felt proud to have so closely remembered what he'd learned and felt a new sense of power in watching the reaction in Frankie.

"Shit! Who the hell are you?" Frankie gasped. "You've had twelve years of Catholic schooling and then chose to come to a Catholic college, and you hate God? You've been fucking me for four months, and you tell me you don't believe in relationships or commitment? Jesus, Anthony, who are you, and how did I get mixed up with you?" Finally, he looked Anthony square in the eye. "Perhaps you can't tell, but I love you, Anthony!" Tears streamed down Frankie's cheeks.

"If you love me, then grab whatever happiness there is for us today, because I don't believe in tomorrow."

"Do you love me, Anthony? Do you care at all?"

"Love is a commitment to be wounded—if not today, then tomorrow. I enjoy what we have, and I'll enjoy it until it's over, and then I'll have great memories. If it never ends, if we spend our lives together, it will be nice. But it will be on these terms, Frankie. This is *who I am*."

Frankie's speech became broken, and he tried not to sob as he spoke. "I have more to offer than you'll take from me, and I need to demand more from you than you have the courage to give." Leaving his beer on the bar, Frankie slid off the stool and walked out of the bar. His shoulders were heaving as he stepped out into the late-afternoon light.

"You're one of those fucked-up assholes who's going to do just fine in life," spat the bartender as he cleared the beer glass from the empty place where Frankie had sat.

Frankie and Anthony barely spoke the rest of the semester, and just before final exams, Anthony heard that Frankie would return to New York to finish his final year of undergraduate work. On the last day of the semester, as the halls were loud with the dismantling of dorm rooms, Anthony stopped by Frankie's room and was met with the angry glare of Frankie's roommates. Frankie, holding a box of books, stood looking at Anthony, no words to say.

"Just because this was all I had to give doesn't indicate that you didn't mean anything to me, Frankie. For the rest of your life, how many other people will give you everything they have, however limited that may be?" With that, Anthony turned and left, feeling somewhat sick to his stomach yet reinforced in his resolve that he had held true to his values.

Seventeen

A nthony returned to college in the fall of 1977. Only one of his previous-year roommates returned. He found, to his surprise, that there would be only three men in his dorm room this year and that he was to have one of the suite's bedrooms to himself. He later figured out that when the registrar heard that a student was gay, no roommate was assigned. With a quieter living arrangement, he settled into the new semester, pulling good grades and limiting his partying to the weekends at the gay bar in Green Bay. He auditioned and was accepted into Sweet Harmony, taking Frankie's spot.

Anthony's second and third years at St Norbert's became steady and predictable. His grades were good. The rehearsals, performances, and travels associated with Sweet Harmony kept him grounded in a routine. This musical group was like the St. Veronica's Youth Choir in that musical excellence was important—that message was the same. But the method was so very different. No ranting, no swearing, and no drama. The group was well run by a senior professor in the music education department who had little interaction with the members outside of official group business. Sweet Harmony occupied Anthony's time, which allowed him to separate more from his family and his hometown. That was comfortable.

As he began his third year, Anthony declared himself a business major, deciding that music was a wonderful hobby that would no longer be fun if it were his job. He no longer went to Milwaukee for weekend visits. In November of 1978, after Annie's repeated calls and demands, he returned home for Thanksgiving. On the eighteenth, the news reported the story that 918 Americans had followed cult leader Jim Jones into mass suicide in Jonestown, Guyana. By Thanksgiving, the papers were filled with details about the theology and philosophy of the Peoples Temple Full Gospel Church and of Jones, who was influential enough to take nearly a thousand souls with him when he was ready to die. One of the reports on the television on Thanksgiving morning detailed how Jones used sex to control members of the group. According to the report, he had proclaimed everyone to be gay and had forced both men and women to have sex with him while proclaiming himself the only true heterosexual. Members were taught that the apocalypse was imminent and that only today mattered. Sexual plurality was encouraged, and commitment only to Jim Jones was required. "How could anyone follow such a horrible view of life?" Annie Conway said as she passed yams around the table that afternoon.

Anthony knew exactly how it could happen.

Finishing school in four and half years after switching majors, Anthony Conway graduated with a degree in management in December of 1980. By then, he had not heard from Ron in three years, although his mother still exchanged infrequent letters with Judy. When Ron and Judy returned to Wisconsin for annual visits, they spent most of their time in Oshkosh. They would usually plan a day or two in Milwaukee, always having dinner with the Conways. Anthony was not in attendance at any of these dinners, although he'd always been invited.

Taking a supervisor's job with a market research company in Chicago, Anthony moved to the Lakeview neighborhood just north of the Loop after graduation. He found an apartment on Surf Street, near Diversey and Clark, only eight blocks from the developing Boystown area of Halsted Street. A crime-filled area in the early 1970s, the neighborhood was being gentrified by the affluent gay community. The resultant rejuvenation was well under way when Anthony settled into a second-floor, two-bedroom apartment in an English Tudor–style apartment building. In thirty minutes, he could walk to the Magnificent Mile of Michigan Avenue; in ten he could be in Boystown. He spent weekends at Sidetracks, the new gay bar in the area that would become an anchor in Boystown in the decades to come.

Anthony had no trouble finding tricks at the bar, but no relationship lasted more than three months. All ended with the same speech—"no one can really commit to anything; there's only today." Keith and Annie asked Anthony if he was gay, telling him that they loved him either way. He denied the possibility and began dating women again, taking them to Milwaukee for an occasional dinner with his parents. However, he had not had sex with any woman but Claire. Lynn married and settled in the Milwaukee suburbs, producing the first grandchildren. Alan lived with a series of women after moving to Cincinnati to work for Procter & Gamble. He married at thirty, to the first woman he found who didn't want to have children.

Whenever Anthony returned home for the holidays, the family would talk of the glory years of the choir. Thanksgiving was his favorite holiday. There were no presents and hence no pressure to provide them and no disappointment in receiving something that was less than perfect. Thanksgiving was about today—no legend of a savior to honor and no church service to attend. It was about the important people in his life and about food. He hated Christmas and Easter, although he continued to come home for the family traditions. At each holiday, there would be stories told of the choir—never new ones but only the favorite ones that could be told endlessly. His brother always told of the hysterical time the hamsters got loose from the classroom of the school where the choir was staying during one of the trips. Although he never admitted it, clearly he had released the rodents. His mother and sister laughed, describing over and over again the sight of fifty young women trying to tease and curl their hair in an old church bathroom and the time Ron had them try to sing a difficult piece a cappella in a religious grotto on a tour and how the tenors got so far off-key the entire piece collapsed. His family laughed about the parties, the rehearsals, the trips, and the teens sleeping on the floor of the Conway living room nearly every weekend. Eventually the topic would turn serious, and Annie would talk about the profound positive impact that Ron and the choir had on her children, how it kept them connected to their church and their faith and gave them love for music and for one another. Anthony always remained silent, watching his siblings and parents nod in agreement. Annie's continued devotion to Ron served to reiterate to Anthony that he was left unprotected during his most formative years. He recognized that, even ten years later, his mother was blind to anything that might have happened, never considering the possibility that Anthony might have required any protection from anything. This realization was a fork in the road on Anthony's continued development as an adult. One of two things was true—either the relationship with Ron was good and had good results or his parents had abandoned him to a monster in order to feed their own interests. The latter being far too much to consider, Anthony continued to develop his own value system based on what he'd learned from the good teacher.

Two years after moving to Chicago, Anthony heard that Claire had graduated from Central Michigan and entered the Peace Corps. She was living somewhere in Africa, making a difference. It hurt Anthony to think of Claire. Although he had short relationships with a dozen men and had platonically dated a couple of women since high school, nothing approached the connection he had had with Claire. He wondered what she was doing in Africa. He wondered if she had replaced him. Later that year, Anthony was home for Easter weekend and ran into John, the boy from the high school concert choir with whom he'd had his first age-appropriate sex. John had graduated from the University of Wisconsin with a prelaw undergrad and was now finishing his JD at Marquette. He cheerfully introduced Anthony to Rich, his partner of two years, and talked about his family's adjustment to having a gay son and brother. John asked if Anthony was "out to his family" yet, and Anthony felt embarrassed to say no. John placed a hand on Anthony's shoulder. "All in good time, all in good time, my friend. I wish you the best. You were important in my development, and I hope your life goes well." Anthony could not look into John's eyes but felt their pity as he and Rich turned to walk away.

It was the summer of 1984, when Anthony was in Milwaukee, that his mother told him that she'd heard from Claire. Returning from a Peace Corps project in Ethiopia, Claire had come home to spend some time with her mother, who was dying at an early age of adult-onset leukemia. Claire had called Annie to ask what Anthony was doing with his life. She hadn't left a number, and Annie had enjoyed the conversation too much to realize when she hung up that she hadn't asked for it. It took two days for Anthony to dial the old number he had for Claire's house. He had waited until he returned home to Chicago, wanting there to be a safe distance between him and Claire when they were reconnected. The automated message told him that the number was no longer in service. A week later, he went to the public library, where he found phone books for the major American cities. In less than five minutes, he had a new number for Claire's parents, but he waited three weeks before using it.

Her mother sounded frail when she answered the phone. Her mind sharp, she instantly recognized Anthony's voice. "How nice to hear from you. Yes, I have been feeling a little under the weather lately. I understand that you're working in Chicago. Do you like city living? Do you ride that loud train system? I couldn't be comfortable sitting on a train that's riding fifty feet in the air!" The old, happy, friendly Mrs. Williams was there, underneath the pain of a death anticipated if not imminent. "Yes, Claire was here for nearly a month—it was so nice to have her home. I'm so sorry that you missed her. She left just yesterday for Ethiopia for another six-month project. She had the opportunity for a much better assignment this time, but it required a one-year commitment, and she didn't want me to have to hold out for a whole year to see her again. The doctors told me that would be unwise. I can give you her address. Let me see—I have it right here. Oh yes, here it is." There was some shuffling of the phone, and then she was back, reciting the address for the Peace Corps national office and relaying the codes required to get a letter from there to a field manager in Ethiopia. Anthony quickly jotted down the address, realizing the immeasurable distance that had been built between him and Claire. "Write to her soon. It takes a month or so to get a letter there. If you'll give me your number, I will give it to her when she comes home at Christmastime." They talked a few more minutes, and then Anthony hung up. The conflict in him was heavy. Claire was the one person who understood that everything about Anthony and his life was bullshit but who was interested in the real him anyhow. Now she was in Africa, and there was no one in this hemisphere who knew him. He never wrote to her.

When December came, Anthony stopped answering his phone, allowing calls to find their way to the answering machine. Claire called twice. She sounded wonderful and optimistic the first time and more pensive and sad the second. "My mother has a month at most, Anthony. I need to be present for her—focused on the moment and here when she needs me. I can't pursue you right now, but I'll be happy to hear from you. After she is gone, I will move to San Diego. A friend I met through the Peace Corps has a marketing position for me with her consulting firm. She's holding it until I am...well, finished here. I was hoping that finishing things in Wisconsin would include some time with you, but I understand if that isn't going to work for you. I love you—always will. But I think it was you who told me to live for today, to find happiness where it can be found now and not await a future that may never come. So I am not waiting for you. Good-bye."

Anthony never returned the call but heard that Mrs. Williams died just one week later.

Eighteen

On his twenty-eighth birthday, sitting at the smoky U-shaped bar at Sidetracks in Boystown, Anthony decided that his life was stalled. It was early, and the bar crowd was sparse. Five or six friends were due at nine o'clock to celebrate the birthday boy, but Anthony had arrived at seven thirty to get a head start. On his third gin and tonic in thirty minutes, Anthony was reviewing his life and concluding that it was no different now than ten years earlier. He was popular and outwardly successful but felt entirely fraudulent. A cubic zirconium—not to be too carefully inspected. Regardless of what had happened—his promotion to divisional manager at the firm, his ability to get a date anytime he wanted, and the ownership of his apartment, which had gone condo a year earlier—he was always only a breath away from thinking to himself, "If only they knew."

Across the bar, two friends greeted each other with a hearty hug, the overhead pin lights illuminating their genuine joy in seeing each other. Anthony set about eavesdropping on the reunion. It was apparent that they had not been together in some time and that perhaps one or both men lived out of town. After a few minutes of pleasant catch-up, the topic turned serious. The taller man, a decent-looking blond in his early thirties, told of the progress he had made with his therapist in the past year. "It's funny," he said. "None of the facts of my life have changed. Just how I look at them. It's not a matter of what is right or wrong, what is good or bad. It's just a matter of what's productive for me. I need to have a life that's productive, that *works for* me. I've learned that I am not my experiences. My experiences are just things that I've had. I don't have to 'be a certain way' because of what's happened to me. I don't have to categorize my past as good or bad. I just have to look at how to use the information to make a better today—to make things productive for me." Anthony was intrigued. You are not your experiences; your experiences are something you've had. He wondered. A few minutes later, a third man joined the two—apparently the boyfriend of the shorter guy. The three discussed dinner, paid the bar tab, and left.

Anthony's friends arrived on cue, and the birthday party began, running until closing time at three in the morning. Glad to have scheduled the following morning as a vacation day, Anthony slept in. It was one of the few times he had gotten drunk at the bar and awoken alone. It felt good to have a hangover in private. By noon, he was up, with only a slight headache, standing motionless in the shower until the hot-water tank was empty. He thought about the conversation he'd witnessed the night before and about the therapist's office he passed walking home from work on nice days when he skipped the train. "Milford—something Milford," he thought. With a towel around him and hair still wet, he grabbed the phone book and found it in short order. Dawn Milford, PhD, *located across from the Lincoln Park Zoo at Clark and Fullerton*, according to the short ad in the book.

Although his usual practice was to sit on cathartic phone numbers and messages until it was too late to make the calls, he reminded himself that "he was not his experiences" and dialed Dr. Milford. He got the answering machine, which made sense. A psychologist—*a good one*—would be in session, not sitting by the phone. Dawn was in private practice and therefore had no office personnel to answer the phone. She returned his call near the end of her workday, sounding pleasant and comfortable. "Of course she's comfortable," Anthony thought as he briefly explained in the most general of terms that he was feeling stalled in his life and wanted to "get some tips" on setting a new direction. Dawn made an initial appointment for late the next week, explaining that he should spend an hour with her, feeling no obligation to continue if he didn't sense a connection or think she could be helpful. In addition, she would place a long questionnaire in the mail that day, and he was to complete it and bring it to the session. She made it clear that she did not take insurance, and Anthony assured her that this was not a problem. Privately he had already decided that he would take no chance of producing an insurance record of this treatment for the human resources staff at work to see.

The questionnaire arrived two days later—to say it was long was an understatement. It took nearly two hours to complete. Anthony felt exhausted, having entered historical information about his parents, grandparents, and siblings on the form in addition to providing pages and pages about himself—childhood, schooling, sleep habits, drug history, medical record, and his feelings about everything from relationships to hobbies. Paperwork in hand, he met with Dawn a week later at her office.

She listened patiently for nearly the entire session to Anthony's history—as he presented it. His childhood, high school, college, and career. He was not dishonest in anything he said, but he clearly shaped his statements carefully, which she probably knew. He touched on his relationship difficulties, briefly describing himself as bisexual but more interested in men these days than women. She took no notes, and it comforted him to think that there was no transcript being produced. Asked if he had ever been in a relationship or had sex with a woman, he answered honestly—yes, but not since high school. She seemed to sense Anthony's discomfort with discussing his sexual past. Although he continually indicated his desire to analyze his current relationship difficulties, she stated plainly that she needed to understand his past. At the end of the session, he made an appointment for the next week, intending fully to cancel once he escaped the office.

He didn't cancel. He felt fearful yet strangely drawn to the danger of exploring how his past shaped his present. Returning the following Thursday, he was surprised that Dawn was able to pick up exactly where they left off. "So, I want to understand your early sexual experiences and your feelings about your sexuality. I think that may help me provide insight into the relationship challenges you want to explore. We'll want to talk about your family and childhood as well." She was direct and kind, about forty, and wore a wedding ring. She dressed professionally—a little prudishly. On both his visits, Dawn wore a starched white blouse buttoned all the way to the neck, with a long skirt and knit cardigan. He would learn in the months to come that the white blouse was as reliable as the session time—only the skirt and sweater colors changed. At this second meeting, her skirt was navy, and the sweater was sky blue. It was as if she were truly no fun or wanted to make it clear that she would be interested in no fun with her clients. She had short red hair that was probably not natural, dark eyes, and exceptionally red cheeks.

On his second visit, Anthony was able to better take in his surroundings. The office was on the top floor of a nondescript three-story office building full of dentists, accountants, and a few psychotherapists. Anthony was bemused, wondering in which office he would find the most pain. Dawn's space was quite nice, considering the vanilla nature of the outside of the building. Dark cherry wainscoting ringed the office, accented by a deep-green Oriental rug on the floor. Her desk in the corner faced the wall, the room dominated by a love seat and two wing-backed chairs plus a leather armchair on wheels that served as the desk chair. Dawn sat in this leather chair for the sessions. Anthony claimed one of the wing-backed chairs, where he could see a painting on the opposing wall that was interesting. It was an abstract in deep greens, burgundy, and muted gold, and it reminded Anthony of the abstract stained-glass windows he had seen in the cathedral in downtown Chicago. Although he had not attended mass there since he moved to the city, he remembered that church in particular because it contained the men's room where Anthony's mother nearly caught him and Ron having sex. If the abstract design and colors were supposed to evoke feelings from the patient, it was a success.

"Why do you think that you are bisexual rather than homo- or heterosexual?" Dawn pulled no punches, yet there was no accusation in the question—just the request for information. Turning uncomfortably in his chair, Anthony answered, "Well, I am open to sex with both men and women. I don't see that changing."

"Have you had opportunities to have sex with men in the past five years?"

"Yes."

"How often have you turned down an offer to have sex with a man you were attracted to?"

Anthony paused, staring at the painting.

"There's no accusation here—you'll find no judgment from me, regardless of your answer."

"Probably never." Anthony chuckled.

"What about with women? Have you had the opportunity to have a sexual relationship with a woman you've found attractive in the past five years?"

"I don't really meet many women outside of work, and I don't get involved at work."

"Not my question" came a quick reply. She was not about to let him off the hook. Anthony had always understood that psychologists listened to whatever you said and then asked how you felt about it. He admired this therapist's fearlessness. Two women came to mind. One was a very attractive blonde who lived in his building; another was the sister of a friend. The blonde made it clear she was interested in Anthony, and the sister had said point-blank that she had a fantasy about converting a gay man.

"Yes, I've had a couple of opportunities I can think of."

"Why no sex with women, then?"

Anthony laughed nervously. "Aren't you just supposed to be asking me how I feel about that?"

Dawn laughed in return. "We'll get to that."

Anthony had to tell her honestly that he didn't know why he had not acted on any opportunity for a heterosexual roll in the hay and then nervously mused aloud that perhaps he wasn't bisexual after all. He felt caught in a lie he hadn't told.

"Are you saying that you think that you might not be bisexual because you haven't had sex with women?"

"I guess so—I never really thought about that."

"Is it sexual contact that determines sexual orientation? Anthony—did you feel like you had sexual orientation when you were young, before you ever had sex?"

"I don't know what you mean," Anthony stalled.

Dawn clarified, "A child, even before understanding sex, has sexual feelings. When you were a child, do you remember your interactions with playmates, with adults—do you remember any sexual feelings?"

"I remember feeling different. I know that I was afraid I was gay when I was little—maybe ten years old. I remember a few times wishing I was a girl so a boy in my class would like me."

"So perhaps you felt attracted to boys even before you understood what sex was?"

"Yes."

"What about masturbation? Did you masturbate as a young man? Was your first sexual release from masturbation?" Dawn seemed completely comfortable with the topic, although Anthony was sure she could see him squirm in the chair.

"Yes. I was about twelve or maybe thirteen the first time I tried masturbation," Anthony answered, feeling immediately stupid for the way he stated it—like he had taken self-gratification for a test-drive to try it out.

Dawn didn't really react to the exchange of personal information. "And do you remember what you thought about when you first started masturbating?" she asked.

"Um, I don't really remember," Anthony replied. In reality, off the top of his head, he didn't really remember his thoughts that first amazing day when he experienced orgasm.

Dawn continued, "And when did you first feel attracted to girls?"

"High school. I was jealous of the boys with girlfriends. I wanted to be like them. I wanted to have a girlfriend, like everyone else did." All at once Anthony stood. "This is a mistake. I'm sorry. I don't want to do this. You say you're not judging me, but you are. You're making me tell you that I'm gay, and I'm not."

Dawn remained calm and seated. "Indeed, perhaps this is a mistake, Anthony. You get to decide that. I'm sorry if we've gone in a direction that you don't want to go. We can end if you like. But I am not trying to make you anything. I want to understand you so I can be helpful to you. Whether my style or goals fit you is your decision to make. I won't be offended if this isn't what you want."

Anthony sat. They were quiet for a long time. Finally he spoke with composure. "I can't help you understand me, because I don't understand me."

"Fair enough," she replied. "All you need to decide between now and next Thursday is if you want to understand yourself better and, if so, whether you think I can help you. If your answer is no to either question, just let me know. But don't be disappointed in yourself. There is no failure here. It's okay to not be completely finished with yourself, and it's okay to feel that my style doesn't fit you."

"Fair enough," Anthony responded, and the session was over.

Nineteen

Anthony did return the next Thursday. Dawn was pleased to see him. "What would you like to talk about?" she asked as they settled into their chairs. Anthony had thought of nothing else but this question all week long. "I don't think I want to spend time discussing whether I like boys or girls—it doesn't matter. I have failed in all relationships. I'd like to focus on understanding that."

"Are you willing to talk about when you were young?" Dawn asked. Anthony nodded, and she paused, waiting to make sure.

They spent the session talking about family. Dawn had noted a deceased sibling on the questionnaire, and Anthony talked about Kathleen's illness and death. He was surprised that his most emotional moment in talking about that event came in describing how guilty he felt entering his name into the third-grade textbooks, thereby "passing" his sister. He had not previously shared that with anyone and hadn't considered the impact of the event on him until that day. They discussed his observation that life had simply continued after her death, in spite of the tears and emotions that told Anthony things could never be the same.

"What would you have expected your parents to do?" Dawn asked. Anthony hadn't really thought of that, and now in retrospect, it was clear that there was no other course for them but to continue. His father clearly needed to work; his mother naturally had to care for the remaining three children. "Is it possible that your parents were indeed permanently changed by the loss of this child yet found a way to go on?" she asked. "Could both be true?" Indeed they could. In the weeks after that session, Anthony began to understand that his parents had surely been devastated by their daughter's death and had gone on, not because it was easy but because it was necessary. This realization helped him and forged trust between Dawn and Anthony. This was a beginning, but it took months to build the trust necessary to begin talking about Ron.

One crisp fall day, Anthony sat down in his chair at Dawn's office and had no immediate response to the question "What would you like to talk about this week?" Seeing the opening, she asked, "May we talk about the choir?" Anthony had told her that he'd been in the choir and that Ron Wilcox had been a huge part of his teenage years. Allowing silence to convey his agreement, Dawn began with some easy questions—names and places mostly. Then she forged on. "When did Ron Wilcox come to St. Veronica's? How old were you? How old was he? What were the rehearsals like? Did you like the choir? What was your first impression of Ron? What kinds of things did the other choir members say about him? What did you like about the choir?" These questions were fairly comfortable, but it was clear that the two were dancing around something much bigger.

"You've said that Ron had a big impact on your teenage years. Don't tell me what the impact was. Don't tell me what he did to have impact. Tell me *why* he had impact."

Anthony thought for nearly thirty seconds. "He was powerful."

"Powerful over you or over many people?"

"Over everyone."

Dawn probed further. "What was the source of his power?"

Anthony thought more. "Rules didn't apply to him. He broke all the rules and was continually exalted. It didn't matter what he did—whether he changed music, swore in church, gave kids beer, or told people God was an asshole—he got away with it. People couldn't hurt him, couldn't affect him. I wanted to be like that."

Dawn asked one more question. "How close did the two of you become?"

This was it. Anthony took a deep breath, but Dawn's countenance didn't change. If she knew something big was coming, she played it well. "He was my first lover. We slept together for years—basically from when he came to Milwaukee to when he left." Anthony paused, and Dawn waited, in no hurry to move on. "I've never said that to anyone before. I don't want to talk about it today."

Sensing the magnitude of the words just spoken, Dawn shifted the discussion back to the choir, and they talked about Anthony's feeling that his mother got too involved, that she paid more attention to other kids than to her own children, and that Ron built one of the finest youth choirs anyone had heard. It was two weeks before Dawn probed further on the topic of Ron the lover.

It was the day of the first snowfall of the season—Thursday, November 13, 1986—when the truth of Ron began to unfold. Anthony sensed it coming and foolishly felt prepared. They talked about the age difference between Ron and Anthony, particularly when they first had sex. Anthony talked about riding in the new Camaro, the playful lead-in, and the act itself. When asked, he was unsure about whose idea it was to have sex, admitting that he had thought about it before it happened. He shared the comments Ron made after the act—that he knew Anthony wanted this and was doing it for him. That he thought

Anthony was special. She asked if he thought the experience was good for him. He was sure that it was. She listened patiently as he repeated *the speech* for her: "There is no future pleasure to wait for—you must enjoy pleasure whenever it is available without demanding definition or moral judgment."

"What positive impact did Ron have on your life?" Dawn asked.

Thinking of a favorite quotation from a book by Japanese author Kōbō Abe, Anthony replied, "'I could not forever take shelter from the rain under another's eaves.' Ron taught me that you must be independent, that you cannot believe that there is a permanence to love or relationships that will cover for something missing in your own life—you must provide for yourself, because the only thing reliable in your life is you. I've watched all my friends and family suffer because they expect from the people around them things that those people can't give. I don't do that. I enjoy what there is today and don't expect any future from anyone. I learned that from Ron."

This statement led to a discussion of how that philosophy might have impacted the relationships Anthony had attempted. "Did you trust Ron?" Dawn asked.

"Ron made his intentions and plans known, and he did what he said. Yes, I could trust him."

"So you *could* trust him. But *did* you trust him?" Silence. Dawn waited.

"I don't know," Anthony answered.

"If I'd just met Ron, would you tell me that I should trust him, say, with a valuable possession?"

"Ron never stole, so yes, I would say he could be trusted with your valuable possession."

"Would you recommend that someone trust Ron with his or her son or daughter?" Silence again. Longer this time. Dawn was patient.

"I don't know. I think it would depend on the kid—Ron was an intense personality, and I don't think every kid could deal with him."

"But special kids could?"

"I guess."

"And you were special?"

"He said I was."

"And were you? What was special about you? What was there before you met him that Ron saw that was special? What made you special to Ron?"

"I don't know."

"Well, let's just say, for argument's sake, that you were an average kid—that you had good points and bad points, hopes and fears, but that you were essentially typical of kids your age. Why did Ron choose you as a lover? Why didn't he choose your brother or the kid next door?"

"I think we chose each other. You're making this out to be a one-way street, and it wasn't. No one forced me to sleep with Ron. He didn't threaten me or hold a gun to my head or even demand anything from me. We found each other."

"Next week I want to talk about why you found Ron. If you have time this week, think about that topic."

Anthony thought about almost nothing else for the next week. He arrived at Dawn's office the next Thursday armed with evidence of the mutual nature of the relationship. "I was questioning my sexuality by the time I was in sixth grade," Anthony began as soon as he sat in his chair and focused on the abstract colors on the wall. "I was attracted to his power, his ability to excel even when the rules said he couldn't. I loved the way he could make the sum of the choir so much greater than the parts of the choir. He's a musical genius. He also listened to me, and he thought things through. He helped me understand my parents, and he challenged all those around him to improve themselves, whether it was singing or under-standing faith. He was and still is the most powerful man I've met. It was easy to pursue his attention and friendship, and I felt lucky to get it."

Dawn sat back and smiled. "Well, you are certainly ahead of the curve when it comes to taking my homework assignments seriously. Now, answer some questions for me. First you said he listened to you. Early on in the relationship, what kind of things did you share with him—what did he listen to?"

Anthony thought for a minute. "Mostly I talked with him about my mother."

"Did you mention to him that you resented your mother's involvement in the choir?"

"No."

"Did you talk about your feeling that she paid more atten-tion to other teens than to her own?"

"No."

"So, what did you share with him, and how did he help you?"

Anthony thought. "Mostly I told him that she was a bitch."

Anthony and Dawn both chuckled. "We probably all needed someone we could say that to as teenagers!" Dawn quipped. "But think about it carefully. Was there anything seri-ous that you took to Ron? Did you ever talk with him about your sexual-orientation questions, or about events at the high school, or about where you would go to college?"

"I don't think I did," Anthony admitted after some thinking.

"Did Ron share things with you?"

"He talked about choir music, his classes at the conserva-tory, his new car—things like that," Anthony said triumphantly.

"Did he ask your advice or simply inform you about these things? Were you involved in picking his classes or choosing the color of his car?"

Anthony had to admit that he was not.

"And how did he help you improve upon yourself?"

Anthony recounted the "philosophy of life" speech.

"You've told me about how Ron challenged you to approach relationships without any expectation of commitment or permanence, how he helped you to prepare for the disappointments that may come when you trust your heart to another. I guess the question I have is this—how is that working for you? Is there a correlation between the philosophies you adopted through your relationship with Ron and the challenges you've said you've had with relationships as an adult?"

Wow. Anthony couldn't believe that Dawn was going to try to pin his current dissatisfaction in building relationships on the valuable and true lessons that he learned from Ron. "I don't see that as a major factor in my current situation," Anthony said coldly.

Dawn paused but maintained eye contact. "One last question. Do you believe that Ron's ideas about people and relationships came genuinely from his own heart—that he believed as much as you do those things that he discussed with you?"

"Absolutely."

"You said you went to his wedding, right?" Anthony nodded. "Is he still married?" Another nod, and Anthony felt suddenly nauseous. "Why do you think he married?" There was no answer. Marriage seemed to Anthony to be the most optimistic thing a person could do. It was an acknowledgment that permanence was possible and that a person believed he or she could have it. He'd always wondered how Ron could make such a statement, such a commitment. It was such a betrayal of everything he stood for. Everything Anthony had come to stand for because of him. He could hear his life cracking open and felt a tear he was unaware of roll down his cheek.

"Anthony, tell me how you're feeling right now."

"Undone." Anthony stood and left without another word, fifteen minutes remaining in the session.

The next morning, Dawn called Anthony at home as he was packing his lunch for work. Answering her inquiry, he told her he was fine. She asked that he take the week off in terms of their work together—no homework assignment to consider.

Twenty

O ver the next two weeks, Dawn whittled away at the relationship between Anthony and Ron, providing breaks
in the heavy discussion by using some sessions to talk about
less stressful topics. It was exhausting work, and Anthony knew
where it was heading. Just after another Thanksgiving with his
family—another holiday that featured a happy discussion of
choir years—Anthony sat in Dawn's office. "I'd like to start this
session with the questions you told me I should always be asking when we first started working together. How does everything we've been doing make you feel?"

Anthony smiled. "Funny you should ask, because I was
thinking about that this week after another holiday dinner of
'choir talk' with the family."

Anthony recounted how he felt when his family talked
about the good times with the choir and then turned to how he
had been pondering the last time that he and Ron had sex at
the apartment, just before Ron left for San Francisco. He told
Dawn about the music Ron played and how he never would
know if the same music from their first experience had been
played by coincidence or not and about Ron telling him that
he had slept with his sister.

"When I left his house, I drove down to the lakefront and
sat there for hours, watching the waves. I was totally filled with

relief that he was leaving and totally filled with sadness that he was gone, all at the same time. I was angry at him and hurt. I wanted him to still be mine so that everything I believed would still be true. That's how I feel today. I think we're heading somewhere that I need to go, yet I am afraid that I won't like where I end up."

"I think that's a good analogy," Dawn stated matter-of-factly. "But just like the whole story wasn't over on the day Ron left for California, our work won't be done until the realizations that make you sad are put into perspective. I am not going anywhere, Anthony, and you're making tremendous progress."

Anthony started the conversation. "I know that you've thought all along that the relationship with Ron wasn't healthy. So, maybe it wasn't. But then, what was it? I have to believe he cared for me. I was special to him, and he was special to me."

"You say that you *have* to believe he cared for you, Anthony. But *do you actually* believe that he cared for you? What if he didn't really care the way you imagined. What would that mean?"

Anthony paused a very long time. He knew the answer, but the thought of verbalizing it was terrifying. Dawn waited but maintained eye contact, as if to say that she knew it was time. Anthony's eyes welled with tears. Still he remained silent. It was as if his twenty-eight years were passing like a fast-forwarded video in his mind. He felt hot and sick. This was too much. He didn't want to cry, but even as he told himself that, he realized it was too late. He was already slumping over, sobs coming uncontrollably. After an undetermined amount of time, Anthony sat up, dizzy and drained. Dawn was coming back into the office, and as she closed the door, he could see a young woman leaving. Anthony then realized that the session had expired, and Dawn had apparently rescheduled her next patient. "It's fine, Anthony. Today is an incredible day for you. Talk to me."

All at once, it gushed. Anthony's thoughts and statements were disjointed and blurted through sobs. "Why did this happen? Am I *that defective* that someone like Ron can just pick me out of a crowd and screw up my life? Why did Ron take away my youth? He lied to me. Did he ever really believe anything he told me, or was it all a ploy to have sex with me? Was he gay? Would I feel gay if it weren't for Ron? How could my parents just let this happen?"

The realization that Ron had been a manipulator at best, a child abuser at worst had always been in Anthony's mind. But now it was stated plainly. He cried for nearly half an hour more.

As he cried, Anthony realized that the pain he was feeling had been there all along. He wasn't special. He wasn't even ordinary. He was defective—vulnerable and easily manipulated. Even his first sexual experience was fraudulent. It wasn't about love. It wasn't even about attraction. It was about a sick man and a stupid kid. Hadn't he always known that? A cracked vase can never hold water—it might be pretty on the shelf or be useful for some lesser purpose, but it will always be inferior—unable to do what vases do. From the time he was young, Anthony knew he was cracked, that he could only ever reside on the shelf next to the more important, more useful vessels. Ron could never have made Anthony special or even conforming. He would only use the cracked vase for a lesser purpose.

"You knew all along," Anthony said when he finally took his sweaty head out of his hands.

"You're not alone, Anthony," Dawn stated gently. "There are a growing number of men coming forward with tales of abuse at the hands of church leaders. I don't know where it will lead—right now the church seems to be ignoring it or quietly dealing with anyone who raises public scrutiny. I've worked with a number of patients with your history, and there is life after this, Anthony."

"You know what the worst thing is?" Anthony began crying again. "It doesn't matter if I am gay or straight. I had two genuine loves—a woman and a man—fucked up by this. *By him.*"

"We'll talk more about that next week. Right now, I think I may be as drained as you, Anthony. Let's break for today."

In the weeks following the breakthrough, Anthony talked about Claire and about Frankie. He talked about the psychological and emotional connection he felt with Claire, how she listened and considered his viewpoints—some that seemed silly now—and how she always debated the issue, not the person. He knew that she truly loved him and told Dawn that she had contacted him just a year earlier. He admitted that he loved her as well. They also talked about Frankie and the feelings Anthony experienced when he was in a "gay relationship"—how comfortable it was, even when Anthony was uncomfortable with the label. Anthony talked about the acceptance he felt from Frankie's roommates, who weren't particularly interested in him as a gay man and who in the end disliked him for what he did, not who he was. Anthony wasn't sure if he had fallen in love with Frankie but felt that his history had prevented him from seeking what may have been a wonderful relationship.

Eventually the sessions returned to Ron and the course of action that might be taken. After some weeks of pondering, Anthony decided that he did not want to see or confront Ron and that he was not ready to tell his parents. He worked hard to see his mother as a person who did indeed have her own issues that perhaps impacted her raising of the children but who ultimately loved her children, even if imperfectly. Anthony struggled with the fact that in not confronting Ron he allowed Ron to perhaps continue his behavior. But he simply didn't feel strong enough. He did tell his sister, who listened, cried, and supported Anthony. She was clearly shocked that this had happened to her brother, but did not appear to be surprised that there was a sinister side to Ron. He swore her to secrecy, and she kept her word. She also added some perspective to all that was Ron with her own recollections and admitted sleeping with him, although she bore no ill effects. The two siblings now had a closeness born of shared secrets. But it was not enough to break through Anthony's walls.

A year and a half after beginning his therapy, as he approached his thirtieth birthday, Anthony decided to cut his visits to once a month—a maintenance schedule that recognized the hard work completed while honoring the need for continued support. Dawn told him that she was seeing new patients whom she suspected had suffered the same type of abuse as Anthony. She had talked to colleagues at a recent conference who said that it appeared sexual abuse by priests was somewhat rampant in the church in the sixties, seventies, and perhaps still. There had even been talk among the psychologists at the conference that support groups may form and lawsuits may eventually be launched. She promised to let Anthony know if such a support group formed in the Loop or Near North Side. Anthony could only ponder the irony of the situation. If abuse was widespread in the church and being perpetrated by priests, it figured that Anthony's damage had come at the hands of a lowly choir director. He could immediately picture sitting in a circle of "victims" and finding himself on the fringe of acceptance, since his abuse wasn't as "official" as others'. Old feelings of insufficiency would never leave Anthony.

As they entered the "maintenance stage" of therapy, Dawn asked Anthony if he'd consider contacting either Frankie or Claire or both. "What would I tell them—that I'm as screwed up as ever but now know why?" Anthony joked. "I still don't even know if I am gay or straight. Who would I tell them that I am?"

"Why don't you forget the labeling, move slowly, and see what happens?" Dawn challenged. Anthony resolved to do just that.

Twenty-One

Six months after the suggestion by Dawn that he do so, Anthony began looking for Frankie. It had been two years since he'd begun therapy. In an effort to feel healthy, he'd turned down some, though not all, meaningless sexual encounters. He had not pursued any women, although the offer from his friend's sister was still quite open. Anthony still felt stuck in the idea that straight people had real relationships and gay men could only have short-lived affairs. Frankie had seemed to be an anomaly in this regard, and Anthony needed to find him. It had been ten years since they had spoken; thus Anthony had no idea if New York would still be Frankie's place of residence. He began there, pulling the fattest of phone books from the reference shelf at the Chicago library, stirring dust that reminded him instantly of Ron's Forty-Seventh Street apartment. He cursed Ron aloud at the notion that dusty smells would forever haunt him. No Frankie Bohne. No Frank or Francis either. Over a period of two weeks, he pulled out and perused dozens of books, hitting the library after work twice each week. Armed with a pocket full of change, he was ready to make a call immediately upon finding the listing. His propensity to stall with phone calls and letters had been to his detriment in the past, and he wasn't about to take a chance this time. Finally he found a listing for Frank Bohne in Pittsburgh. He went immediately to the payphone, hands shaking as he dialed. Although it was only five thirty in Chicago, Pittsburgh would be an hour ahead, and he hoped to find Frankie at home. He gasped when the phone was answered by a child. Having to ask "Is your father there?" hadn't entered Anthony's mind before the call, but he recovered quickly enough to say the words.

A few moments later, the phone was picked up, and a voice said, "This is Frank."

The memorized speech rolled off Anthony's tongue. "Hello, my name is Anthony Conway, and I am wondering if you are the Frankie Bohne who attended St. Norbert College in Wisconsin in the late 1970s."

The response was friendly and immediate. "No, I'm sorry. I've never lived in Wisconsin." The two men chuckled at the chances that there would be two people in the United States with this rather unusual name, and this wrong Frankie wished Anthony luck in locating the right Frankie. It was only when he hung up the phone that Anthony realized just how much he was sweating. He went home exhausted.

Three more trips to the library proved futile, and now all of the phone books had been studied. Anthony remembered that Frankie had an older brother named Leonard. He recalled teasing Frankie more than once about two brothers with such uncommon names for the 1970s. Anthony and Frankie often ate dinner together at college. Acting motherly, Anthony would call down the corridor at McCormick Hall, "Frankie, Leonard, time for dinner!" Frankie was always good-natured about it and would whisper in bed at night, "Who's your big Frankie now?" Starting again with New York City, Anthony was surprised to hit pay dirt in the first book—Manhattan. There was a Leonard Bohne listed among the thirty or so Bohnes in the book. It was an early night for the library, and Anthony could see the staff beginning to close up. He jotted the number down and rushed home, pausing only to throw his jacket on the sofa before picking up the phone.

Anthony had actually talked to Leonard once from the college dorm. He was the supplier of the lyrics to a song that settled a bet between Anthony and Frankie. Anthony could no longer remember what song it was. He did recall that while Frankie preferred the slang version of his given name, he'd been told that Leonard bristled when called Len or, worse yet, Lenny. He also didn't like being called *Len-erd*. Rather, he pronounced it *Lee-o-nard*, as in Da Vinci without the final syllable. This characteristic caused Frankie to tease his family about who was actually the fussy queen.

Anthony dialed the phone and immediately recognized the voice that answered. "Frankie!"

"No."

"I'm sorry. Is this Leonard?" Anthony said, carefully pronouncing the name. He hadn't remembered that the two brothers sounded so much alike.

"Yes, this is Leonard. Who is this?"

Anthony launched into the prepared speech, inserting "your brother" at the appropriate places.

"Yes, my brother attended St. Norbert. Who is this again?" Anthony reintroduced himself, realizing that he had been racing through his greeting.

There was a pause before Leonard answered. "I remember you. You broke my brother's heart." This was said matter-of-factly, not accusingly.

"A long time ago, yes. I'm afraid I was a rather bad friend as well. I was wondering if you could put me in touch with your brother. I'd love to catch up on things with him and perhaps do a better job of being a friend this time."

"I am sure he would have liked that. I'm sorry to tell you that he passed away, about a year ago. He never forgot you,

Anthony, and had talked about trying to find you a time or two." He sounded hurt but finished flatly: "It's sad that you two waited so long."

Anthony was overwhelmed. His sadness at this turn of events was counterbalanced by an immediate rage. He couldn't help but feel that Ron had taken Frankie from him. Holding back tears, he told Leonard the things he had planned to tell Frankie—how important he was to Anthony's life, how kind and loving he was, how much he taught Anthony, how Frankie was a whole person who just happened to be gay rather than simply a gay person, and how Anthony was only recently able to see what a great influence Leonard's brother had been in his life. "I appreciate you saying that. He was indeed a great brother, a joy for me right up to the end. After our mother died in eighty-four, we brothers were the only family we had—you may remember that our dad died when Frankie was really young."

Anthony felt suddenly guilty about the way he would mock Frankie's mother when calling for dinner back in the dorm hallway.

"We had so much fun until he got sick. He had AIDS. They just don't know what to do with it, and it was a horrible last year for my brother. But he smiled, right up to the last few days. He pined for you, Anthony. For years, he said there would be no other. He dated some, which obviously is how he got sick. But he never had another true love, in my opinion."

The weight of the words hit Anthony hard in the gut. He struggled to recover, giving Leonard a brief overview of his life—his career and living in Chicago—things that Leonard probably wasn't interested in. But Anthony didn't know what else to say. Finally Leonard interrupted, "Would you like me to send you a picture of Frankie? I have a really nice one of him and me walking down Fifth Avenue after the Easter parade the year before he got really sick. I had about twenty made and sent them to his close friends. I'm sure he'd want you to have one." Anthony had no pictures of Frankie. Thanking him profusely, he rattled off his address, and the call ended.

Anthony cried, softly at first, then with great sobs. The opportunity to know him again, perhaps more honestly, was gone. Lost forever. The chance to repair the damage that Ron had done in someone else's life through Anthony—gone. Anthony lay awake all night, smiling at good memories and crying about the loss. He called in sick the next morning, got his car out, and drove to Milwaukee. He told no one he was there and had only two destinations. He stopped first at St. Veronica's, a stern security guard nodding in his direction as he climbed the limestone steps to the church building. Apparently, while God was still available, he now had protection.

Anthony sat in what he was sure was the same pew, half expecting to see his elderly soul mate in the pew across the way. Surely she was gone now, hopefully to the reward she worked so hard to earn. It had been more than ten years since he'd been there for anything other than a holiday Mass with his parents. The glass saints watched, unchanged, unchangeable. In fact, nothing seemed different. The play of the light through the colored glass, the slight scent of Murphy Oil Soap on the pews and hot-wax smell of the candles. It was as timeless as the traditions of the Mass itself. He didn't pray, didn't even really consider the possibility. He simply wanted to know how it would feel to go back.

Turning his eyes heavenward, he considered the saints. It was early afternoon and gray outside. The saints were illuminated, thought not brightly. On his left Thomas, Paul, Barnabas, Joshua, and Moses stood patiently and seemed unimpressed by his return. Turning to his right, Peter, James and John, Joseph, Elijah, and Abraham were likewise strangely uninterested. Anthony had always thought that the saints of these windows pondered him, as he did them. But he now recognized that their expressions of joy, pain, and anger were not expressions about him or even directed his way. The relationship had changed. These were no longer his saints, his advisors and judges. These were simply windows. Beautiful works of art. What Ron said was true: faith is the creation of the weak-minded, those who need something greater to believe in. "Believe in yourself, take control of yourself, and the spiritual comes into focus for what it is—myth." Ron's words rang in his head. These colorful saints were simply pretty glass.

Anthony was lost deep in thought when he was startled. The organ began to play. Someone was in the loft practicing. Turning in the pew, Veronica greeted him. His thinking of the saints as nothing more than pretty glass vanished when he saw her. With an organist in the loft, the staircase would be open, and Anthony wondered at the irony—after being held at a distance by Veronica during his last visits to the church years earlier, was this happenstance a peace offering by the saint? Standing, genuflecting out of habit, Anthony walked back into the foyer and approached the stairs, which were indeed open.

Reaching the loft, the young musician was frightened to see Anthony. He clearly understood that the security guard outside on the steps was of no help at the moment. "I apologize for scaring you," Anthony offered. "I grew up in this church and sang in the big youth choir in the seventies. I happened to be in town and thought I'd take a trip down memory lane. I know it seems odd, but do you mind if I just sit up here for a few minutes while you play?" The organist nodded cautiously, and Anthony took his seat to the far right of the loft. "My name is Anthony, and I was here when Ron Wilcox was the director."

The director responded, "I never knew a Mr. Wilcox, but I think there have been a number of directors here in the last fifteen years. I've only been here three months, and we don't have a youth choir. St. Veronica's is much smaller than it probably was when you were a kid. Most Catholics are in the suburbs now. We have an adult choir, but I guess I knew there was a youth choir in the past. I think there are some youth-choir record albums in a box in the music room."

"Well, if you ever have reason to listen to them, you'll find my solo in the third song on side B of one of them. I think I was seventeen when we made that album."

"Pleased to meet you, Anthony. I'm Bill Parnell." With that, Bill directed his attention to the music, and the organ began to play softly again. It was clear that the piece he was rehearsing was large, to be played with much more volume and gusto. Bill was obviously learning it now and saw no reason to blast his mistakes for the passersby to hear.

Closing his eyes, Anthony could almost feel the presence of the choir. He remembered that there were indeed good times in the loft—rehearsals when tough passages finally came to life and performances that filled the church with beauty. After a few minutes, Anthony turned in his seat and silently greeted Veronica. Her colors soft and dappled as ever, she remained sweet, her eyes lowered to view the image of her savior on the bloodied towel. This downward pose made it easy to feel her stare. He imagined that she was returning the greeting, but he wondered what she was really thinking about him. And about her place in history—he had always wondered about that. He silently asked her, "What do you think of me?" No answer came.

He thought again about her place in church lore. Veronica was apparently one of hundreds, perhaps thousands of ordinary citizens who lined the streets to see three condemned men dragged to their deaths on a hill outside the city. These onlookers were all nobodies. She became somebody simply because she stepped forward and wiped the face of the right prisoner. If she had wiped the face of one of the two thieves, she'd have remained anonymous. But she chose wisely, wiping clean the face of the one all the controversy was about. And she was rewarded with a lasting image of the savior's face on the towel and with the lasting tribute of the church he created. So here she was, the passerby saint who did nothing more important than live for the day. Something attracted her, and she stepped forward. Then she stepped back into the shadows, and the church that grew to world prominence remembered her. "Does your power to wipe clean remain?" Anthony asked silently. "Can you wash away the stain in me? If you do, will the imprint of my foul life ruin your towel?" People rejoiced in the imprint left by the bloodied savior on Veronica's towel. But if she were to wipe away his stain, what would he leave behind with her, and would anyone find it beautiful? After all, Jesus was thought of as the ultimate misunderstood innocent, while anyone who understood Anthony would think him anything but innocent. He stared carefully into her gaze, mesmerized. Was she simply a single-event saint, impotent to wipe the stain from anyone else? Was Veronica special in her ability to take the image of the Christ onto her towel, or was it the Christ who decided where to leave His image? Who was special on that terrible day? Anthony felt no solace in Veronica and wondered why. Was she lacking power, or was he lacking favor?

He turned and sat back in the seat. Bill eyed him cautiously from behind the organ console. Clearly Anthony didn't belong there. In fact, he wondered if he would ever return to this building again. There was nothing here for him—neither judgment nor forgiveness. Only pretty glass.

Standing, he thanked the organist and walked to his car. It was a chilly day, typical of late October. The brisk breeze at odds with the warm sun. Driving slowly, Anthony headed east, past Ron's house on Forty-Seventh and onto the freeway.

Following the same route as the night he first rode in Ron's new Camaro, he passed the baseball stadium and headed for the lakefront. He opened the window to hear the seagulls and the waves. It was much cooler on the shoreline, and Anthony turned the blower up on the heater. He drove into Lake Park and left the car in the lot, walking to the flowering crab apple tree under which he and Claire had first made love. The blooms had come and gone months ago, and the leaves that had not fallen looked tired. Claire had called this tree *their tree* in the months after that first night, and they had picnicked under it more than a dozen times. Anthony envied the tree, which had stood the test of time without flinching, while people and relationships had come and gone for him.

The brush on the bluff had grown tall, obscuring some of the view of the water far below. Anthony sat in what he was sure was the exact spot where he had held Claire. The chilled breeze told him there were tears on his cheeks, and he smiled at the realization that he could still have feelings about the place. He sat until the cold ground became uncomfortable, then walked slowly around the tree in a large circle, hands behind his back, looking like a Buddhist monk in contemplation. He concentrated on thinking about nothing. About just being there, his problems and doubts and guilt suspended. Aware of nothing but the now. "You are not your experiences. Your experiences are simply something you've had." These words by the guy across the bar had driven him to therapy, and his therapy had brought him to where he was. But he knew that no one could actually walk away from his or her experiences. "Perhaps you are not your experiences in totality," he pondered "But they absolutely shape who you are. You are, at least to some extent, your experiences."

He circled the tree perhaps fifty times in the next twenty minutes before he looked up and saw a father with his two bundled children assembling a kite about thirty feet away. "I'm sorry if we're disturbing you," the man called. "This just happens to be the one place I can always get the kite up for my kids." Anthony smiled, opened his mouth to speak, and realized that emotion would not allow for words. He waved kindly to the man, smiled at the two children, and walked a few more laps around the tree.

He returned to Chicago in the late afternoon and went to the library to begin looking for Claire. He knew that this could be a more futile effort, since marriage would have likely changed her name. If her name hadn't changed, then her childhood surname—Williams—might as well have been Smith or Jones. The San Diego book, which was where he started, had nearly five hundred Williamses. Luckily, *Claire* was a little less common. In fact, there were no Claire Williams entries in the San Diego book. The library lights were dimming, the time near the six o'clock closing hour. Anthony replaced the phone book and drove home, unsure of all he felt and didn't feel.

Three days later, an envelope arrived from Leonard Bohne. Anthony carefully placed it in the middle of the kitchen table and turned away, attending to boiling some pasta and cutting some vegetables. Only after he'd sat down with his dinner did he touch the envelope again. He turned it in his hand, looking for a clue of what was inside. He knew it was the picture, of course, but was hoping to see it a little at a time. Setting it aside again, he reviewed his electric bill, which had been in the mailbox as well. Although he'd never done it before, he studied the bill, noting the usage this month in relationship to one year ago. When he placed his dish in the sink, he had to admit to himself that nothing else would mean anything until he saw the picture he knew the manila envelope held.

Carefully slicing the flap away from the packet, he slid out a white sheet of notebook paper, folded neatly in half. He could feel the picture tucked inside. On the paper were written a few words. *Thank you for calling. My brother cared for you, and I am glad to know that you cared for him. Leonard.* Unfolding the paper, the picture looked up at him. It was a white-rimmed snapshot of the two brothers. Frankie, on the left, was slightly taller than Leonard, whom Anthony had never seen before. They stood on a plaza, with a bed of red and yellow tulips on Frankie's left and a large fountain—not yet filled for the summer—on Leonard's right. There were people around them in the distance, and parts of tall buildings filled out the snapshot. Frankie was smiling cheerfully, his brown hair tousled by the apparent breeze that Easter Sunday. He wore a blue blazer with a white shirt and tie—probably his Sunday-service attire—while Leonard was clad in a sport shirt and had no jacket. Leonard's arm was around Frankie in big-brother fashion. Flipping the picture over, he found written *Easter Sunday 1986, Fifth, near the Plaza Hotel.*

The last time Anthony had seen Frankie was on that final day of freshman year at St. Norbert's. He had been stern and wounded and had not spoken a single word to Anthony. Seeing this picture reinforced for Anthony that life had gone on—Frankie had found happy days in New York, even if what his brother had said about him pining for Anthony was true. Seeing that Frankie had enjoyed happy days after Anthony and then knowing that he had also died since their time together, Anthony could not process his feelings. Ron could be blamed for Anthony's inability to build the relationship with Frankie. Could Ron then be to blame, through Anthony, for Frankie's death? What if Frankie had stayed in Wisconsin? What if he had moved to Chicago with Anthony or if Anthony had been with Frankie in New York? It was easy to suppose that a lasting relationship with Anthony would have kept Frankie from AIDS. Kept him alive.

Anthony carefully placed the snapshot on the table and sat back, feeling profoundly ill and sad. This was *his* fault. Not only did Ron ruin Anthony, but Frankie was dead because of Anthony's inability to overcome Ron. He said aloud the first thing that came to him, a portion of the Catholic Litany of the Saints:

> Lamb of God, who takes away the sins of the world,
> spare us, O Lord.

> Lamb of God, who takes away the sins of the world,
> graciously hear us, O Lord.

> Lamb of God, who takes away the sins of the world,
> have mercy on us.

His chair tipping onto the floor, Anthony lunged for the kitchen sink in time to avoid vomiting on the floor. Sobbing as he wretched, he was sure his neighbors would hear him. The weight of the tragedy—the theft of Anthony's youth, the loss of Claire, and the loss and ultimate death of Frankie all bore down, his sense of well-being collapsing. He was unsure how long he hung onto the counter and heaved into sink. It was long after his stomach was empty. Finally he slumped to the floor and whimpered. It was after dark when he went for a walk through the neighborhood, repeatedly mumbling, "Who will wipe away my sin?" as he stumbled up and down curbs, too nicely dressed for a street person but otherwise exhibiting all the traits. When he returned home, he carefully placed the picture and note back into the envelope. He did not look at it again.

Things were different after that. The realization that much of his life was lost—wasted—caused his focus at work to wane. His appetite left, and he stopped calling his friends. He continued only his weekly calls to his mother, simply to avoid her calls to him. He was short and polite in his conversations with her, blaming a cantankerous new client at work for his distraction and lack of energy. Outwardly, the signs of significant dysfunction were unapparent. Had anyone close to Anthony seen him regularly during this period, it would have been obvious that a line had been transgressed that put him dangerously close to an abyss.

Over the next two weeks, Anthony was at the library six times. He started at one end of the first shelf, with Atlanta, and was working his way through the dozens of phone books. He'd found two Claire Williamses listings in fairly short order—Dallas and Denver. He connected with the Claire in each city, only to find that neither was the Claire he sought. It was many books later when he found a third listing—this one in San Francisco. He cursed himself for going alphabetically instead of geographically. Had he stayed in California, he would have found this listing much sooner. He went to the phone booth at the end of the hall and dialed.

A man answered the phone. "Hello?" Anthony began. He provided a brief description of his reason for calling—not wanting to alarm a husband as to why a strange man would he calling and asking for Claire. It seemed that this man would probably not be Claire's husband, however, since the listing was in her name. But he sounded too old to be a child. "My name is Anthony Conway, and I grew up with a Claire Williams in Milwaukee. I am hoping to reconnect with Claire and am wondering if Claire is available to talk with me." This explanation, he hoped, would satisfy the needs of the male answerer and get him connected with the potential love of his life.

"Claire doesn't live here" came the terse reply. Anthony began verifying that he had dialed the correct number but was interrupted. "This is the right number; she just doesn't live here anymore."

"Can you tell me if Claire once lived in Milwaukee?"

"Yes, I think she lived there before she went to college." Anthony's heart pounded. It flashed into his mind that she might not live there anymore because she, like Frankie, was dead.

"Can you tell me where I might reach her?" he said, trying to sound friendly and not as panicked as he actually felt.

"I don't know where she is. She moved out of town a couple of years ago. We lived together, and when she moved, I just kept the phone number."

Anthony thanked the man and hung up, with perhaps a dozen unanswered questions: "Who are you, and how did you know my Claire? Is she okay? How can you not know where she is? Did she ever mention me?"

Anthony sat back down in the reference section. Looking over at the shelves of white pages, he assessed that he was already about 80 percent through the section. Still, there were some books to go—Scranton, Seattle, Spokane, St. Louis, Stockton, Syracuse, Tampa, Toledo, Tucson, Tulsa, Washington, DC, and Wichita. Once through these, he'd have checked the largest metropolitan areas, which was the extent of the library's resources. Of course, there was no way to know if she lived in a metropolitan area or even in the United States. Perhaps she'd gone back to Africa, for that better Peace Corps assignment she passed up to be available to her mother years ago. Anthony was tired and walked home.

Two days later, he sat back down with the remaining phone books and found another listing for Claire Williams in the fourth book he checked—St. Louis. He went to the pay phone and dialed, getting an answering machine with the voice he remembered. Cheery, optimistic Claire warned him not to hang up, to leave a message because, the message said, "I want to talk to you." Anthony hung up without speaking. Looking at his watch, he realized that Claire might still be working. Jotting down the number, he went home and waited.

Twenty-Two

O ver the next three hours, Anthony played the anticipated phone conversation over and over in his head, as if it had already taken place. Hoping to take his mind off the call, he made a peanut butter sandwich, which he didn't eat. Everyone knew Anthony as one of those people who could eat a peanut butter sandwich anytime, any day. Not today.

At seven o'clock, his phone rang, and he panicked at the thought that he wasn't ready until he remembered that she couldn't possibly be calling him. He was laughing at himself as he picked up the receiver. It was Annie Conway, calling to express her concern for Anthony since she hadn't heard from him in more than a week. The reality was that Anthony had called his parents just three days earlier. This was a game played out about once each month. Anthony called his parents every week without fail. Yet Annie called him with some regularity to express her concern at the lack of contact. At first, this worried Anthony, and he had enlisted his sister to spend a day with their mother and assess her mental state. With the all clear delivered, Anthony then grew angry, recognizing this mock concern from his mother as a ruse to incite guilt in the son who had moved away, never married, and wouldn't spend the night in his childhood home when he came to visit. Finally, he had reached the stage of amusement, taking pleasure in ignoring the accusations and then counting how many times in the conversation they would be reintroduced.

"I was just thinking about you," Anthony lied. "I was at the library after work and was trying to remember the name of that book you said Dad liked." His father liked murder mysteries, which Anthony hated. But it was interesting to steer the conversation in a new direction in order to see how long it took for the guilt talk to reappear.

"Oh, you mean the Detective Ransom series? Yes, your dad's read every one of them. They're by Clark—Will Clark."

"That's right—I should have written that down. Next week I have to go to Detroit for a conference, and I want to take a book to read in the evenings. I leave on Saturday, and the conference starts Monday. My friend Josh lives there, and we're going to the Detroit Symphony on Sunday. But after that, I'll be alone at the conference, so I thought I'd take a book."

Annie rattled off the titles of a few of the books—Keith's favorites from the series. Anthony pretended to write them down. After a few more minutes of visiting, Annie wound down the conversation. "I just wanted to be sure you were okay—we hadn't heard from you in a while. A mother worries, you know." Yeah, right. "Will you be coming alone to Thanksgiving dinner?" The holiday was just two weeks away.

"I think so," replied Anthony.

"I worry about you—" started Annie.

"Mom, I need to let you go. I'm expecting a call from work—they're installing some new software on the system, and they'll be calling me any minute to let me know if I have to come in to test it."

"That's why you come home alone, Anthony. You work too much. Let them get someone else to work at seven at night."

With a few more biting comments, Annie was satisfied that the damage was done and hung up.

At precisely eight o'clock, Anthony dialed Claire's number. On the second ring, the cheerful voice of Claire answered. "Hello. Hello?"

Anthony paused and then gathered himself. "Hello, Claire. This is Anthony Conway." Now the pause was on Claire's end.

"Well, I'll be damned! Anthony Conway. How the heck are ya?" Her tone was playful and cheery. The same Claire.

"I'm good. How are you?"

"I can't believe you called me! I'm great. I was just eating some tomatoes and wheat germ. I worked late tonight."

Anthony pictured her. She still looked like a teenager in his mind but now in the kitchen of a little, cottagey place, bare feet on the chair, knees tucked up under her chin, eating fresh vegetables. Healthy, happy, young.

"You were hard to find," Anthony began. "I can tell you every city in America—well, up through the Ss—where a Claire Williams lives!"

"How many of me are there?"

"There's only one you, but there are three or four Claire Williamses!"

There was a pause. "My God, Anthony Conway. Where have you been, and why have you surfaced today?" The tone was friendly but suspicious. Perhaps with a hint of bitterness.

"I live in Chicago. I moved here right after graduation from Norbert's. I'm a divisional manager at a marketing company here. I live near the Loop and love it. My apartment went condo last year, and I bought it. I get back to Milwaukee a few times a year—my folks are still there. So are my sister and brother in-law and my two nephews. My brother is in Cincinnati with his wife. So I guess I've been in the same place since college. I understand you've moved around a lot."

Claire could sense the shifting of focus, although she had more questions. "Well, let's see. After I graduated from Central

Michigan, I did two Peace Corps tours, both in Ethiopia. I guess you knew that. Then I went to San Diego and worked in marketing for a consulting firm. I really enjoyed it there but moved to San Francisco to be with a guy I'd met who got transferred there. We lived together for a year—"

"I talked to him!" Anthony interjected. "I called your number in San Francisco and talked to a guy who said you didn't live there anymore, but the phone listing was still in your name."

Claire continued without comment. "Then I moved here for a really great job I got through a client I had in California. I'm doing fund-raising for nonprofit organizations. Right now, I'm raising money for a hospice in Creve Coeur."

Wheat germ. Charitable fund-raising. It was all *so Claire.* "Do you have a family?" Anthony ventured.

"I had Chester, my yellow lab. He was the best family I've ever had! But he died last year. And who do you come home to?"

"I come home alone. I was thinking about getting some houseplants, but the commitment seems too serious." Anthony laughed at his own pitiful joke.

"I'm not surprised," Claire said with a hint of pity. "So, how did you find me?" Anthony explained his library phone book search. Then Claire asked further, "And why now?"

"Well," Anthony began, "I guess I'm too young to be having a midlife crisis, but I've spent a lot of this year looking at my life. I tried to catch up with a good friend from Norbert's and found that he had died. That got me thinking that I should connect with other people who were important to me before I lose other opportunities."

"Opportunities for what?"

"I guess they're opportunities to tell people—to tell *you*—how important you were in my life. I need to tell you that I'm sorry. I know I hurt your feelings. I think it's logical for you to think that because I acted the way I did—cutting myself off from you—that I didn't care. But the reality is that you were really important in my life. I have never found anyone who I could talk to who would listen to me like you did. I wish that I had been able to listen to myself back then, but I appreciated how you listened so patiently to all my crap."

"What would you have heard if you had listened to yourself back then?" Claire was always one to dig deeper into a comment or opinion.

"I'm not sure. I haven't fully worked out all that was going on in my head back then. I just know that you were valuable to my life, and I didn't treat you that way."

"Thank you, Anthony. That means a lot to me. Have you worked out what's in your head now?"

"I'm getting there!" Anthony laughed.

"I'm glad for you, Anthony."

The topics turned lighter for a few minutes. Claire wanted to know about Annie and Keith Conway, about Alan and about Lynn and her children. They reminisced about high school—the musicals, the football games, their dates.

"I was in Milwaukee last year and went for a walk in Lake Park," Claire said. "Our tree is still there, and I sat under it for an hour and thought about our picnics."

"I was there last week! I was standing near the tree daydreaming, and a guy came with two kids to fly a kite, right where we used to. He said it was the best place to put a kite up."

"Anthony, do you fly kites anymore or picnic?"

"I haven't flown a kite since you and I did, although I helped my brother-in-law assemble one last summer for his kids. It got caught in the neighbor's TV antenna. My friends and I usually walk down to the lake here in Chicago for the fireworks on the Fourth of July, and we sort of picnic. No grills—more like sub sandwiches from the shop we walk by and martinis from a thermos! But I think it still qualifies as a picnic."

"I'm really glad you called." Anthony could feel the conversation ending and dreaded it. "I am curious to see if you'll call again. I have a yoga class in a few minutes, so I'm going to let you go. But call back if you'd like—I'd love to talk with you more."

They said their good-byes, and Anthony considered the conversation and its end. Years before, Claire had left a message on his answering machine saying that she wouldn't chase him but would be happy to hear from him. He hadn't followed through. Claire seemed to be giving him the same message now. Anthony wondered where to go with the challenge.

He didn't sleep well that night—the beginning of many sleepless nights. He would toss and turn, getting perhaps two or three good hours of sleep in a night. He'd be in bed by nine thirty, setting his alarm optimistically for seven. But he'd spend most of those hours fixated on Ron, about the damage and destruction that lay in the path of time behind him. As Anthony had become more and more despondent about his own life, he'd felt more and more heavily coated in guilt about doing nothing to stop whatever havoc Ron might be wreaking wherever he was now living. He couldn't escape the feeling that his weakness had left Ron unchecked. And he was convinced that he could not stand one more Conway family holiday dinner and its accompanying discussion of the good days of the choir. Ron had taken his family from him. He had taken Frankie. He had taken joy, and peace, and optimism.

But there was one hope—reclamation of Claire. Anthony followed through. He called Claire the very next evening, and she seemed genuinely pleased to hear from him. They talked for an hour. Mostly about the past ten years. Taking turns, each told the other mildly interesting facts about their lives.

No deep thoughts or emotions shared. Anthony said nothing about his sexuality or lack of definition where that was concerned. He simply indicated that he'd had no relationships since high school. But the conversations were the beginning of what he hoped was a road to redemption.

He was to leave the following day for the Detroit conference and opted to drive, which took about five hours. While on the road, he thought mostly about Claire and what this reunion could mean. Near Battle Creek, he hypothesized that he had the ability to enjoy sex with members of either gender and that he had favored men simply because he'd never had a connection with anyone that measured up to the psychological connection he had with Claire. Near Jackson, he was convinced this was the case and determined to pursue Claire in order to dispel the null—the notion that there was no correlation between the loss of Claire and his attraction to men. Heading past Ann Arbor and into the western suburbs of Detroit, he was feeling optimistic that his life was taking a positive turn and that the investment in therapy had been well made.

Following the directions he had scrawled on a half sheet of paper, he made his way to Farmington Hills, the Detroit suburb where his friend Josh lived with his partner, Rick. Josh had done some consulting work for Anthony's company some months back, and Anthony had shown him the Boystown area of Chicago in the evenings. They had exchanged personal information and talked by phone a few times since then. For Anthony, Josh had been a successful foray into a nonsexual relationship with someone he'd found attractive. When Josh heard that Anthony would be in Detroit, he offered to return the favor of showing him around. He had also offered to get tickets to the Detroit Symphony Orchestra's Sunday matinee performance the day after Anthony arrived.

It was nearly five on Saturday evening when he pulled in to Josh and Rick's driveway. It was a typical suburban subdivision with curved streets and no sidewalks. The din of the freeway less than a mile away dispelled the illusion of country living. It appeared to be a planned development, with no more than four distinct house plans. The varied use of brick colors, false dormers, and window styles were meant to provide individuality in a neighborhood designed to conform. It was a nice home: a white, pillared, two-story colonial with an attached three-car garage that dominated the view from the street. It was everything Anthony hated about suburban living. Somehow the gritty street noise of urban living was much more musical than the drone of the freeway system in the suburbs. He was sure that Kmart and Red Lobster were just around the corner. In the suburbs, cookie-cutter houses were always surrounded by cookie-cutter retailers.

Josh was happy to see Anthony, hugging him in the driveway. Rick was introduced, and it was announced that wine was chilling and dinner was in an hour. The three enjoyed the evening, and near nine o'clock, Anthony left for his hotel. Rick offered to make brunch before they left for the symphony the next morning, and Anthony felt obliged to accept. He wasn't a breakfast eater, but that was more a matter of time than menu. If served late enough, Anthony enjoyed the heavy breakfast foods—French toast, omelets full of meat and cheese, fried potatoes. They agreed on ten o'clock, a little early for Anthony. But it allowed plenty of time for brunch, some conversation, and the hour-long drive into Detroit for the symphony.

Having heard the famed Chicago Symphony Orchestra on many occasions, Anthony was a bit predisposed in his thinking that the afternoon would be a disappointment. However, Detroit's Orchestra Hall was gorgeous. Their seats were on the main floor, halfway between the stage and the balcony overhang. Being the Sunday matinee, the hall was as filled with retirees as the parking lot was jammed with Buicks. The best heeled occupied the private boxes, which ringed the hall between the main floor and balcony. The orchestra was superb, and guest violinist Itzhak Perlman was as spectacular as his reputation implied. Anthony had perused the program before the concert but didn't recognize any of the pieces to be presented.

After the intermission, the symphony began the fourth piece in the program—"Méditation" from *Thaïs* by Jules Massenet. It took less than four bars of the piece to ignite Anthony's memory—it was the piece Ron played on the night he took Anthony's virginity. Instantly everything came back—the ride in the new Camaro, the smell of oil heat and dust, the statue of Moses, and the loss of his innocence to Ron that cold night near the end of the Christmas break of 1972. Tears streamed down Anthony's cheeks, and he feared at one point that he would break down completely. "Will Ron never leave me? Who will wipe away this stain?" Anthony remembered that on that night he had noticed how large the moon looked rising low in the horizon over Lake Michigan. It wasn't until years later that he learned the trick of perspective that caused the huge apparent proportion the moon takes on when low in the horizon. The moon isn't any larger when low in the horizon; it simply appears larger because it has context—because other objects on the horizon give it perspective. Time marches on, and once it rises into the dark sky, the moon appears smaller simply because it is alone in the vast sky. "This thing with Ron is like the moon," thought Anthony. "It seemed huge back then—low in the horizon of my life. It's supposed to be smaller now—just a memory. But in reality it's never going to get smaller. It's all perspective. He'll never be gone; I'll never be through with this."

As the piece ended, Josh turned to Anthony and saw his tears. Josh seemed proud of his Detroit Symphony Orchestra—that it could evoke such a response in this seasoned Chicagoan. "Have you heard this piece before?" Josh asked during the applause.

"I've heard it twice but never live. I didn't know what it was called, so I didn't realize I would hear it today," Anthony replied.

"Must be one of your favorites?" Josh asked as he turned toward the stage to acknowledge the rise in applause as Perlman stepped forward. Anthony didn't answer.

Anthony stumbled through his conference the rest of the week in Detroit, wondering where Ron would appear next. Would the conference hall have the same dusty smell? Would there be a sculpture in the hotel lobby that reminded him of Moses? It would never end, Anthony concluded. The hall didn't smell dusty. There wasn't a sculpture in the hotel lobby. But it would never end.

Twenty-Three

After returning home from Detroit, Anthony talked with Claire every day for a week. She quickly became hope. Recovery. Sanity. She asked probing questions about Anthony's life, about his relationship with his family and his lack of meaningful relationships since adulthood. "You seem so bitter toward your family. You always have," Claire observed on the second evening's call.

It was so difficult to dodge Claire. When Anthony replied that he'd just "always been different from them," she asked how. He couldn't explain it. When he implied that he had dated a number of women but didn't find a good relationship, she asked for a description of the last woman he'd dated. "What did she look like? What did you most like about her? What would you have changed about her?" He fabricated a story about the woman in his building. The more he tried to construct answers, the more difficult the road became. He wanted to be transparent but feared what she'd see.

On the fourth night—the Tuesday before Thanksgiving— Claire asked about Frankie. "How did your college friend die?" she asked.

"His name was Frankie, and he had a blood disease—something like leukemia. But his brother didn't say too much, and I guess it doesn't really make much difference. I lost my chance to reconnect."

"Why did you guys fall out of touch after college?"

"We had a disagreement just before my third year." It had actually been at the end of his first year, but Anthony lied, wanting the friendship to seem longer than it had been. "Then he didn't return that fall. He was a year ahead of me, and he went back to New York to finish his last year."

"Because of you?"

"I'm sure that wasn't it—I think he missed home or got a scholarship or something."

"Anthony," Claire started. He knew he was in trouble. "You're not being honest with me. There's more to all of this—more to Frankie, more to college, and more to your life since college. There's more to the time you and I had together. I know you don't want to tell me. But you can. When you're ready. Until then, we shouldn't talk as much, because you're damaging our friendship. I'd rather miss the you I once knew than try to befriend a you that's fabricated." Claire would have gone on. She had more to say. She simply paused to take a breath.

"Ron molested me."

Anthony could not believe the words had escaped his soul. It was the last thing he intended to share. In that instant every-thing changed, but neither he nor Claire knew how it changed. Anthony had never spoken those words directly before, never even thought them aloud outside of therapy. Now he was in a limbo of anticipation, knowing nothing of what would come of his revelation. These moments happen so rarely in a per-son's lifetime. The doctor says, "It's cancer," and there's that moment between the news and the outcome. That moment when you don't know if it means six weeks until death or treat-ment with a high probability of success. It's that instant when you fall off your bicycle and don't yet know if you can laugh or cry because your brain hasn't assessed the damage. It's one of the few moments in life without emotion, because your mind hasn't yet processed enough information to dictate any. You're in limbo. Anthony was in that moment.

"I know" came Claire's reply.

"You *know*?" Anthony searched for the event from his past that could have made this statement true.

The word *how* was forming in his throat when Claire spoke again. Gently, calmly. "I guess I didn't know for sure until you just told me, but I was sure that something went on between you and Ron, and I was convinced that you were being abused—physically or mentally—maybe both. Talk to me about it, Anthony."

"I guess I was just a stupid kid—" Anthony began.

Claire interrupted. "There's no reason to qualify what happened. Nothing you tell me about it will change my feelings for you."

"It started when I was first in the choir. I was fourteen, I guess. He didn't hold a gun to my head or anything—it wasn't like that. I guess I said yes."

"You were too young to say yes, Anthony. It doesn't matter how it happened—only that you were too young for it to be good for you."

Claire always understood. Anthony wondered why she had never asked about Ron or what was going on.

"Was it still happening when you and I were dating?"

"Yes."

"I'm so sorry that this happened to you and that I wasn't there for you."

"You were there for me, Claire. *I* wasn't there for me. *My parents* weren't there for me. *The church* wasn't there for me. And you were just a kid, too." Anthony paused. "How did you know? You didn't go to St. Veronica's; you weren't in the choir. You hardly ever even met Ron."

"I came to a lot of your concerts, and I saw him a few times at your house. I always hated him, Anthony. I remember that you went alone to his wedding, as if you didn't want me or anyone else to know him. I always thought he was bad for you. But I didn't know exactly why. I suspected this, though."

"He took you from me, Claire. He fucked up my head. Still fucks up my head."

"And what about Frankie? Did Ron take away what you had with Frankie?"

"Frankie was a great guy, Claire. But he wasn't you." Anthony felt the need to protect himself from what little truth hadn't yet been shared. "I'm not gay, Claire."

There was a long silence. Because neither of them had anticipated the conversation going in the direction it did, each was unsure where to go next. After a moment, Claire spoke. "I still love you, Anthony. What happened to you doesn't change my thoughts about you. You don't ever have to worry that what you tell me will make me feel differently. I am here for you."

"You're not here. You're there. St. Louis. It might as well be Ethiopia."

Claire responded, changing focus, "Do you have off for Thanksgiving this weekend?"

"Yeah. I'm supposed to go to Milwaukee. My brother is coming in with his bitchy wife, and we'll all sit around and talk about the glory days of the family—how great the choir was, how great Ron was, and how proud my parents were that we all stayed in church during our teenage years—protected from the evil world." Anthony spoke with discernible bitterness.

"You've never told your parents about Ron?"

"I've never told anyone but my therapist and my sister. It took a year with a therapist. My sister's been great about it—she listens, and she doesn't ever ask questions."

"Come to St. Louis," Claire suggested. "I'm invited to a friend's house for Thanksgiving. You can go with me, and we will spend the whole weekend together. I want to see you. I don't mean to pressure you, and you can say no. But I think we've been given a chance to know each other again—wherever that might lead. We both have four days off; let's have some fun with them. I might even be able to arrange for a kite!"

Anthony thought. The only thing that could get him off the hook with his parents would be a girl. He assembled the plan in his head, even as he answered Claire. "Okay. I can leave right from work tomorrow and be there by, what, nine o'clock or so? Or I could wait and come on Thursday morning."

"Come tomorrow night. That will give us time to get used to how old we look before we head to my friend Maria's house on Thursday." They both chuckled, grateful for the return to an easy conversation. "She's planning dinner at three, and I think there'll be about ten of us. All friends—no family."

"Okay, I'll come," Anthony repeated. "I need to go now. I feel like I just ran a marathon. I'll pack tonight and take my car to work in the morning. A lot of people will be out, so I should be able to get a parking space. Can I call you in the morning for directions?"

"Yes. I'll be up before eight. Call me in the morning, and sleep well tonight. I can't wait to see you, Anthony. Good night."

Her voice was as sweet as ever. Full of reassuring calm. Anthony said good night and hung up. He sat in the same spot for nearly thirty minutes before he picked up the phone and told his mother that the girl he'd been dating in Chicago had invited him to go to St. Louis for Thanksgiving with her family.

Annie was full of instructions and opinions. "Who is this girl? When will you bring her here? Your brother and sister will be so disappointed. We'll miss you. It won't be the same. Where will you stay? Make sure you take a gift for the host—take some wine or flowers." On and on and on. There was, as anticipated, little criticism and little guilt. The prospect that Anthony had a girl outweighed the transgression of shirking the family holiday tradition.

Twenty-Four

I t was well after midnight when Anthony fell into bed with no hope of sleeping. His bag was packed except for the things he'd need in the morning—toothbrush, razor, and allergy pills. Surprisingly, he did sleep, taking only an hour to drift off and not waking until his alarm called for him at six thirty. Oddly, he dreamed about Ron. They were in the park where Claire and Anthony had first made love. It was summer, and as they walked amid the trees, they paused and kissed. It felt like kissing Claire—the lips soft and feminine. But when he opened his eyes in the dream, it was Ron holding him. As they turned to walk on, it was gray and cold, the leaves were gone, and Anthony was alone. Sounds from outside the park intruded. The alarm broke the spell.

Although puzzled by the dream, he felt refreshed and optimistic. His biggest secret had been shared, unloaded in the safest place he could have left it. Claire was releasing him from the burden.

He showered, finished packing, and threw his bag in the car before coming back into the apartment to call Claire at seven forty. He knew the route to St. Louis—Interstate 55 out of Chicago and all the way across Illinois. He only required directions to her house. Claire gave him her address in University City, a neighborhood in the heart of St. Louis near

Washington University. The area was diverse and urban, and Claire had fallen in love with it while raising money for the University City Residential League, a nonprofit group founded in the 1960s to preserve the changing neighborhood around the college. Claire lived just off Delmar Avenue near Forest Park, the historic site of the 1904 World's Fair. Much of the original fairgrounds was now a park and included the St. Louis Zoo and the art museum. Finding the neighborhood seemed easy, and the two talked for less than ten minutes.

"I'll wait until you get here to eat," Claire offered. "There are some great Lebanese restaurants we can walk to. I really appreciate you coming, Anthony. We're going to have a great weekend."

Anthony agreed that the weekend was going to be fun and hung up.

Parking in the Loop was abnormally easy, as predicted. The office was quiet and half empty, the phones silent. Anthony was wholly unproductive. At four thirty, half an hour before quitting time and nearly two hours before he normally departed, Anthony exited the parking structure and made his way out of the city heading southwest. He was well on his way by the time the sun set.

It was a little over three hundred miles to St. Louis, but Anthony stopped only once for gas and a Diet Pepsi and was parked in front of Claire's house on Pershing Avenue at nine twenty. She lived in the upper apartment of a two-story, two-family home on a street lined with ancient elms. Although the leaves were gone, you could see that the streets were fully covered by a canopy of lush green in summer. The house was a white stucco Tudor with a long driveway on the right that led to a three-car detached garage at the back of the lot. Red brick accented the corners of the building and the arch over the single door on the front of the house. There were four windows, on the front of the house, both upstairs and down. The windows on the two floors were identically placed, indicating that the apartments were the same. A single, wide brick chimney ran up the left side of the structure and past the hip roof. Through the leaded glass on the outside door, Anthony could see an inside foyer with two doors, one leading into the lower unit and the other leading to a staircase to the upper. It was strangely like Ron's apartment in Milwaukee, except the layout hinted that the door to the upper unit was on the right, the opposite of how it was for Ron's building. Bag over his shoulder, Anthony rang the bell and heard Claire descending the staircase into the foyer. She threw open the inside door, crossed the foyer in a single stride, and pulled open the outside door. She beamed and quietly breathed, "Oh, Anthony!" as she threw her arms around him. She held him close for a long time, during which Anthony tried to process the greeting. He hadn't really seen her face. Certainly she looked different. She was still thin and fit—he could tell that by the way his arms wrapped so completely around her waist.

Claire released him and stepped back into the doorway. The foyer light caught both their faces. In an instant, they both made the same observation—they were looking at a face they knew obscured by the unremovable costume of time passed. After a few seconds, they both burst into laughter. "My God, we're old!" Claire laughed.

Anthony knew better than to simply agree. "But you still look great, Claire! I'd have known you anywhere." Claire reached toward him, and Anthony thought another hug was coming. Instead, she slipped his duffel off his shoulder and took it from him, turning toward the open door behind her. "Put your car in the driveway, all the way back, in front of the right-hand garage door." With that, she ascended the stairs, leaving the door open. Anthony followed the instruction and then locked both the outside and inside door and climbed the stairs to the apartment.

There was another door at the top of the stairs. Anthony closed it behind him and stood in the living room. Although not exactly like Ron's apartment in Milwaukee, this house was clearly built in the same era. There was a fireplace on the wall opposite the door and beautiful, dark wood flooring. Anthony had recently had the red oak floors in his condo refinished. These floors were darker, perhaps cherry or walnut. The living room led to a formal dining room but without the room-dividing built-ins that served as home for Moses in Ron's place. Instead, the far walls held corner cabinets with leaded glass doors.

Anthony half expected to smell oil heat and dust. Instead, he smelled the varnish of the apparently recent floor refinishing and garlic. "I'm in the kitchen," Claire called, and Anthony moved in the direction of the voice. The kitchen had been updated, with wood cabinets and newer appliances. The pantry, no longer needed for dishes and groceries, had been converted to a small laundry room. Claire stood in the doorway of the pantry turned laundry room, and Anthony could see a microwave oven on a counter next to a stacked washer-dryer unit.

"I thought you might be too tired to go out walking, so I went to the restaurant earlier and picked up dinner. I've got spinach fattoush feta salad, some hummus, pita bread, and chicken kabobs."

Anthony had no idea what the fattoush part of the spinach fattoush feta salad was but replied, "Sounds good!"

As the microwave hummed, Claire took the salad and hummus from the refrigerator. She turned, and her eyes met Anthony's. She smiled. "I can't believe you're here. Sit down. This will be ready in a minute." They were rushing to dinner, using the task to eliminate any unease.

Anthony took a seat at the small round café table situated in front of the kitchen window. Gazing out, he could see his car sitting in the driveway. He wondered what Claire drove—probably a Subaru or Honda. Claire slid into the chair across from him as she set the salad and hummus in the middle of the table. The fattoush part of the salad appeared to be toasted pita bread—seemingly the only extra ingredient. She opened a cellophane bag and pulled out four pitas, handing two to Anthony. "I buy these at the Middle Eastern bakery on the corner. I love the texture so much that I hardly use silverware anymore." With that, she tore a corner of the pita off and used it to pick up a small mouthful of salad. Anthony did likewise, dipping a corner of his pita into the hummus. He looked around the kitchen and then back at Claire. The apartment and the meal—it was all *so Claire*. Simple and elegant at the same time. Different yet easy to assimilate. He smiled at her. "Tell me what you're thinking," she ordered.

"I'm thinking that this is so much better a place to spend a holiday than my parents' house. I'm thinking that you're so different and so the same. It's like you're the finished product of the Claire I knew—you're grown-up and self-sufficient, yet you're really exactly the same as you were in high school."

"What a nice compliment!"

As Anthony took the time to really look at Claire, he could see that she was still the same person—the blue eyes, the small, slightly upturned nose, and the teeth that were white but not completely straight. But her skin displayed the evidence of her time in the hot sun of Africa. She had lines through her cheeks and around her eyes. It was odd to see the wrinkles of a woman ten years older than Claire on the healthy, bright skin of this young woman of thirty. The conversation turned light, focusing on the trip from Chicago, Claire's job as a fund-raiser, and the plan for Thanksgiving dinner at Maria's. She ran through a short description of the anticipated guests. Claire and Maria's best friend, Terry, and her new boyfriend, Bob, whom Claire hadn't yet met. Maria's elderly neighbor Minnie, whom Claire described as the coolest old lady she'd ever met. Eric, Maria's friend since high school, and his partner, Jeff. "They've been together for nine years," Claire said. And finally, a couple Claire did not know who were spending their first year in the United States and who knew nothing of American Thanksgiving. She couldn't remember their names but knew they were from Wales. Maria had met them at an art class she was taking at the community center.

"That's ten including us, right? I think that's it," she said. "So, what did your parents think about you spending Thanksgiving here? Did you tell your mom you were spending it with me?"

"I told her I was invited to St. Louis for the holiday by a woman I knew, but I didn't tell her I was spending it with you. My mother has been on a mission to find me a woman to marry, and she always loved you, Claire. If I'd told her I was going to see you, she'd have probably come along to make sure I didn't screw up!"

"I think I liked your mom better than you did in high school."

"I think everyone liked my mom better than me back then! Maybe even now."

There was a pause, and the edge of discomfort seeped into the room. Claire suddenly pushed back from the table. "Oh, there's chicken!" No one had heard the microwave bell, which had probably sounded ten minutes earlier. She crossed the room and pulled the kabobs from the oven, touching one to verify that it was still warm. She set them onto the table, sat back down, and reached across to take Anthony's left hand.

"I'd like to say that I'm not going to ask you a lot of questions this weekend, but I know I could never keep that promise. I always ask questions." Claire smiled. "But you can change the subject anytime you want to. You don't have to talk about anything you don't want to, as long as you are honest with me."

"You really see me as dishonest, don't you." Anthony said this more as a statement than a question.

"You are the most wonderfully dishonest person I've ever known, Anthony. You were wholly dishonest in high school, and I guess I have come to understand why. And you are now, although I don't know why. You can tell me anything, Anthony. I don't have any preconceived notions about you or about us. I'm just glad to have the opportunity to see you and to get to know who you've become."

They smiled and set to work on the kabobs, although no one was hungry. After a few minutes of distracted eating, Claire spoke. "It's not too cold out. Do you want to go for a walk?"

"Sure," Anthony replied, and they cleared the table, Claire remarking that the remains of the takeout food would be a good snack in the morning.

"Maria cooks like an Italian mama. Be prepared to stuff yourself tomorrow afternoon."

They walked for nearly an hour around the neighborhood. It was warm for late November, still over fifty degrees even though it was after ten o'clock. They passed a few other pedestrians either redeeming the unseasonably warm opportunity or dutifully walking their dogs. Claire greeted each passerby warmly. The conversation was about their lives over the past ten years—Claire's work in the Peace Corps, Anthony's career progression through his company, their leisure-time activities. They laughed at how different they were. Claire loved folk music, yoga, and Eastern thought. Anthony enjoyed opera, racquetball, and political strategies. It was half past eleven when they walked up the apartment steps. Anthony yawned as they dropped their jackets on the living room chair and collapsed onto the sofa.

"Well, let's talk about sleeping." Claire sighed contentedly. "You have three options. I don't have a guest room—my extra bedroom is my attic. You can sleep here on the couch; I have blankets and pillows. I also have an inflatable mattress for the floor, and I have sheets for it. We'll just have to dig it out and set it up. Or you can sleep in bed with me." She provided that third option in the same matter-of-fact way as the first two.

Anthony paused. The idea that he would have sex with Claire this weekend had crossed his mind, but he wasn't prepared to drop into town after ten years and fall into bed after two hours. She sensed the question in his pause. "I don't mean it like that," Claire said, knowing how Anthony interpreted the suggestion by the look on his face. "I'm not ready to have sex with you; I just thought the bed might be more comfortable."

"Oh, that's what I thought you meant," Anthony replied playfully, then turned serious. "I'd like the chance to sleep next to you. It's something we've never done—spent a whole night sleeping in bed together."

In twenty minutes, they were climbing into the queen-size feather bed in Claire's bedroom. Teeth had been brushed, and both were in sleeping clothes. Claire wore panties and an oversize T-shirt that fell midthigh. Anthony had on a T-shirt and boxer shorts. As quickly as they got into bed, Claire shut off the light, kissed Anthony on the cheek, and laid her head on his chest. It all seemed so natural to Claire. She appeared comfortable and secure, as if sleeping with a bed partner— sleeping with Anthony—were a regular occurrence. Claire had lived with someone a few years back, and Anthony assumed that she had had other relationships. So perhaps sharing a bed was comfortable for her. Anthony had spent precious few nights with a bed partner, and on the occasions he had, sleep was always preceded by exhausting sex.

He liked having Claire close. It felt full circle—a return to what should have been. What could have been. He searched his feelings. He thought he was aroused, although his body didn't exhibit the evidence. He felt scared and excited. Perhaps this was the beginning of achieving victory. Over Ron. Over confusion. Over questions. Surprisingly, they were both asleep in fifteen minutes.

Twenty-Five

Anthony awoke early, morning just beginning to show its face outside the window. It was not yet seven o'clock. He was on his back, and Claire was on his right, turned away from him on her side, with her backside tight against him. Her left arm trailed behind her and onto his torso, her hand resting over his bare navel as if keeping track of him. His shirt had ridden up during the night, and he could feel his boxers bunching in his crotch. He was used to sleeping naked and alone. Claire slept peacefully, and Anthony spent a few moments listening to her smooth, quiet breathing. He perused the room, noting the African tapestry that hung over the dresser, the only art on the wall in the room. The walls were sage green, the trim glossy white. Narrow cream blinds hung over the double windows, but they were not turned closed. He could see the peak of the house next door through the window, barely illuminated in the predawn darkness.

His right arm slowly alerted him to the fact that it was hopelessly asleep at his side, pinned partially under Claire's body. Anthony realized that his hand must be against or under her buttocks. While that seemed sexy, he had no feeling in the arm and, therefore, could take no advantage of this high school–like opportunity for a "quick feel." He wondered if he had snored, something he'd been told by overnight guests that he did when he slept on his back. He normally drifted to sleep on his side but always awoke on his back. As was his typical first priority in the morning, the realization came to him that he needed to urinate.

With as little movement as possible, he slipped out from under the quilt and went to the hallway bathroom, right arm tingling. Not wanting to be heard relieving himself, he sat on the toilet and sighed quietly at the relief of the first morning pee. He brushed his teeth, considered himself in the mirror, and decided it had been a good idea to keep his hair short this year. It had been longer the year before and garnered a fair amount of daytime compliments but was prone to the really bad morning hair that had plagued him as a child. His short haircut was perhaps not as flattering, but it was easy and looked better pre–morning shower.

When he'd gotten up, he hadn't considered where he'd go from the bathroom. He decided not to return to bed but rather walked up the hallway to the living room. The sun was beginning to trail above the house across the street, and Anthony looked down on the frost-covered lawn below. He wished he'd brought slippers, although he didn't own any. The wood floor was cold on his feet. Hearing activity at the back of the house, he went to the kitchen to find Claire filling a teapot. She was wearing her nightclothes, along with thick white gym socks. She turned and spied Anthony looking at her feet.

"Sexy, eh?" She giggled.

"Good morning," Anthony returned. Claire set the chrome teapot on the stove and turned the gas flame high before crossing the room and hugging him. "Good morning, sunshine!" she said with her usual lyrical flair. "How did you sleep?"

"Actually, I slept really well. I am not used to having a bed partner. I wasn't sure whether I would lie awake more on a couch I wasn't used to or with a sleeping partner I wasn't used to, but I made the right choice. Your bed is comfortable, and I don't think I woke up at all last night."

"You snored!" Claire laughed.

"I should have taken an allergy pill before I went to bed. That usually keeps me decongested, and I don't snore as badly. Did I keep you up?"

"No, I only noticed it once. It was cute."

"Hopefully not my cutest quality!"

The kettle began to rumble as Claire took two mugs from the cupboard and set them on the table with spoons and a jar of honey labeled *Missouri Heartland Organic Honey.* As the kettle started to squeal, she took the hummus from the refrigerator and the pita bread from the counter and grabbed the teapot, filling both cups with boiling water. "There's tea in that cabinet on your left—get me an orange pekoe and grab whatever kind you want."

Finding a large plastic bowl, Anthony sifted through the individual packets of tea bags. There were names he'd never seen before. As he was concluding that he'd be choosing blind, he spied a single packet of Earl Grey. Meeting Claire at the table, he handed the orange pekoe to her. Spying his choice, she laughed. "I knew you'd pick the safe one!"

Light was streaming through the kitchen window as they drank tea and ate the bread. Claire's breasts were clearly outlined through the thin T-shirt, a fact that seemed to cause her no consternation. Anthony considered the fact that he had seen her naked before, years earlier, yet this really didn't seem like the same body across the table from him. He'd remembered Claire the girl but sat opposite Claire the woman. Beautiful still but different. She was totally relaxed and totally in control of herself and the situation. That hadn't really changed over the years.

"It is supposed to be nice again today—in the fifties," Claire offered. "I thought we could take a good walk in the park before we go to Maria's. I'll need to exercise early, because after dinner, I won't want to do anything but feel fat!"

"That would be great," Anthony replied. "I walk a lot in Chicago. I usually don't use my car at all during the week. Most of the time, I take the bus downtown for work, but sometimes I walk home, which is about two miles. And I walk everywhere else during the week—the grocery store, the drycleaner's, even the bar."

Claire rose and got the teapot, adding more water to her mug. "Why don't you shower first? You can use the bedroom to dress. I'll put this stuff away. If you're still in the shower when I'm done, I'll come turn the water cold!"

Anthony laughed, remembering that his sister had done that to him regularly when he was a teen. Lynn would sneak into the bathroom while Anthony took his long showers and reach into the stall, turning the water cold. Anthony's response to the shock was always the same. "Fucking bitch!" he would yell, half-angry and half-amused. It became a somewhat loving ritual between them, occurring once a month or so, until the day Anthony's mother thought she'd get in on the action. Sneaking into bathroom, she reached into the shower, turning it cold on Anthony. As was his practice, Anthony called out the same curse to whom he thought was his sister. To his shock, the curtain flew open, and there stood Annie, completely undaunted by her sixteen-year-old son's nakedness. "What did you say?" she scolded, both indignant and bemused. The story was one of the memories Annie, Lynn, and Anthony all laughed about years later, and apparently Claire remembered it, too. "Do that, and I'll have to curse you!" Anthony laughed.

Anthony showered—quickly—and dressed. He sat in the living room while Claire showered, pleased at how well the visit was going. It was amazing how they had settled into their old groove of easy conversation. There was no prying, no accusation, and no recriminations about the past. Thus far, the visit was perfect. There was no pressure for sex, yet it was clear there was chemistry. "Three more nights," Anthony was thinking as Clair emerged in jeans and a heavy sweater. Anthony had anticipated walking in the cold weather and had brought his corduroy jeans and some nice sweaters as well.

"I've got layers on, because if it gets warmer later, I will need to take this heavy sweater off," Claire said.

"Good idea," Anthony replied. "I should do the same thing—then I won't need to wear a jacket." He returned to the bedroom, pulled a blue T-shirt and long-sleeved Henley out of his bag, and changed clothes, wearing them under the heavy sweater he'd had on. When he returned to the living room, he found Claire looking out the window, a large bag in her hands. The creaking floor betrayed his arrival, and she turned. "Here. This is my contribution to the weekend." She handed the bag to Anthony. Inside was a poly bag with the unassembled components of a green and blue kite, along with three balls of kite string.

"Wow, this is a much nicer model than we ever flew in high school," Anthony observed.

"My income's a little better now!" Claire chuckled.

At nine, they left the house, walking eight blocks to Forest Park. A bronze plaque at the entrance told the tale of the park as the site of the 1904 World's Fair. It was chilly outside, but the sun was bright and warm. They entered the park on Lagoon Drive and walked through the golf course, where a few diehards were already frustrating themselves. At the Y in the road, they bore left onto Fine Arts Drive and walked to Art Hill. There were some geese here and there, soaking up the remnants of warmer days. Although the breeze was noncommittal, the kite went up fairly easily. The grassy area was large and was situated across from an art museum, overlooking a lagoon. Forest Park was huge—five hundred acres larger than Central Park in New York. There were joggers and strollers enjoying the morning, and many returned Claire's waves. As the kite bobbed and wove its way through the sky on the second ball of string, the two took turns at the helm. Without the steady breeze at Lake Park in Milwaukee, the kite required more attention to stay afloat. As they watched the spectacle, Claire talked about her work and then about her relationship with Tom, the man she lived with in San Francisco. "I loved him, but I don't know if I was *in love*," Claire explained. "He didn't want children, and I wasn't ready to commit to giving that up. In the end, we were just in different places. What's been sad is that he hasn't spoken to me—taken my calls or answered my letters—since I moved out." Anthony realized that if she'd written him and called, then he would have known that she was in St. Louis when he asked. He wondered if Tom had ever heard of Anthony before their phone call. She talked about her love for St. Louis and the life she'd built there. Then she turned serious.

"Anthony, I understand some of what happened to you in high school and how that affected you. But tell me what's been happening in your life in the past ten years."

"You really don't understand about high school, because it took me years to understand. I think the impact of Ron was really not about the sex. It was about the things that he filled my head with. I don't know if I'll ever recover from that. Even though I understand the destructive nature of my approach to people and relationships and I understand how Ron planted those values in me, I can't escape them."

"Why?"

"Because they're true. They may be negative, and they may prevent me from connecting with people, but they are proven true over and over again. People who say they care don't. People who say they'll never forget do. People who say they'll commit can't. I am alone. You are alone. Sometimes that's hard. But there's no escaping the notion that connection is painful. People who disagree with that get into relationships and get connected and committed and get hurt. Every time. I wish I could prove the theory wrong, but I can't."

"So tell me how this theory has been reinforced in you in the past ten years. Tell me about your relationships, about your life."

Anthony felt a need to avoid this conversation. But he didn't know how. "I'm not ready to verbalize my feelings on that, Claire. I guess I've avoided that topic for so long that I am not sure how to describe my feelings on my adult relationships. Can I think about it for a while before I try to tell you about my past ten years? Or perhaps we could take it a year at a time?" The last statement was made humorously, with the hope that his resistance would take on a softer air.

Claire thought for a minute. "Okay. But I will ask again tomorrow. Let's walk some more. I want to show you the park." Claire said this cheerfully, effectively changing the subject and letting Anthony know that it was okay. There were two young boys riding their bikes slowly past them, eyeing the kite in the air. "Would you guys like to fly this kite?" Claire called. "Then you can take it home and keep it!"

The boys stopped short and looked at each other. "Yeah!" came their reply in unison as they dropped their bikes at the side of the path and ran toward Claire. She handed them the string, and they looked at her in awe, the kite a prized possession left in their care.

"Have fun!" she called as she handed the third ball of string to the boys, took Anthony's hand, and walked them toward a trash can fifty feet away. As she dropped the bag for the kite into the can, she released Anthony's hand and hooked her arm through his. "This way." She steered onto the path that led deeper into the park. The two boys called out their thanks one more time as they immediately set to work on tying the third ball of string onto the line to put the kite higher in the sky.

They walked for another hour before turning out of the park onto Lindell Boulevard. Heading back toward Delmar Avenue and Claire's street, they stopped at a corner coffee shop and split a cinnamon roll—the first indication that Claire's healthy lifestyle might have some vices. She was a regular at the shop, as evidenced by the greetings of both staff and other obviously regular customers. It was just after noon when they walked back into Claire's apartment. "I need a nap!" Claire announced as she tumbled onto the couch, stripping off her sweater. Anthony took the other end of the couch and let his head fall back on the overstuffed arm. The next thing he knew, Claire's head lay against his chest. "We've been asleep for an hour!" She laughed. "I feel totally lazy!"

The phone rang, and Claire got up to answer. Anthony could tell it was Maria, asking her to pick something up on her way over. The two women talked for a few minutes, and Claire told Maria about the morning walk, the kite flying, and the decadent cinnamon roll. Hanging up, she instructed Anthony to help her remember to get whipping cream on the way to Maria's. "We should leave in half an hour," Claire instructed.

They changed into fresh clothes only slightly dressier. Anthony emerged from the bedroom in black jeans and a lightweight burgundy sweater, and Claire came from the bathroom in the same jeans she had been wearing but with a pink sweater set. She'd put on makeup. Not heavy but noticeable. She looked fresh and shiny, like a *Seventeen* magazine cover. A girl next door kind of pretty.

"You look great," Anthony offered. "I look better just being next to you!" Claire placed her hand on his forearm as she passed him and kissed him on the cheek. No words were spoken, but Claire smiled as she turned from the closet with both their jackets.

They arrived at Maria's at two thirty, two cartons of heavy whipping cream in hand. As promised, Maria had cooked up a storm, and the dinner was expansive. All of the guests were happy to meet Anthony and seemed to know the story of the reunion when they arrived at Maria's, causing Anthony to conclude that the reconnection with Claire had been the topic of some conversation among Claire's circle of friends. The guests fawned over both Anthony and Bob, Terry's new boyfriend, while they fielded questions about the holiday from the guests from Wales. When the party broke up at nine o'clock; it had been an enjoyable evening—nice people, great food, and lots of wine and dessert. Anthony had learned a few things about Claire. Apparently, she couldn't help but give money to the homeless on the street corner but not without also delivering a lecture on taking responsibility for one's life. Recently she had converted her typically cash handouts to McDonald's gift certificates in order to prevent the vagrants from using cash unwisely. She bought gift certificates each week and had them ready when a beggar asked for spare change. This had gotten her more than a few dirty looks and some curses, but she was not dissuaded from her cause. Also, she was apparently a very funny drunk who typically was the life of the party until the instant she fell asleep, regardless of where she was. Everyone roared at Maria's story of Claire sleeping through a very loud rock concert and hearing only the encore after a ninety-minute nap.

They returned to Claire's just before ten and decided to take a short walk. There was a mist in the air, and the night was moonless. They walked for an hour and came home wet but feeling less bloated from the heavy dinner. Together on the sofa, they watched the news and then changed for bed and pulled the quilt over them at midnight. Claire curled up next to Anthony, head on his chest, and slid her hand under his T-shirt and onto his chest. "I'm tired but not sleepy," she said. Anthony paused for a minute and then pretended to snore loudly. They both giggled. "I get the message," Claire chided.

It took longer to fall asleep. Claire's body was against Anthony's right side, with his right arm under her pillow. She slowly moved her hand back and forth across his chest, stroking his thin chest hair. Anthony was not as rail thin as he had been in high school but was still in good shape. "I always loved this part of you," Claire said as she ran her hand over the protrusion of his lower rib cage down onto his still flat stomach. Anthony knew exactly what she was talking about. His ribs had always seemed to stand out obtrusively when he lay on his back. Even when he had slept with thinner men, he noticed that the transition from their chests to their stomachs was not as pronounced. In realizing what Claire was referring to, Anthony noted to himself that Claire had obviously run her hand over a number of other men's chests and made the same observation. He was silent, obviously having no ability to tell her he knew from his own experience with men just what comparison she was making. Claire sidled up closer, kissing Anthony tenderly on the cheek twice and holding her face against his neck and cheek. "This feels right" were her last words for the evening. Anthony lay awake until after he could hear the smooth breathing that told him she was asleep and content. He felt wholly content as well. He felt at home. He didn't feel the presence of Ron. He knew he and Claire would share themselves completely before the weekend was through.

Twenty-Six

They slept later on Friday morning, Anthony waking with his right arm aching from two nights of Claire's incursion into his side of the bed. The couple moved through the morning routine of showers, dental hygiene, and dressing as if they'd lived together for years. It was so easy to find a comfortable place with Claire.

The day was busy and filled with light conversation. It drizzled on and off, but they took umbrellas and jackets and walked back to Forest Park, this time aiming at the art museum. Their approaches to taking in the art were radically different, and they split unintentionally from time to time. Claire favored modern art, Anthony the portraits and landscapes of Renaissance Europe. Claire enjoyed taking in a whole room at once, standing back and absorbing the mood and interplay of the works. Anthony tended to stand at length and consider the single piece that struck him when he entered each gallery. Both, however, enjoyed hypothesizing the story behind each piece. They were sure that *Mary, Lady Guildford*, captured in a 1527 portrait by German artist Hans Holbein the Younger, had been robbed of an afternoon with her secret love by the requirement of her landowner husband that she sit for yet another portrait by some boring but rising artist. And they decided that the hooded man in the center of

Max Beckmann's *Young Men by the Sea* was actually not visible to anyone but the artist, and that the shrouded character was actually death, come to take the seated youth, who was about to go for a swim. They laughed at the mystery surrounding the painting, and that none of their theories were based on a shred of evidence.

They had dinner near Creve Coeur, after Claire stopped to check the mail at her office. With a steadier rain taking the fun out of the idea of a walk, they were home by eight o'clock. Claire tuned the stereo to an easy-listening station and set the volume low. Leaving him in the living room, she went to the kitchen and returned with a bottle of Sonoma County merlot that she had neglected to take to Maria's on Thanksgiving. They settled into the dark leather sofa. It was a dry red wine, which Claire explained was not the right wine for turkey anyway. She served it in small juice-size glasses, as was the custom in Italy, where Claire had been twice. It was momentarily eerie for Anthony. Claire's apartment was not dissimilar to Ron's old place in Milwaukee, and here Anthony was, sitting on the couch under the front windows with a glass of wine offered by a host he was terrified of but wanted to sleep with. And he *had indeed* wanted to have sex with Ron, hadn't he? It may have been forbidden by the rules of age and faith, but he'd wanted it. And now, here he was with Claire, who'd stated that she was uninterested in sex, hoping that the forbidden would happen. *Could* happen.

"Tell me about the most important relationship you've had since you and I graduated from high school," Claire stated without a hint of hesitation. "It's time for me to know you." She clinked her glass against Anthony's, retreated to the far end of the couch, pulled her legs up to her chest, turned the floor lamp over her shoulder off, and settled into a gaze of anticipation at Anthony.

"I think I might need more wine to bolster my courage," Anthony quipped.

Claire was ready with a reply. "Wine doesn't make you do brave things; it makes you do stupid things. It's having no choice that makes us brave. And you have no choice, my friend. There will be no sleep until you fess up!" She laughed warmly. Anthony sat frozen, facing forward, like a patient on an examining table. Claire seemed content to wait. He found himself searching for a clock, as he'd relied on the predictable ticking in Ron's house as a mental focal point when he felt off-balance. There was none. Finally, he turned toward her, brought his legs up onto the couch and crossed them, and made eye contact.

"This will take me some time, and it will come out with all kinds of poorly constructed sentences that would make my seventh-grade English teacher Sister Joyce's head explode." He settled back against the sofa arm opposite Claire. She exuded neither excitement nor dread at the idea that "something big" was coming. She was simply there. It was simply time. If there was to be a *Claire and Anthony*, he quickly assessed, it needed to be built on full disclosure.

"I've never been in love," Anthony began and then paused. "Not since you," he added, turning to gaze out the window at the street below. "After Ron finally moved to California and was out of my life—well, not out of my life, but at least gone from my sight—I really struggled with my sexual identity. I think one of the things that drew me to the possibility that I would turn out gay was the idea that it would kill my mother. I was so resentful. Anyhow, I started hanging out some at a gay bar. It was called the Depot." He looked over to check for a reaction, but there was none. "I feel like you're about to say you already knew this!"

"Whatever I thought or felt is unimportant, Anthony. This—sharing. That's what's important."

"Anyhow, I hung out there pretty often, and I did some experimenting. Actually, I did a lot of experimenting! I don't think I really considered whether I was gay or just playing around. I just did it. Then I went to St. Norbert's, and I met Frankie, who I am sure you've guessed was gay. He was different than the guys I met in the bars. At the bars, everything was about being gay—about sex. But Frankie was a whole person, and we became friends. More than friends, I guess. He was really good to me, but I wasn't really able to handle it. I didn't trust people, didn't want relationships. And I was careless with his feelings. Even if he was gay and I wasn't, even if we weren't going to be lovers, I was careless with his feelings, and I really hurt him." Anthony felt the pang of guilt germinate deep inside even as he was betraying Frankie by minimizing the emotional component of the relationship. "Even if I wasn't gay, he was a person worth loving, and he offered me love and friendship, and I squandered it. I guess it was the most important relationship because it could have been significant on a number of levels. If I was gay and wanted a partner, Frankie could have been that. Even straight, Frankie could have turned out to be the best friend I ever had. I suppose it's sad to say that Frankie was my most significant relationship, because what makes it significant is not what I had—it's what I mishandled."

There was a pause. Anthony could feel emotion welling up in him—the thought that Frankie was dead, that he would never know that Anthony felt this way, felt this regret, and in telling someone else about it, he had mischaracterized the relationship and thus betrayed Frankie once more. He felt sad. Claire got up from the couch, kissed Anthony on the cheek, and said, "Thanks." Grabbing the wine bottle off the end table, she filled her glass but noticed that Anthony hadn't taken more than a sip from his. Setting the bottle on the hardwood floor next to the sofa, she reclaimed her end.

"Now, fast-forward to today. Are you gay?"

"No. I am not gay. Perhaps I have the ability to enjoy sex with whomever I find attractive. But sexuality is about more than sex. It's about connection. I'm not gay. I'm straight. But I don't seem to be able to connect with a woman either. I'm attracted to attractive people. But I'm broken, in terms of connection. I feel like a two-pronged electrical outlet in a world full of three-pronged plugs. No one can really get inside here." With that, he ran his left hand in front of his face and down his body. "I think I've been better alone." Anthony wasn't sure she would buy the idea that a guy who'd had sex with no one but men since high school, who'd just stated that his most important relationship had been with a guy, and who'd slept next to her for the past two nights and hadn't tried anything—that this guy was straight. But he knew that *he* needed to buy it. Survival depended on it.

"What do you mean you're broken?" She seemed to be ignoring the question of sexual orientation, at least for the moment. Claire was always one to look for the deeper, more psychological path, leaving the more practical questions for later.

"I guess I mean that all the stuff that Ron filled my head with has broken my ability to believe in people. And I realize it's stupid, because Ron himself went and got married, so I guess even *he* didn't believe his bullshit. I know in my head that it's a dismal view of the world, but the problem is that it's not my head that's broken: it's my soul." Anthony looked away from the window and settled on Claire's beautiful face. "Can you fix me, Claire? There's no point to all this sharing, to all this 'wanting to know me,' if you can't do something with the information."

For the first time since they'd begun talking on the phone weeks earlier, perhaps for the first time ever, the spotlight had been moved from Anthony to Claire. She stirred uncomfortably on the sofa cushion as she poured herself a third glass of wine. Perhaps stalling for time, she moved toward Anthony with the bottle as if to refill his still-full glass. Taking note that he hadn't made a dent in his wine, she settled back into her space and set the near-empty bottle on the floor again. It was quiet, and Anthony returned his gaze to the world outside the window.

"I love you, Anthony," Claire began. "I've always loved you, and even though I've loved others, it's never diminished my feelings for you. Now you're here, and we've both grown up, both changed. You're different but still really the same. I still love you. I can't fix what you say is broken in you, because it's not in my power. It's in your power. But I can be here all along the way. If you want evidence that Ron was full of shit, evidence beyond the fact that he himself chucked his philosophies in the end, then consider that I've loved you for nearly half my life. I'll go on without you, like your parents went on without your sister. But I'll keep loving you. So, I can't fix you, but I can be part of your healing. I can be here, be with you, love you, and be your friend. That's the exact same offer I made to you over ten years ago, and you walked away. The real question here, Anthony, is this: will you step up to the plate this time? I'm here, on this end of the couch, and you're there on your end. We're close but not truly connected. It's the same thing emotionally—you've got this space between us. I'm not going anywhere, but will you maintain the empty space between us?"

"I'm not sure how to respond." Anthony got up, his legs cramped from sitting. He took a sip of the wine and set the glass down before pacing across the living room. Claire was silent. Turning back toward the stereo, he heard a song from high school on the radio. It was one of those syrupy love songs, a homecoming dance song to be sure. The sugar-sweet song was called "Dream Weaver," and Anthony remembered that he had owned the album by Gary Wright.

He turned the volume up and faced Claire, hand outstretched. "Dance with me?" Claire finished her wine in one swallow and stood to join him. As they danced, Anthony buried his face in Claire's shoulder. He felt joy and release as he held her tight. "I love you, Claire," Anthony whispered, tears on his cheeks. They kissed deeply, their slow dance coming to a halt. When the song was over, Claire seemed a little uneasy on her feet, and they tumbled together onto the couch. Reaching down for the bottle, Claire held it up to the light to see that it was nearly empty. Turning it upside down, she drank the last of the wine, and they both giggled like high schoolers.

It was only ten when they went to bed. Anthony was scared, hoping that all would go well. However, Claire was fairly intoxicated, and she began to doze soon after hitting the pillow with her back to him. He spooned her and put his arm around her, his hand falling onto her breast. It startled him, and he moved his hand to below her chest. He wasn't sure what to do next, and the thought crossed his mind that he didn't want to be accused tomorrow of taking advantage of her drunken state. He lay awake for a long time, listening to her even breathing. He felt energized. Scared. He was heading into uncharted territory. Although he'd not been truly honest, he'd shared more in the past two days than he'd shared in his life, outside of therapy. Claire was a friend, partner, lover, and therapist all rolled into one. He felt in awe of her, listening to his heavy confessions and then sleeping so peacefully. He wasn't sure what scared him more—that ultimately he wouldn't connect with her or that ultimately he would. He didn't know how she'd fit into the world he'd created. Everything about him would have to change to accommodate Claire in his life. But it was exciting to think about.

He awoke as the light was coming up over the house next door. He'd slept fitfully, anxious about the chance to have sex with Claire and anxious also that he might not. The answer came when Claire sensed that he was awake and rolled over, laying her head on his chest. Her hand found its way under his T-shirt, and she began stroking his chest, as she had done two nights before. This time Anthony responded, curling his arm around her and gently rubbing her back. After a few moments, Claire raised her head and kissed Anthony on the lips softly. The room was still dimly lit, but the sun was beginning to greet the morning.

"Can I touch you?" Claire asked. Anthony had only ever been formally asked for permission to be touched once before, and it was by Claire, in high school, the first time she recipro-cated his sexual advances. Her touch was tender, less aggressive than he was used to with his one-night stands. But she didn't seem to know exactly what felt good. Anthony realized that she would certainly have less point of reference on this topic, being female. Slowly they became naked, helping each other undress. Anthony's hands seemed to go everywhere on Claire's body except to those most secret places. He wasn't afraid, just incredibly intimidated. Gradually he found himself touching her intimately, and he heard her breathing change.

It was exciting, not just sexually but in all regards. Anthony had returned to a heterosexual life, and it was with the woman he had loved many years before. He wanted to feel everything—the emotion, the connection, and the sexual arousal. And it was all there—sort of. He also felt horribly uncomfortable. It seemed clumsy, as it had those many years before. Claire didn't seem to notice anything odd, so Anthony assumed that it was all going well. He had no point of refer-ence regarding his performance. He entered her tentatively, as if he wasn't sure what he expected to find. It felt good, and instinct seemed to take over. They kissed and held each other as they both felt the coming climax in Anthony. She held him close, wanting to feel all of him against and inside her. He lay atop her long after it was over, then finally turned onto his side and held her.

After a few minutes, she got up and went to the bathroom. It was only then that Anthony opened his eyes, and as they drifted down onto the sheet, he noticed a trace of blood. Looking at his body, he found that his penis was red with blood. His reaction was fear, knowing that blood associated with sex could be a death sentence in the world from which he came. As he was sitting up, Claire came into the room with a towel. "I'm sorry. I thought I was over my period," she said. Anthony was confused, having spent his life so far away from the cycle of a woman.

"Did I hurt you?" he asked.

"No," she replied. "I guess I was just still bleeding a little." As she spoke, she settled on the bed and gently began cleaning Anthony with the towel.

Still missing full comprehension, Anthony stood. "I can just hop in the shower."

As the hot water ran over his body, Anthony inspected himself. Once he caught his breath, he realized what had happened. Women had menstrual periods, and Claire was apparently not quite over hers. Her words that she "was not ready to have sex" with Anthony on that first night now took on a whole new meaning. He wondered what Claire had actually meant and what she thought *he* meant when they each had said on Wednesday night that they were not ready to have sex. It appeared that they may have had two different reasons for their similar statements. Inspection verified that he was not wounded—the blood apparently innocuous. Still, he inspected himself once more.

Claire apologized again when he came out of the bath-room. Anthony was more composed and assured her that everything was fine. This unfortunate by-product of lovemak-ing with a woman overshadowed the experience itself, and Anthony would have been content to avoid considering the whole experience as he dressed. But the thoughts were there, nonetheless, and he began a silent conversation with himself as he moved to the kitchen and sat in the chair looking out at the yard below.

"How was it?" he asked himself. It had felt good—the inter-course. And he had had an orgasm.

"Why are you sick to your stomach?" This was a huge step. Claire was clearly going to become the center of his life, and that was huge.

"After all your searching, have you found home? Is Ron gone?" His mind raced ahead. Would they live in St. Louis or Chicago? Who had the higher income or would have greater difficulty replacing his or her job?

"What will you tell your friends in Chicago? That you're straight? That the phase of dating women in high school wasn't really a phase at all? That the past ten years were the phase, and now you've emerged from it?" This wasn't about what his friends thought. This was about Anthony and Claire and what was right for them. It was about forever banishing Ron and the poisonous lie that he was gay.

Claire walked into the room, clean and dressed, and handed a penny to Anthony as she sat down opposite him. "For your thoughts," she said with a smile and then reached across and took his hand in hers. "This wasn't what you planned. You said you weren't ready for this. So talk to me, Anthony. Let me know what you're feeling."

"You said the same thing," Anthony countered, hoping for an escape.

Claire was prepared. "You have a sister, Anthony. I think we know why I wasn't ready on Wednesday evening."

Anthony would probably never know if Claire was being truthful, but he had no grounds on which to question her. "It's been a long time for me, Claire—since the last time I made love to you. You were the most important woman in my life and the only woman I'd ever made love to. If this was going to happen again, it would have to be because you were again the most important woman in my life. I wasn't ready to make that statement on Wednesday night." He paused and turned the rod on the blinds to close out the world outside. Looking back at Claire, he felt tears forming in his eyes. "I need you, Claire. You know me better than anyone, and yet you love me. I can't walk away from that. I wish I could say that I am madly in love with you, but I don't know anything about being madly in love. I do know that you make me want to be who I think I should be, who I could be. I can't walk away from that. But I don't know where to go from here. My mind is completely overloaded."

"Then let's just agree that we've made a start and enjoy this last day we have together. Tomorrow you'll go home, and we may each need to take some time to process all that's happened this weekend. I don't understand it all either, Anthony. But I don't need to. Not right now. I am having a great time with someone I love. Let's not waste the day trying to answer the unanswerable." She stood and kissed his forehead, then held his head against her chest and rocked him gently.

Twenty-Seven

I t was a nice day. Everything was dipped in light frost, glisten-
ing new in the morning sun. Future thought was suspended, and Claire had planned a fun afternoon. After breakfast at
her favorite coffee shop and a walk around the neighborhood,
they left the area in the bright sun and chilled air and spent
the afternoon at the Magic House, St. Louis's children's museum. Anthony had never been in a museum that encouraged
patrons to touch everything. Housed in the three-story, turn-
of-the century Victorian mansion, the museum had opened
in 1979 and was expanded in 1985. Even the area designed
specifically for children under seven was interesting. Anthony
played with the exhibits but spent a good deal of time watching Claire. Considering her. She was completely comfortable
acting childlike as she moved from exhibit to exhibit. Anthony
was more tentative, always worried about how he looked to
these people whom he would likely never see again and who
themselves were wrapped up in the childlike, wonder-invoking
nature of the museum. He did many things that he would have
spurned in all other situations, including trying his hand at
spinning a Hula-Hoop around his uncoordinated waist while
watching a video about gyroscopes. As the hoop dropped again
and again around his ankles, he spied Claire laughing with joy
as she kept her ring spinning. He wondered if he could stay this

spontaneous in the long run with someone like Claire, whose very being expressed no intention of ever fully growing up.

Claire reciprocated the Thanksgiving invitation by having Maria over for dinner, along with Terry and Bob, whom Anthony had met at Maria's house. It was clear that Maria, Claire, and Terry were as close as three high school girlfriends, disappearing as they did into the kitchen and giggling. Anthony could tell by their bemused looks that Claire had told them even before dinner about the lovemaking and probably even about the blood with which it was tainted. Anthony felt proud, like a high school boy who'd scored with the popular cheerleader, knowing that their sexual intimacy was the topic of conversation. As the women kept to themselves, he visited mostly with Bob, a nice guy who had spent some time in Chicago earlier in his career. This allowed the two men to share stories of their favorite restaurants and Michigan Avenue stores.

Terry had brought the ingredients for her famous beachcombers, a rum drink with a fruit-punch essence. Although they were months from beach weather, they drank two pitchers of them as they laughed and told stories throughout dinner. Claire was an eclectic cook. She had prepared, with little apparent effort, a lemony chicken dish with quinoa. Pronounced *keen-wa*, it was something Anthony had never even heard of. It was akin to fine rice, looking somewhat like tapioca. He was corrected when he made that comparison.

"This is a much more complete protein than rice," Maria stated plainly as she explained the side dish. Apparently the food had an Incan origin, although Anthony doubted that the ancient natives prepared it with vegetable stock, garlic, scallions, and white wine as Claire had done. The dinner was good and obviously nutritious and was thankfully followed by a completely contrary dessert of Maria's making, apple cobbler—sweet and rich.

There was an ease with which the group enjoyed conversation with one another over dinner. Topics ranged from serious political discussions to the retelling of embarrassing stories from the girls' past foolishness together. Anthony forgot himself at times and then wondered with fear if he'd been too demonstrative, too feminine in gesturing or joining in on a joke. But no one seemed to see him any differently from Bob. If he tried, he could feel straight, sitting there with his new/old girlfriend. The guests seemed accepting, even embracing, of Anthony as a member of this group of special people. He felt *in the circle.*

As Maria was helping to clear the table, she laughed about Eric's and Jeff's help with the same task at the Thanksgiving dinner the day before. "Eric started clearing plates—did you notice that? He was so cute. I don't think he's ever washed a dish in his life! He'd be helpless at home without Jeff, but there he was last night, being mister kitchen assistant! I was about to dog him about trying to look domestic, but Jeff beat me to it."

"Oh, is that what Jeff was poking him about in the kitchen?" Claire asked with a smile.

"Yeah, he was saying he'd never seen Eric with a dirty dish in his hand; he'd only seen him emptying his plate, then retiring to the bathroom while Jeff did the dishes. It was so funny! They may be two guys, but they bicker about their roles just like any married couple!"

Bob offered his observation. "I suppose it doesn't matter whether you're gay or straight; when you've been with someone nearly ten years, a relationship is a relationship."

"It's funny. Eric is definitely the husband, and Jeff is definitely the wife in that relationship," Terry added. "I suppose all the gays are like that—one's the dumb husband who has to be beaten into submission, and the other is the poor but brilliant wife who has to do the dirty work!" The three women laughed in unison as Bob rolled his eyes at Anthony.

"Well, isn't it always Jeff who sits with us girls at parties?" Claire laughed. "I love Eric with all my heart, but I'd never ask for his advice on anything, relationship-wise." The three women nodded again in agreement.

Anthony felt the need to give the guy perspective on this joke. "Hey, you three are stereotyping!" He laughed. "Maybe I'll call Eric the next time I come to town, and he and I will make a gourmet meal for you—no girls allowed in the kitchen!"

Terry laid her hand on Anthony's arm and smiled. "If the meal turns out, it will be because you make a good wife! Then Jeff will be furious!"

Anthony felt his face flush as the friends roared with laughter, influenced by both the joke and the beachcombers. Before he needed to think of a comeback, Maria was there.

"Well, I've known Eric since high school, and I wouldn't change him—he's got a huge heart, even if he can't dust and vacuum." The three women nodded once more, and the topic changed to the need for more drinks.

As Terry mixed the third pitcher of beachcombers at nearly ten o'clock, the three women decided it was time to quiz the men. Questions flew at both Bob and Anthony about their families, their jobs, and their past relationships. Anthony, feeling intoxicated for the first time that weekend, was up to the challenge. When asked why he hadn't been in a relationship in ten years, he smiled and said, "Because Claire left me alone in Chicago." The giddy girls were sufficiently touched by the sappy answer to pursue him no further on the topic. It was nearly midnight when the guests left—Bob being the most sober and able to drive.

Anthony helped with the last of the cleanup, Claire nearly asleep on her feet. Climbing into bed a little after one, Anthony awaited Claire's arrival from the bathroom. He was surprised when she crawled into bed naked and sidled up next to him, only to drift off to sleep in what seemed like thirty seconds. Anthony, still in his T-shirt and boxers, had trouble getting to sleep, already anticipating the clash of worlds he would feel when he got home the next day.

They made love in the morning for the second time that weekend. Claire's menstrual period was over; he'd been assured of this as they began. But Anthony was suspicious as he touched her. This time he initiated the sex, made easy by her nakedness beneath the quilt. He enjoyed the touch of her skin—so soft and smooth. Not like the male bodies he usually touched but interesting still. He loved the body hair of the men he usually slept with—hairy chests, beard stubble, and the trail south from the navel—it seemed gross to him that a woman with such smooth and pretty skin would have pubic hair. It was natural that men would be hairy, but Claire's sparse body hair seemed a defect. A turnoff.

He was sure his foreplay was clumsy. There was really nothing there for him to touch. He entered her with his finger but wasn't sure what to do once he got there. And frankly, it seemed uninteresting. You could see a man's response to your touch— see the evidence of your work right before your eyes. But this was a mystery, a blind alley. After what was only a short time of foreplay, Claire drew him to her and guided him inside. As with the day before, it felt good. Instinct again took over, and there was perhaps a better rhythm between them. When it was over, he longed to lay his head on her chest and hold her hand, as he had done many times with Frankie years before. But her chest was not comfortable, encumbered by breasts. As they lay there, he tried to glimpse the future. If they were together, and if every relationship had a husband and a wife, regardless of the genders of the partners, who would Anthony be? Could he ever really be the *guy* in the relationship? He felt so inferior to Claire. She was so *in charge*. When he thought of the future with her, he saw himself being cared for, being supported. It made him shudder to think that in the Jeff-and-Eric equation, it was Claire who could fulfill both roles. Where exactly would Anthony fit into her life?

He was sick to him stomach as they rose, and he went to the shower. He'd had such high hopes. Claire was so wonderful. But there was something clearly missing in their physical lovemaking. She wasn't Frankie. She didn't incite the animal reaction in him that even his tricks from Sidetracks Bar had. He didn't crave her. It was incomplete. As he packed his bag to leave shortly before noon, the thought had already entered his mind and taken root. "Could it be that I am a gay man whose one lifelong soul mate is a woman?" If so, it could be nothing but the cruelest of tricks.

When they said good-bye, it was clear that Claire would now lie back and see if Anthony could "step up to the plate." She said as much and said it plainly. They agreed that it had been a wonderful weekend, a wonderful reunion. They talked about the things they'd seen, about Claire's great friends, and about the laughs and the wonderful thing it was to be reconnected. There was no reference to their lovemaking or even to the serious discussions they'd had. As they stood hugging, it was all good thoughts and good words. But there was an edge already beginning to form—expectations and the fear that they might not be met. Claire had expectations and would accept nothing less than all of him. She was optimistic, but that feeling was perhaps tempered by the fact that this was, at the heart, the same Anthony she'd always known and loved. She was sure that the space between them was not yet closed.

Twenty-Eight

The last six weeks of 1987 were a dichotomy for Anthony. He was living in two worlds, and it felt just like his first semester in college when he spent time with Frankie at school but returned to Milwaukee on the weekends to see Claire. He told no one of his reconnection with Claire and continued his life in Chicago. But he talked with her at least three times a week, discussing everything from the day's events to their future together.

His phone conversations with Claire were sometimes invigorating but usually stressful. He loved talking deeply about careers, politics, religion, friends, and a host of other things. She debated the topics but never the person. And she listened completely before assessing Anthony's position. He hadn't known anyone else like that. She was willing to consider other viewpoints, and she forced Anthony to do the same. They would debate for an hour on a single, unanswerable topic—the trends in child rearing, the environment, or the existence of life elsewhere in the universe. He loved those debates and always felt refreshed rather than worn out when they were over.

What made the conversations stressful was that it was also clear that Claire had expectations. She was waiting for a "stepping up to the plate" by Anthony that she never attempted to define. Whenever he mentioned the difficulty he would have in leaving Chicago or his job, she would always say that she wasn't asking that. Yet she offered no clarity and never suggested that she might move to bring them together. She did, however, seem to express in her tone an underlying desire to be with him. And Anthony could not be completely honest with her. Nearly all of his friends were gay, so he couldn't fully describe them. He still spent a night or two each week at Sidetracks and couldn't talk about that. Since coming home from St. Louis, he was living an inauthentic life—one foot in each of two worlds, with the gap between them widening. He was sure that he'd only be able to maintain his posture for a short time, because the situation was just like his first semester in college, and that had ended his relationship with Claire the first time.

Two weeks before Christmas, he met Bill, an arbitration attorney from Libertyville who showed a genuine interest in Anthony. Bill had been married for five years and had a four-year-old daughter. They met at the bar and then attended a play together later in the week and had dinner in the Loop that weekend. It was after dinner that Anthony offered to show Bill his apartment and Bill spent the night. This being the first time he had sex with anyone since Claire, Anthony was attentive to the feeling, the texture, of the experience. To his disappointment, it was eminently more comfortable and satisfying. It wasn't that making love to Claire didn't feel good. It was just all so clumsy. Bill was familiar territory, and Anthony was excited during his time with Bill, although devastated upon reflection. He found himself drawn to this man he had just met and pulled in directions with him that he couldn't make himself go with Claire, whom he'd known for years. Bill's touch—his feel. The grain of his skin and the substantial hands and masculine features. These were attractive in a way Anthony couldn't find with Claire. It was disquieting. Normalcy was so close—Claire was back and available; Ron could be dismissed finally. Goals so reachable and unattainable.

Christmas came and went, with Annie Conway visibly disappointed that he didn't bring a girl to the family holiday celebration. After he explained that she had gone back to St. Louis for the holiday with her family, Annie expressed in plain terms that relationships could not be so one-sided, that this woman would need to spend some holidays with Anthony's family. He could only roll his eyes at his mother. The reality was he was entering a new relationship, with Bill, and couldn't talk honestly about it. This "girl from St. Louis" was probably never going to emerge, but Bill would have been happy to meet Anthony's family. The thought was depressing to him. So he spent another family holiday as the only member of the family with no one to meet under the mistletoe.

When the inevitable discussion of the past came at three in the afternoon on Christmas Day, Lynn was quick to change the subject, understanding now the pain associated with the topic for her brother. She winked at him as she got up from the table to chase a toddler around the living room of the Conway house. The topic was shortened also when Annie announced that they were thinking of selling the house and buying a condo. Alan thought it a great idea, but Lynn thought it sad that her children would lose the continuity of the Conway family home. Anthony didn't think he cared but spent a few minutes in his old bedroom after dinner before going home depressed.

Two weeks into the new year, the evening news crew reported that a dog had fallen through the ice on the Lincoln Park Lagoon. It had been a warm January thaw, and the dog had wandered out onto the ice to bother the resting ducks. A crowd gathered, and the authorities were called as the panicked dog tried desperately to get back onto the slippery ice. Laying a ladder across the ice, a fireman crawled tentatively out to the dog, talking calmly and encouraging the exhausted and flailing animal. As the fireman reached out to grab the dog's collar, instinct took over, and the terrified animal bit the man. Not seriously injured through his heavy coat, the man persevered, hauling the dog onto the ice and saving its life. The dog, in its fight to survive, would have turned away its only hope because instinct gave the wrong instruction. Anthony knew that he was that dog—destined to follow his instincts to destruction rather than allow Claire to haul him out of his turmoil.

He became resentful. The world, and perhaps forces beyond the world, seemed to have conspired against him. Against his peace of mind. Against success. Resentment toward himself, Claire, Bill, Ron, and God built. Claire was so sweet, so patient, and so connected to Anthony. Yet he was never going to meet her expectations. He would disappoint. He would hurt her. He would fail. Just as Ron had promised so long ago. She wanted nothing less than all of him, and he simply could not be complete with a woman. He knew this now.

He met once more with Dawn, explaining his reunion with Claire, the lovemaking, and the failure to connect with her as easily as he was finding himself connecting with Bill. She asked him to consider that he was gay. That he had always been gay, as he feared. That it was okay. That it was not because of Ron. That Claire perhaps already knew and could be there for him in another form. That there was life after Ron, even if Anthony was ultimately gay.

It was all too terrible to consider. He left without making another appointment.

Claire understood that the relationship was failing. The distance between them was growing, not vanishing. In mid-January, she and Anthony had a quiet phone call. After some minutes of near silence, Claire spoke.

"I need to talk with you less, Anthony. I need to protect myself. I need a break."

"I understand," Anthony replied. "Let's take a break, then."

"Call me when you want to talk. But I am not going to invest emotionally in this anymore."

Those were the last words they spoke to each other. Anthony did not call her again, and as happened the first time he lost her; she never came looking for him. Anthony was promoted at work—a highlight of the winter of 1988, which turned bitterly cold after the January thaw. National Director of Market Research. He now had six managers and nearly fifty employees under him. The raise and bonus potential were substantial, and his parents were proud. Even adjusted for inflation, his salary was now higher than his father's had ever been, and he was financially better off than either of his siblings. He found that comforting, for some unarticulated reason.

Things with Bill developed, and they were good. Bill's office was near the Sears Tower, and he took the Metra train from Libertyville into the Loop each day. At least once each week, he would stay the night with Anthony, and he spent nearly every weekend in the city as well. They began to be seen as a couple, which was odd for Anthony. Bill had faced the difficult task of coming out to a family that had no reason to believe he could be gay, since he'd been married. He was well-adjusted and took pride in the success of his difficult transition. He marveled that Anthony, who from Bill's perspective had probably always been seen as gay, had not come out at work or with his family. But he was patient and kind. Anthony envied him and wondered if Bill could be the new Frankie in his life. He started to see that perhaps there could be love in a gay relationship. Still, there was a discernible space between the two men, structured by Anthony and observed by all. They were together but not. A gap undefined but obvious.

As spring approached, Anthony got a birthday card from Claire with a short message wishing him the best for the year. She included a quote by George Bernard Shaw: *Life is a constant becoming: all stages lead to the beginning of others.* Beneath the quote she wrote simply, *I wish you joy—Claire.* He picked up the phone to call her and replaced the receiver halfway through dialing. He knew there was nothing he could tell her. This was new for Anthony. Claire had always been the one he could talk to, the one with whom he never ran out of topics for discussion. But there were no more topics. Instead, he called Bill.

"When you come for the weekend, bring clothes for the week. Let's spend my whole birthday week together. I don't need any other present. My new job is tough, and I want to come home to you every night next week." Bill agreed and arrived on Friday night with two suitcases and two presents. The small jewelry box contained silver cuff links. Anthony was in the minority of men who still wore French-cuffed shirts to the office. The other package contained a book entitled *Joshua.* It was a novel by a retired Catholic priest, Joseph Girzone. Anthony read the book over the weekend, sitting comfortably with Bill in the apartment. It was a moving tale of Jesus, told without all the rules and regulations of the church. Anthony found it comforting—a different view of God. Not unlike the special view he'd always held of St. Veronica—a saint not like the pontificating and judgmental heroes of the church. The two men had a quiet week, living comfortably together.

Toward the end of the week, as they were discussing plans for the weekend, Bill expressed an interest in attending church on Sunday. He belonged to the Episcopal Church and held his faith deeply. That seemed an enigma to Anthony. "Why would you have interest in a God who hates gays?" he challenged.

"God doesn't hate gays, Anthony. People in some churches hate us. God has simply been misrepresented. I am not going to allow people to keep me from my faith."

Anthony ran through his list of complaints against God, including his poor track record and his absence from view.

"You're looking outside for him, Anthony. He's inside— he's personal. He's not God as someone else defines him for you. He's God as He defines Himself inside your soul. Look for Him there." His advice was much like Claire's had been.

The two began attending services at St. Peter's Episcopal on Belmont, just six blocks from Anthony's condo. Being only a few blocks from the steadily growing Boystown district, there were more than a few gay parishioners there on Sunday morning. It was gratifying to find that the congregation seemed entirely disinterested in Bill and Anthony as a gay couple. They were simply worshippers among other worshippers. The building was beautiful, with small, elegant stained-glass windows. Each pane was a beautiful mosaic of color—no saints in the glass.

Try as he might, Anthony didn't find God within his soul. Weekly he searched for the cathartic moment when the presence of God would appear within him—the salve to sooth the pain inside. By spring, they were regular enough attendees to be asked if they'd like weekly collection envelopes. The church family had come to recognize and reach out to him when he was there on Sunday, but God had yet to make an appearance. A woman from Anthony's office attended there and had seen him with Bill on many occasions. The story that Anthony was gay and attended church with his partner made its way around the office. Although the story told by the woman was not malicious and no one in the office seemed particularly interested, Anthony blocked her promotion when it came before the senior management team, stating plainly that he saw her as untrustworthy because of her participation in negative office gossip. Her supervisor told her that her promotion had been blocked by Anthony and why. She came to him, apologizing for hurting him in mentioning that she'd seen him at church. Her apology was genuine and nearly tearful. She appeared more concerned that she'd hurt Anthony than that she'd been denied promotion. Anthony sat silently until she realized he had no response for her and left his office.

By June, Bill began talking about the advantages of living together, perhaps in Anthony's apartment. The suggestion left Anthony feeling trapped. It was only Ron who had never asked for more. Frankie, Claire, and now Bill. Everyone wanted what couldn't possibly work—commitment. He was panicked by the suggestion and explained that he was not ready for that and had in fact meant to tell Bill that he should consider himself free to date other men, as Anthony himself was seeing some-one else in addition to Bill. It was a lie but successfully allowed him to reclaim the space between him and the world that Bill had transgressed in recent months. They continued to see each other but less often. And Anthony stopped attending church with Bill.

Twenty-Nine

I n July of 1988, Annie Conway called to say that Ron and Judy had moved back to Milwaukee. Judy's father was in failing health, and they'd returned to the state to be closer to her family. Ron was to begin work at St. Matthias Church in the suburbs in two weeks. They had rented a house near the church. Judy had already started at a large twenty-four-hour emergency clinic in town.

"It's a clinic that does abortions, but Judy assured me that she has no part in that small part of the business," Annie had offered. "She was a trauma nurse in California, and the new clinic has an urgent care practice." Anthony found it once again interesting that his mother always defended the imperfections in everyone but her own family members.

Judy had called Annie to renew their friendship with the Conways, and there was a family dinner planned for Sunday after mass at St. Veronica's. Ron had asked about Anthony, and Annie very much wanted him to be there. He was to come up to Milwaukee on Sunday morning, attend church with the family, and come back to the house with Ron and Judy for a family lunch. Lynn and her family would be there, although Alan and his wife would not.

There were so many reasons to say no. Feeling sixteen again, utter rebellion came to mind first. But also the fact that

Anthony was still sorting out the demise of his almost renewed relationship with Claire and his feelings about Ron's part in that. He was back in his *alone phase*, having rid himself of Bill for no particularly good reason. He was a much less frequent member of the Sidetracks group on Friday nights and was rarely taking phone calls, preferring to screen them through his machine and call back with measured, preplanned conversations. But for reasons inexplicable—perhaps because he was already resigned to the fact that Ron would never truly be gone—Anthony accepted the invite, already regretting that he'd not chosen to screen this call. Annie was delighted.

As the week wore on, the weather mirrored Anthony's increasingly conflicted feelings. Every day was both sunny and rainy, sometimes simultaneously. He got soaked three times, twice going to the office and once coming home, each time because the sunshine just minutes before the deluge convinced him he didn't need an umbrella. On Friday, he came into the apartment wet and angry that he'd been tricked yet again. Pondering the weekend, he knew he didn't want to sit at his mother's table while Ron was exalted by his family. But he didn't want to miss it either. It might be a cathartic reunion, he hypothesized. Like the weather. Sunny and raining at the same time. But he had to admit that the reunion was likely to leave him without immediate resolution. He might find no attachment to the present-day Ron, nothing interesting or remotely attractive. Or the connection between the two—the connection that Anthony had come to question over the years—could be reestablished. As the sunshine had lied to him about the coming downpour, Anthony knew that his feelings at any moment during the week could not adequately predict how the reunion would go. He spent the week at his desk preoccupied with the possibilities. He was sure he was different now—different from just a year or two earlier. Perhaps Ron would have no hold on him. Of course, the historical Ron did have a hold on him—always had. But the *Ron of today* might not. It seemed important to Anthony that Ron had asked about him. Was there a chance that they could be together in some way? Did Ron indeed still feel something? If he was available, did Anthony want Ron in his life? Was Dawn wrong in all those sessions in which she maligned Ron? It was certainly Dawn who did the vilifying. He remembered that it was she who made Anthony believe that there was something wrong. In the end, even if there was some impropriety in the original relationship, they were both adults now, the years separating their ages inconsequential. Counting on his fingers while gazing out the office window at the drizzle, he figured that Ron was now nearly forty. While a relationship between a twenty-three-year-old and a fourteen-year-old was perhaps unwise when they'd first met, their current ages—forty and thirty-one—would barely register. Anthony realized in making his calculation that he didn't really know when Ron's birthday was. All those years in the choir, he didn't remember ever hearing of a birthday. Ron was too big for the celebrations of the common folk.

He decided that he needed to make an entrance on Sunday, to be rebellious enough not to be there at the appointed time. Frankly, he didn't want to return to St. Veronica's. There was nothing there for him. On Saturday morning, he called his mother.

"I've been attending church here, Mom, and tomorrow there is a special choir performance that I don't want to miss. I think I'll come after church for lunch."

Annie was conflicted. She didn't like anyone messing with her plans, but it was good news to hear that Anthony was attending church. She was full of questions. "Are you going to the cathedral? That was such a beautiful building. Do you remember when we sang there?" As always, he paced as he talked on the phone, the habit made easier by the recent purchase of a cordless phone. He still resented her reference to choir activities in the *we*. She was never part of the choir, only an overage wannabe.

Sighing as he looked out the front window toward a sugar maple, he focused on the task of getting out of going to church with the family. "I remember the cathedral, Mom. I'm attending a church in the neighborhood here. It's much more convenient, and I like the smaller congregation. I don't really even know if the cathedral has a congregation, so to speak. Cathedrals aren't parishes, are they?" Without awaiting an answer, he continued. "Anyhow, I am going to St. Peter's—it's only about six blocks from here." He assumed she wouldn't dream that St. Peter's was anything but Catholic, and she didn't.

"Maybe we'll come down there sometime and go to church with you. Is that where your girlfriend goes?"

He hadn't thought of involving her in the story, but he'd become such a comfortable liar. "Yep, and it's funny, because she went to a St. Peter's when she was a kid in St. Louis, too." Should Annie ever come down to Chicago to go to church, which was unlikely, since he never invited his parents down, he'd have to create a number of new lies to cover those just told.

There were more questions about logistics—what time was Mass at his church? What time would he get to the Conway house? Should she hold lunch until he got there? And there were warnings—it would be impolite to make Ron and Judy sit and wait for his arrival, the portion of the afternoon they could spend with the family was unknown, and it was possible that he would miss them if he ran into construction on the interstate.

"Judy works nights," Annie explained, "and may have to leave for work."

He had said that he was going to Mass at nine. The family would be meeting Ron and Judy at the ten-fifteen Mass at St. V's. Thus, Anthony assured his mother that he could be at the house by noon, when lunch was planned. However, he warned, they shouldn't wait. If he was late, he'd catch up when he got there.

Annie reviewed the menu, as if it were a matter of importance. Ham, scalloped potatoes (Ron had said Annie's were the best!), rolls from scratch, and two kinds of pie. Eventually Annie wore herself out with fretting, and Anthony was able to hang up. He could picture the group around the dining room table, already middinner when he arrived. The plan was set in his head before he placed the phone back on the receiver.

He went for a long walk through Lincoln Park early on Saturday evening. He wanted to review all that had happened, from the choir years to his journey with Claire, and then Frankie, and finally his therapy. But his mind didn't cooperate. Instead, he alternated between visions of his childhood sexual relationship with Ron and the possibility of a renewed relationship with Ron. He tried to consider the chance that this meeting might break him of any need for Ron ever again. But that scenario didn't seem interesting. One thing was clear. Anthony realized that he wouldn't know how to view Ron until he was there in the room with him. It was unsettling.

Toward the end of the walk, he settled into thinking about moments with Ron that had brought him happiness as a teen: hearing the music of Corelli at the first concert he'd attended, riding in the new Camaro on that frigid winter night when they first had sex, and the first time he brought his own record album over and played it on Ron's stereo as if he belonged there. There were good memories. Things not damaging. There was a relationship that surely impacted both of them for life. Of that he was sure.

Later in the evening, Anthony walked to Sidetracks. He saw some familiar faces but quickly struck up a conversation with a stranger in order to avoid anyone who might know anything about him. The bar was crowded, more crowded than the typically full Saturday night. It was smoky and loud. Communication was stilted and difficult with the pushing crowd and loud music. After about an hour, he invited the stranger—Tim—back to his apartment. It was after one, and Tim seemed hurried, as if under some curfew. After some prodding, he admitted that he was married, his wife believing he was at the White Sox game. He was already late in coming home and had called her to say he was going out for a sandwich just before Anthony had come into the bar. To Tim's surprise, none of this bothered Anthony. On the contrary, it meant that he wouldn't have to make breakfast for someone in whom he had no interest. Once at the apartment, the sex was hurried and hollow. The cab arrived a few minutes after the call was made, and Tim was gone by two thirty. Anthony showered and climbed into bed, pushing thoughts of the next day as far away as possible. He began to wish that Tim had stayed, since it would have been a distraction. But he managed to fall asleep, awaking at eight. He watched the light play through the sheers covering the windows and thought about the mornings at Claire's, when he'd also lain in bed and watched the morning come through the window. It had been a cool night for July, and the windows were open. There was a breeze playing through the curtains, the dancing shadows on the wall a distraction. Tim had been fun, but Anthony was not satisfied. He needed to see Ron without any needs. He wanted to assess him from a position of power, if one was available.

Getting out of bed, he grabbed the phone and called Bill, who was up and getting ready to head into town for services at St. Peter's. Although it was a long trip, with many other churches between Libertyville and the Lakeview neighbor-hood, Bill had recently decided to move back into the city so he could continue his attendance at St. Peter's, figuring he'd settle in the neighborhood around Boystown. "I'd like to be with someone special this morning, Bill," Anthony began. "Can I talk you out of church if I promise you a mind-blowing experience in my apartment? You'll scream for God—I guarantee it!"

An hour later Bill arrived, and Anthony took him directly to the bedroom. An hour after that, Bill walked out the door, looking psychologically dazed. It was clear that the only reason he'd been summoned was for sex. Anthony's comment that he "needed someone special" didn't add up. He was almost rude in pushing Bill out the door, assuring him he could still make the late-morning service at St. Peter's. The sex was good. Everything else was suspicious.

Anthony showered for the second time that day and began dressing for lunch. It was eleven ten when he started his car. He couldn't possibly be at his parents' in Milwaukee before twelve thirty, a half an hour after lunch was to begin. It was closer to one when he parked the car. As he got out, he felt the sudden urge to retreat and take a drive past Ron's old house before seeing Ron again, but his mother saw him through the dining room window and rose from the table.

"I'm really sorry," Anthony began as the door swung open. "The Mass was long with all the choir music, and the damn freeway is really torn up. They're painting bridge supports or something, and it's down to one lane just south of the state line."

Annie, not wanting to make a scene in front of guests, hugged Anthony demonstratively, as everyone watched from the table. She smiled. "No one told you to move to that crowded city!" she quipped. Taking him by the arm, she led him ceremoniously through the living room to the adjoining dining room.

There he was. A load of scalloped potatoes on his fork, midway between plate and mouth. He looked rather unremarkable—thin, gawky, all arms and legs. Older but completely recognizable. Smaller and more human.

He was ugly. Anthony had never made this assessment when he was young. But clearly, Ron was not an attractive man. Pockmarks littered his face. His eyes bulged slightly. Scooping the potatoes into his mouth and chewing as he stood, he came around the table, maintaining eye contact with Anthony as he moved. His right hand reached out to shake Anthony's even as his left arm moved to pull Anthony into a friendly hug. "My gosh, you've grown up!" Ron's first words after ten years were innocuous. The tone was the same as he remembered and the body language unchanged. Judy had also risen, and she hugged Anthony and stepped back, considering the two men. In an instant, Anthony realized that she knew. Maybe not everything and maybe not about Anthony specifically. But she knew about her husband. It was clear that she was assessing more than the degree of maturing Anthony had undergone since they'd last seen each other. She was smiling, but through clenched teeth. She had never been thin, but clearly she'd gained weight over the years. However, she was still pretty, with short, curly hair and crisp eyes.

"Sit, sit!" Annie implored. It appeared lunch had started later than noon, as they were still midmeal and it was nearly one. It was gratifying to think they'd waited for him and he'd still not arrived when they'd started late. He had the power to delay them, if nothing else. Anthony's seat was across from Ron, to Judy's left. Keith was to Anthony's left, at the head of the table; he patted his son's shoulder affectionately as he sat. Annie, of course, was across from Judy, next to Ron. The opposite end of the table contained Lynn and her family. Before sitting, Anthony moved around the table and kissed his sister on the cheek, holding her for just a moment but long enough to denote it as a greeting unusual for the siblings. Anthony had considered beforehand that Lynn knew too— and that she would be sitting at the table as a participant in the secret. But now that the moment was upon him, he felt odd in front of his sister.

The platters and bowls made their way politely to Anthony, who was obviously expected to catch up. He wasn't in the least bit hungry but took a single slice of ham and one spoonful of potatoes. Ron reached across the table. "I'm sure you'll want some of this," he exclaimed. In his left hand was a heaping bowl of the family-famous lime Jell-O torte. There was a gleam in Ron's eye—an amusement as he handed the dish across the table. "Could he possibly remember?" Anthony thought. It had always been completely understandable that Anthony remembered every detail, every event. So of course he remembered that lime Jell-O torte was a source of amusement at the first choir party just after Anthony's first sexual experience with Ron. But it never occurred to him that Ron would remember such a triviality. Taking the bowl, Anthony broke eye contact with Ron and felt Lynn's concerned stare. She didn't know specific events of the past and was thus to be suspicious of every reference, every comment.

Annie restarted the conversation that was apparently in progress when he had arrived—a discussion of the choir's trip to St. Louis and whether it took place before or after the trip to Minneapolis. Everyone agreed that Chicago was the first trip the choir had taken. Ron thought that St. Louis was next and that it was the place where hamsters had been set loose in the school where they were lodging, presumably by Alan Conway. But Annie was sure that Minneapolis was the second trip and that it was at the school there where the midnight prank in the science room had taken place. She mentioned to Ron and Judy that Anthony's girlfriend was from St. Louis.

"Which was it?" Annie asked, looking to Anthony.

Lynn interjected. "Oh, Mother, Anthony wouldn't remember—it wasn't that important to him." Anthony appreciated Lynn's attempt to protect him, to establish the ground rule that Anthony wasn't going to play "remember when." Of course, he did remember. He remembered every detail. It was St. Hedwig's school in Minneapolis, it was the second trip, and it was the site of the hamster release.

"I think Mom's right. We went to Minneapolis second." Wanting to qualify why he remembered—that it had nothing to do with Ron—Anthony continued, "The reason I remember is that it was really hot, and we stopped on the way to sing at the cathedral in La Crosse, and the church was cool inside, because it was stone. We didn't go to St. Louis until the fall—"

"Yes!" Annie interrupted. "You have such a great memory of those good times, Son."

Lynn changed the subject at least three times during the lunch, asking Judy about her new job, asking their father about how the HMO craze was impacting the hospital pharmacy, and asking Annie where she'd bought the ham. But nobody bit on the bait to switch topics. Annie would not be denied the opportunity to relive the glory days of her life with Ron. After the third, rather uncomfortable attempt by Lynn, Anthony caught her eye and winked—saying that it was okay with the gesture.

No one seemed to notice that Anthony ate nearly nothing. No one was aware of his discomfort with the reunion. He himself was uncertain of what feelings he had sitting across from Ron after all these years. Was it revulsion at the events of the past now rekindled? Or amusement at the smallness of the man now presented? Or was there a tinge of excitement at the reunion of two long-lost lovers? Lunch ended, and everyone moved to the living room as Lynn and Anthony cleared the dishes and Annie served brownies. Once safely in the kitchen, Lynn took Anthony's arm as she leaned against the counter. Tears filled her eyes.

"I'm so sorry, Anthony. Knowing what happened and seeing him here takes all my memories and destroys them. I want to kill him."

"It's okay. I came here to see what was real about my memories. I was looking forward to this." The two paused, each considering what was real about their pasts. "God, he's really ugly!" They both howled with laughter.

"I know—Jesus, what was all the fuss?" Lynn laughed. The tension broken, they laughed louder and more deeply than the joke warranted. The tears on Lynn's cheeks came from laughter, and the two held on to each other as if they were about to collapse from trying to catch their breath. Annie's voice rose gleefully from the living room. "Hey, you two kids, no fooling around during dishes!" She laughed, expressing pride that her grown children were still close and explaining to Judy how much she enjoyed watching them embrace life. She again mentioned something about Anthony's girlfriend from St. Louis and then finished by stating plainly that it was the choir that kept the kids close as teens. In the kitchen, Lynn rolled her eyes, and the two began laughing all over again, if only to avoid the real emotion of the moment.

The leftovers refrigerated and the dishes stacked, Lynn and Anthony returned to the living room. The platter of brownies sat on the dining room table, and Lynn took one as she passed.

The visit continued for another hour, focusing mostly on Annie and her trip into the past. But even she eventually became interested in the present. Answering her questions, Ron shared that they had rented a house in Greendale, near

the church where Ron was the new music director. They hoped
to buy the house from the owner, but he was not quite ready to
sell, which worked out for them, since they wanted to get used
to the new jobs and neighborhood before making the purchase.
Annie asked their plans for children, and Judy explained that
they'd had no luck in conceiving. Annie encouraged them to
pursue adoption and told a story of the daughter of one of her
card-club friends whose daughter had conceived just as soon
as she stopped trying. "Perhaps the day you adopt you'll get
pregnant and have your family all set," she encouraged.

Ron's interest had piqued at the third mention of a girlfriend by Annie. He asked how long Anthony had been seeing
her, while Judy asked if it was serious. They both seemed to be
looking to determine his availability, perhaps with the same
reason in mind but surely with opposite motivations. Anthony
answered the questions with few words, and the topic changed
quickly. For most of the afternoon, he was much more an
observer than a participant. Ron focused on Annie and Judy,
who did most of the talking, but directed his glances and smirks
at Anthony with some regularity. He couldn't help but wonder
why he'd ever thought of Ron as handsome or sexy. Yet there
was still a draw, a desire to be chosen by this man.

At three o'clock, Judy apologized that they had to leave. She
needed to go home to change and had to be at the clinic for
her shift. She was working from four to one, Sunday through
Thursday. There was much agreement, at Annie's prompting,
that they should all see more of one another. As they all stood
to say their good-byes, Ron spoke to Anthony, perhaps his first
personal message to him during the visit. "I didn't get to hear
about your life in Chicago, Anthony. I love that city and actually looked for a job there, although it would have put Judy a
little too far from her parents. The medical field is so hot that

she can find work anywhere, especially because she likes the odd shifts. I was thinking that after Judy goes to work tomorrow, I could drive down and buy you dinner. I'd love to catch up. Would that work for you?"

Anthony thought quickly. He didn't want Ron in his world. "Actually, I have a meeting tomorrow up near the state line. Why don't I come up after work and pick you up at your house? I've been longing for dinner at Mick's Steakhouse here anyhow." Lynn looked concerned for Anthony as Annie ran to get paper and pencil so Anthony could record Ron's address. The plan made, Ron and Judy left but not before Anthony noticed Judy's troubled look.

Anthony stayed an hour longer to visit with his family, Lynn's husband, Jack, having walked the two children to the nearby playground. The conversation was uneasy, Annie talking incessantly about the choir, Keith retreating to his den in disinterest, and Lynn continually changing the subject. In the end, there was no scolding by Annie about Anthony's tardiness. He felt himself an observer of a family he barely knew anymore—a mother stuck in the past, a father who had never been all that interested, and a sister trying to protect him from something she really didn't understand. When he stood to leave, Lynn hugged him and whispered, "Call me if you want company for dinner. Jack's home tomorrow night and can stay with the kids. He'll understand." The way she said *understand* spoke volumes, but he didn't pursue it.

"Thanks. I'll let you know," he replied.

It wasn't until he was home that he could consider what seeing Ron had meant to him. He was ultimately unsure. He didn't seem like the same hero Anthony had remembered. Amazingly, he had never even finished college, volunteering that he still had one year to complete and might do that back at the conservatory in town. Anthony had passed Ron in school, just as he'd passed his sister many years before. By the sounds of the stories Ron had shared at Annie's prompting, he'd continued to build great youth and adult choirs. These choirs had performed in other cities and had recorded albums. While Lynn had married and started a family and Anthony had completed college and built a career, it seemed Ron had simply repeated his earlier successes. But he didn't seem embarrassed by the telling of old stories with new names, and Annie was completely enthralled as his audience.

In the end, Anthony was excited to have been invited to dinner—to have been *chosen* once again. Not Annie. Not Lynn or Alan. No one else from the choir. He had chosen Anthony. Old feelings were still there.

He ignored two calls as he sat listening to music in his living room. Checking later, he had a message from Lynn telling him that Jack was golfing the next evening but she would get a sitter if he wanted her to go to dinner. The second was from Bill, and he listened to it twice. "Anthony, this is Bill. I'm really puzzled by this morning. It seems like something is going on with you that I don't know about. Of course, there is always something going on in your head that I don't know about. Listen, I still really care about you. I know I freaked you out talking about moving in together. I've got my house up for sale and found a place this past week out near Wrigley. I'm not looking to pressure you, but I'd like to start again. As friends. I really care about you. Call me."

Erasing the messages, he went to bed.

Thirty

Anthony drove into the office on Monday, going in early to ensure he would have a parking space. It was a hot and very humid day, the kind that shrouded the Loop in a brownish haze. The morning weatherman had predicted it to be the beginning of a week of hot breezes from the south. As he drove down Clark, he pondered the fact that while a resident could still picture the skyline, to the novice it would appear that the city had no buildings taller than thirty or so stories, everything impressive about the Loop having been erased by the haze. He parked the car while wondering if this reunion with Ron was the same—an event whose most interesting features were shrouded by the haze of time and denial.

He had a good deal of research to do, as he was assisting his staff with a huge project. Typically he coordinated the research efforts rather than partook. It was tedious and boring to him nowadays but still demanding of focus. As was his practice in his earlier years, he brought out his Sony Walkman and popped in a cassette. Wearing headphones and listening to soft music while doing research kept him focused and undistracted by rattling copy machines and friendly passersby. He spent the morning on task, Ron and the dinner suspended outside his headphones. After some early-afternoon meetings, he returned to his office. Calling Lynn, he assured her that the dinner with Ron would be fine and she did not need to join them. She protested a little and made her brother promise to call her when he got home, regardless of the time. After hanging up, he put his headphones back on and continued the research. At quarter past four, having made good progress, he closed up his work and stood to leave. He felt fully in control, deceived by the day's measured and managed work. Recognizing the impact the music had had on his focus, he grabbed the Walkman and two cassettes to listen to on the way to Milwaukee. His car had a tape deck, but his urge was to keep the world out as long as possible, and the headphones were effective for that.

Although slightly ahead of the worst of the rush hour, he was still snarled by the traffic as he entered the Edens Expressway heading north out of the city. He had told Ron it would be close to seven before he got there. It took an hour to get through the city and out to the suburbs, the traffic moving better from there. It was six o'clock when he passed the *Welcome to Wisconsin* sign and quarter to seven when he pulled up in front of Ron's house. Surprisingly, Ron was on the porch and came down to the car before Anthony got out. Sliding into the seat next to him, Ron sighed, "Ah, air-conditioning. There's no air in this fuckin' house, and I haven't bought window units yet."

As Anthony pulled away from the curb, Ron leaned to one side and extracted the Walkman from the seat on which he was sitting. "I hope I didn't break this. I didn't see it there when I got in."

Taking it from him and setting it onto the backseat, Anthony replied, "It's supposed to be for jogging, so I think it's pretty tough." The reference to being tough brought to mind Ron's abuse of the refrigerator in his house at the first choir party, and Anthony opened his mouth to say, "Remember when..." but thought better of it.

Mick's Steakhouse was not far from where Anthony had grown up and was less than twenty minutes from where Ron and Judy were now settling. There was an uneasy silence after the initial comments when the two pulled away from the house, and Anthony now struggled to find something innocuous to talk about, fearing that there would be a full twenty-minute silence between the house and Mick's. Mercifully, Ron was faster to find conversation.

"You look the same—just older," Ron offered. "You look good. Not so skinny as you were as a kid—you must work out." Anthony didn't really work out very much but knew that he certainly had more of a man's build now than he had as teen. "I think I would have known you if I saw you on the street," Ron continued.

"You haven't changed a bit," Anthony countered. "Course, you were already pretty much grown up when I met you."

"That's funny. I feel like I was such a kid then. But I guess I haven't changed much. The things I thought were true then have just become truer over the years. People are still an enigma and a complete mystery to me. And music is still my constant."

"How so?" Anthony wasn't all that engaged in the topic but didn't want to be responsible for introducing a new subject.

"I don't know. Hmm…there's more structure in my life—that's for sure. We owned a house in California, so I did the painting and lawn-cutting thing, just like my dad did when I was a kid. We'll probably buy a house here, too—maybe the one we're renting."

He suddenly sounded so boring. Cutting the lawn? Just like his dad? Anthony couldn't imagine himself ever breathing those words aloud. His life was nothing like his dad's. And although organized, it would never be described as *structured.* "I don't have a lawn to cut, which I guess is nice. I live in a condo. The extent of my outside work is to buy a couple of potted geraniums at the grocery store and put them on my balcony!"

This comment led to a discussion of where Anthony lived—the advantages of urban dwelling, the minimal need for a car, and the opportunities for nightlife. As the topic wound down, Anthony pulled into the lot next to Mick's. It was just after seven, and the heat of the sun was still on the asphalt lot, distorting one's view through the sweltering waves rising from the tar. Anthony put the car in park, but before he could shut off the engine, Ron spoke. "Are you sure this is where you want to eat?"

Perplexed, Anthony turned toward the passenger seat. "I don't eat red meat very often, and they have great steak. But if you want to eat somewhere else, I don't care." He waited, and Ron smiled the familiar smile.

"I thought we could head down to the warehouse district, for old times' sake." Anthony was confused. The only thing he'd ever done in the warehouse district was go to the Depot, and he'd only gone there with Ron a few times. It really wasn't a major part of their history—not like the house on Forty-Seventh or St. V's.

"What restaurant is down there?" Anthony asked. "We can head down that way, but I don't know any restaurants there." As he spoke, he reached for the gearshift but then paused, awaiting an answer.

"I don't know," Ron began. "I'm really not that hungry. We could stop and get a burger if you're hungry and then see if the Depot is still there—just for laughs."

Anthony was confused. "You want to go to the gay bar?" His mind whirred. Suddenly he wasn't hungry either. Did Ron know? Had he been to Chicago—seen him at Sidetracks? Did he know someone who knew Anthony? The thoughts came too fast for him to put a cogent answer together, so he answered his own question with another question. "Why do you want to go there?"

"Just for old times' sake. We had good times together there, Anthony. I just want to live in the past a little. It will be fun to see if the bar is still there and who goes there now."

"Probably no one on a Monday night," Anthony stated flatly as he backed the car out of the spot and headed for the street. "But we can see." As he turned east out of the parking lot and figured a route downtown in his head, Ron spoke again.

"Even though I am married, I still like to go to bars with friends sometimes. Not always gay bars, but I like to hit them once in a while. It's a different crowd, and I usually find better conversations there. There's this bar in San Fran I really liked— it was really two bars in one. There was this noisy dance bar on one side and a leather bar on the other. The other leather bar in town was the really wild one with a dark back room and all the weirdoes. You could see anything you wanted to there. But this one had a quiet bar with older guys who liked dressing in chaps and leather vests. There were some pool tables, and it was dark. I liked it. Just a lot of guys sitting around talking." Anthony's mind went to an image of Rosco's in Green Bay. No leather-clad guys there, but it was a dark corner-bar kind of a place. His vision was interrupted by Ron's question. "Where do you hang out in Chicago?"

Anthony thought. "I work a lot. Sometimes I meet friends for dinner or a drink. I never go to the really loud places. There are some neighborhood places we meet at sometimes."

"Do you live far from the Boystown area?" Anthony wondered how he would have known about that area of Chicago. It seemed Ron was fishing.

"Actually, I'm kind of close. I'm between the Loop and Wrigley, in a great little urban neighborhood of apartment buildings and brownstones built in the thirties. Boystown is on Halsted, and that's not too far from me. I've been there a few times." As soon as he acknowledged that he knew of Boystown, he was sorry, not wanting to open himself up to more questions. He did not want to answer the "Are you gay?" question.

"It's too bad I didn't come down there. I'd like to check out that area. It's cool that you live there."

"I don't live *there*," Anthony corrected. "But it's not too far. Why are you interested in the gay areas?" He felt emboldened asking the question. Like the one time he had turned the tables on Claire when he was in St. Louis.

"I like all kinds of people. All kinds of experiences. I like to find pleasure where it can be found. The gay scene is a more open scene."

"What about Judy? Does she go with you?"

"She's always worked nights. And she doesn't mind where I go. I behave myself!" Ron laughed and gently patted Anthony's right knee, leaving his hand there momentarily on the last pat.

"Find pleasure where it can be found." Anthony found himself heading back to where he was at fourteen. A one-sided relationship. It had felt good in spite of the imbalance in power when he was young. Was Ron working to establish some imbalance again? Anthony wasn't sure he was as excited about it this time. Even as he reminded himself that he was thirty-one, he saw himself once again standing on the edge of acceptance looking for scraps. If he was going to be Ron's friend, it was going to be on Ron's terms. Perhaps sensing some trepidation in Anthony, Ron changed the subject, running through names of people who had been in the St. Veronica's Youth Choir and asking if Anthony had seen any of them. The names of old choir members were fired off by Ron, and Anthony repeatedly replied that he hadn't seen this or that person since he'd gone to college ten years earlier.

In twenty-five minutes, the two were entering the Depot. It was nearly empty—expected for early evening on a Monday. The fifteen or so in the large bar all looked curiously at Ron and Anthony, as if they had been the first unknown visitors on such an evening in a long time. Monday was regulars' night at most bars, and the Depot was no exception. Ron chose two stools on the corner of the wooden bar and ordered a beer before the bartender asked.

Little had been changed by the years. Just inside the door was the narrow side of the U-shaped bar that ran the length of room. It faced a dimly lit dance floor on the right that was corralled by a knee-high wall of cheap paneling. Beyond the dance area were two pool tables under Miller High Life lamps. Restrooms were at the far side of the rectangular bar. The ceiling tiles looked like the same ones under which Anthony had danced years earlier, smoke stained and dingy. This place, packed on a Saturday night, had been a focal point of Anthony's life when he was eighteen. Now, with a Monday night crowd too thin to hide the shabbiness, it seemed tawdry and boring.

Anthony thought for a moment and then ordered a Tanqueray and tonic. It was his favorite summertime drink. Gin was the only liquor he knew well enough to be discerning about, always ordering either Tanqueray or Bombay Sapphire. He would pass if he had to drink the cheap rail gin. The bartender nodded and returned with the two drinks, taking the time to twist a lime into Anthony's. On a busy Saturday, he would be lucky to have a bartender drop one in the drink, and he wondered if bartenders enjoyed these slow nights when they could practice their craft correctly. A proper gin and tonic should always have a twist of lime. Ron was ready with cash and bought the first round. Surprisingly, he took both drinks, which had been set on the bar, and turned to Anthony, offering him the gin and tonic ceremoniously. Holding up his beer, he proposed a toast. "To our return to the scene of the crime!" he said lightheartedly.

"What was the crime?" a rather disheveled man two stools down asked through a gap-toothed smile.

Ron was quick with an answer. "I haven't seen this guy in ten years," he began, not turning toward the man. Eyes locked on Anthony's, he continued. "He brought me here and showed me a lot of the best times of my life. I'm hoping that today is the first of many new good times."

"If he don't want to show you a good time, slide over!" the new friend said enthusiastically.

"Easy, Mel." The bartender added with a wink and smile. "Don't scare off the new guys."

The two embarked on some additional catch-up, about Ron's work in California, his choirs there, Judy's work, and their decision to come back to Wisconsin to be near family. Anthony talked about his work and about college. He felt some sense of power in the discussion of college, knowing Ron couldn't top him in that area. Ron asked about the girlfriend Annie had mentioned at lunch the day before.

"I wouldn't call her my girlfriend," Anthony answered uneasily. "She's really just a friend. I wanted to spend Thanksgiving with some friends in St. Louis, so I made her sound more important to get out of the family holiday disaster. My mom's determined to get me married off, so she gets crazy when she hears that I'm seeing someone. I don't usually say much about who I date, but this one was convenient."

Ron looked around. There were a few men around the nearest pool table, eyeing the visitors curiously. "Have you been back here since we used to hang out here?"

"I used to come here pretty often, even without you, when I was first eighteen. But after I went up to St. Norbert's, I didn't come home much on weekends. I don't think I've been here in ten years. Hasn't changed much."

"How often do you hang out in Boystown? I hear there are at least ten gay bars on a few blocks there."

"That's probably right. I haven't been in most of them. I've been there a few times with friends. But there are also some great blues clubs near where I live. I go there, too."

"So, no big attraction to gay life?" Ron leaned toward Anthony and smiled. Whether it was an inquisitive or accusatory smile, Anthony couldn't tell. Either way, Ron's question was clear. Perhaps admitting to continuing with gay sexual relationships after Ron left Wisconsin would let Ron know that their relationship was real—that it was not an accident for Anthony. Being straight would indicate that what they'd had was an error. Suddenly he had an urge to let Ron know that what had happened between them was okay. Was good. Was positive.

"To quote a friend, 'I find pleasure where it's available. I don't judge, and I don't wait for the future promise of something better.'" Anthony sat back on his barstool and emptied his drink. He signaled to the bartender that another round was needed. As he set his empty glass on the bar, he pulled an American Express card from his wallet and dropped it on the sticky counter with a planned look of carelessness—as if he did it every day. "Can you just start a tab?" Anthony called to the bartender.

"We don't do that on busy nights, but as long as it stays like this tonight, I can."

Anthony nodded to the barkeep and said, "Bring another drink for Ron's new friend, Mel, too." Mel smiled, at least three teeth missing. Ron shifted with slight discomfort at having been offered as a friend without his permission. Anthony smiled, self-satisfied. "We'll see who's powerful," he thought.

Ron regained his composure and turned fully toward Anthony, perhaps to establish some distance between himself and Mel. "Smart friend who gave you that advice. So, how much pleasure have you found in Boystown?" He leaned in further and smiled. Anthony knew this question was going to keep on coming—in some form or another. He'd known that since he'd laid eyes on Ron the day before. Was Anthony gay? That was the real question Ron was asking. Did Anthony like girls or boys? Hadn't that always been the question?

Anthony responded coyly, "There's a great restaurant on the corner of Belmont and Halsted, right at the beginning of Boystown. Jacques, it's called. I've had some of my favorite meals with some of my favorite people there."

It was clear that what was not said in Anthony's reply answered Ron's questions insufficiently. Yet both sensed an establishment of order in this renewed relationship. Ron already had the answers. For both of them. He would push the envelope; Anthony would follow. Ron would be comfortable in Anthony's discomfort. Nothing had changed. Anthony could toy with control over his destiny, but Ron would ultimately decide for both of them.

The two sat through two more drinks, and at nearly ten o'clock, Ron strolled to the men's room in a zigzag that reminded Anthony of the wedding reception and their stroll to the men's room. Anthony watched him go, realizing that he himself was not exactly sober either. Still safe to drive but not of completely clear thought. He was gone a long time, and Anthony was beginning to wonder about him when he saw Ron emerge just ahead of Mel. Somewhere in their conversation, Mel had gone over to the pool tables. Anthony had lost track of him, but apparently he had gone into the bathroom either just before or behind Ron. He wondered if Ron had chosen his time to use the restroom with that in mind.

Instead of sliding back onto the barstool, Ron put his hand on Anthony's shoulder and remained standing. "Let's go." The bartender had seen the indicators and was already figuring the tab. He brought a charge card and tab to Anthony, who added a twenty-five percent tip and signed, taking the carbon copy of the receipt with the card and shoving them into his wallet. Scanning the sparse crowd, Anthony noted that Mel was sitting on the lap of a drunk pool player.

Heading out of the warehouse district, the two were quiet, the air-conditioning fan in the car providing distraction. As they neared Ron's house, Ron spoke. "I hope it's cooled off in the house. You can only park on the opposite side of the street from the house, so you'll want to come around the block from the other side when we get there." Ron expected Anthony to come inside. Anthony hadn't thought about that possibility until just then.

Obediently, he entered Ron's street from the opposite direction he'd come earlier that evening, parking the car behind a red Pontiac Bonneville with California plates. "That's my car. I need to get over to the DMV and get my Wisconsin plates. I didn't want to renew my California plates before I left, and they're expired now. Yesterday a cop in a parking lot warned me to get it done, but he didn't give me a ticket." Indeed, the blue sticker on the lower-right corner of the plate read *APR*—the month the plates should have been renewed. "Classic Ron," thought Anthony. "Breaking the rules and receiving no penalty."

Although a decent evening breeze had come up and all of the windows in the house were open, it was still warm and stale when they stepped off the porch into the sunroom of the house. The small entry room led into a large living room that ran lengthwise across the front of the bungalow. A fire-place—either originally only for show or later rendered nonfunctioning—stood at the far end of the room. A fern with brown-edged leaves was placed in the opening. Anthony had half expected to see the same furnishings from Ron's Forty-Seventh Street apartment, but everything was different. The room was bright, perhaps the result of a woman's touch. The curtains were light and opaque, the floor covered in neutral carpet, and the furniture of a country style in a blue and cream plaid. The dining room, visible from the entryway, had traditional furniture—a wood table with six matching chairs. No piano or stereo components there. The wall held a four-tiered plate rack, each shelf holding four plates with a different landscape scene—all very Norman Rockwell.

Only one piece of Ron's bachelor pad of the 1970s remained. On an end table next to the fake fireplace stood Moses. "You still have Moses!" Anthony exclaimed.

Ron laughed. "It's the only thing Judy's let me keep, and she hates it. She doesn't want it in the living room but can't stand it in the bedroom. I need to see him every day—he's watched everything I've done for many years."

"He's seen a lot then," Anthony remarked with some melancholy.

Ron went over to the stereo—one of the poor-quality all-in-one units—and pushed play on the cassette deck. It was a symphony Anthony had not heard, and it played from where it had been left, somewhere midpassage. The music was twentieth century—Anthony could tell. His least favorite period of classical music. It always sounded too *Broadway* to him—not *classical enough*. Ron spoke. "I saw this performed live in San Francisco last year. I love it. It's so *dissonant*." He looked toward Anthony as if to discern whether he would understand the term.

"Perhaps that's what I don't like about most twentieth-century symphonies. They're dissonant in a clumsy way. It's too pop for me, too Broadway. Too Bernstein, too *West Side Story*. I guess I am an old-school listener." Ron moved to Anthony and put his arm around him playfully. "Expand your horizons, dear fag. New pleasures to find and old pleasures to rediscover." You could smell the beer on his breath and see the haziness of intoxication in his eyes. His hand slid off Anthony's shoulder and down his side. "You still carrying that tennis ball that you had as a teen?"

Everything raced in slow motion. Nothing had changed for Ron. He was the same—hadn't grown and hadn't changed. He would have been like Moses—frozen in his history and his intentions. Except that it seemed that Ron had been somewhat neutered by his conventional wife. The surroundings had been brightened up. More legitimized. But like the statue, he was still stuck in that old position. For Moses, it was the futility of his quest to bring his followers into a better existence. They could cross the desert, but they'd still be an obstinate and unbelieving people. Cattle, really. Wandering around demanding that everyone acknowledge that they were chosen yet doing everything they could to reject the chooser. For Ron, it wasn't a quest for a better existence for his followers; it was a demand that they support his dysfunctional existence. Moses was righteous and his followers dysfunctional. Ron, however, was clearly dysfunctional. What did this mean for his followers?

Anthony could feel it, had felt it since he'd walked into his parents' house the day before. Ron expected there to be no change in Anthony. In fact, no change would be tolerated. Ron had returned to take up governance of his subjects again. The surroundings might be different, but the structure was the same. It was all to start again, just like it before.

But Ron was ignoring all that had changed in Anthony. He wasn't the same as he had been as a teen, was he? Even as he inhaled, preparing to tell Ron to knock it off, he felt the reaction in his pants and in his soul. Had Ron come back for him? Come back *to him*? If this was a continuation of what had gone on years before, could it now be *right*? Anthony was older and wiser. Ron would recognize that—even be attracted to it. Anthony knew it. Had to know it. Ron had returned to find Anthony. Just as Anthony had gone looking for Frankie. Because it had been good. Because Ron realized that it could be what it was meant to be. Anthony lost Frankie. But it all made sense now, because it was always going to be Ron. Claire, Frankie, Bill. None of them were Ron.

He turned toward Ron and put his head on the boney shoulder. It was all making sense. Anthony could never come to terms with who he was while he was so incomplete. It was Ron he needed to be who he was. In an instant, he could see the future. Coming out. Being with Ron. Beginning life again as the person he was meant to be—Ron's lover.

He expected to be enveloped, to be held by the lover who had returned to him. Ron instead steadied him as he stepped back and then reached down and began to undo Anthony's pants. Anthony wanted tenderness. Wanted love. But Ron couldn't wait. He needed Anthony's body. He felt a trickle of sweat run down his back as the belt was released from his pants. Then he heard the zipper. He wanted Ron to know at least that he'd grown up—that he was now an equal lover and an equal partner in bed. He reached out and took hold of Ron's waist, unbuttoning the fly from bottom to top and then stepping forward to take hold of the top of the pants at Ron's hips, even as Ron was doing the same. Their pants slid roughly down, held by the sweat on both their bodies. They stood unbalanced and awkward, pants around their ankles, touching each other. Ron swayed uneasily. Anthony spotted the gaudy country plaid easy chair and steered him carefully back and into the chair. He knelt to remove Ron's shoes and socks and then slid his pants off. He wanted this to be slow and intense lovemaking. Ron, however, was not erect. Anthony set to work to correct that but to no avail. After a few moments of stimulation, he could hear Ron's breathing even out, calm and peaceful. Glancing up, Ron appeared at first to be in thought. But on closer inspection, he was clearly dozing. Anthony raised himself up and kissed Ron, who appeared startled as he smiled.

"Sorry, I'm still on California time." Glancing down at his nakedness, he joked, "Hey, how'd that happen?"

"I don't know. What do we got here?" Anthony responded as he took Ron's flaccid penis in his hand.

"I don't think it's working. It only works for Judy, and even then she has to give it a lot of encouragement."

Anthony was puzzled. "What do you mean?"

"I don't really do this much anymore. I slept with a woman where I worked in San Fran last year, but I couldn't really get it up for her. Judy doesn't know about it; she'd kill me. She's not that into sex, but when we do it, I can usually get off after a while."

"What about men? Have you been getting it up for them?"

"Haven't really had much sex with men in a while. It's just not that interesting."

Anthony was stunned. He stood, looking down at Ron, who was slumped in the awful chair, wrinkled shirt wet with sweat, penis wilted and inadequate, and then at his face, which was unperturbed and glum.

"What do you mean? You're not attracted to guys anymore? To me?" He felt his voice rise. "Why are you here? Why did you want to go to dinner tonight—to skip dinner and go to a gay bar? Why did we come back here and get naked?" As he asked that question, he realized that his own pants were still around his ankles. Stumbling slightly, he brought them back to his waist.

"Don't get pissed, Anthony. This is fine. We can have sex sometimes if you need it. But you can't expect some kind of commitment from me. I'm not back here just for you. Jesus!" Ron sighed heavily, the smell of used beer permeating the room. Assuming his propitiation acceptable, his head sagged back onto the chair, glassy eyes closed.

Suddenly it was clear to Anthony—the selvage of his life was gone. It could have been different. He could have turned out differently. Claire. Frankie. Bill. All had been possibilities. Ron was never a possibility. Scenes played in his head. A college graduation party where Frankie laughed with Lynn and the rest of the family as Anthony cut his cake, cap and gown shimmering in the sunny backyard. Claire, his best friend, holding his hand as they sat in the Rexton Funeral Home at some future date when his father died. Her support and love unconditional. He saw himself attending last year's holiday party at the office but with Bill, introducing him to his coworkers and boss. Happiness. Peace. Love. None of these things happened. Could ever happen. They had not been simply stolen by Ron. Not entirely. They had been forfeited. Given up. Without a fight. A voluntary offering to an impotent god who had offered nothing and taken everything.

Anthony's mind ran like a lemming toward the cliff, following his flood of emotion over the edge. He turned to step away from Ron, his eyes falling on the reliable Moses who had accompanied Ron through his miserable life. In that instant, Anthony knew. Ron wasn't anything like Moses. The prophet, imperfect as he may have been, had passion. Had single-mindedness. Had love for his followers even in his own worst times and in theirs.

Moses gave. Ron took.

Moses was driven by higher purpose. Ron was driven by his need to control.

Moses wanted better from and for his followers. Ron simply required followers.

A tear rolled down Anthony's cheek as he looked back at the man who'd controlled his life. Seeing him, lying drunk and incoherent in that common plaid chair, it was clear that Ron was thoroughly insufficient for all the pain he'd caused. He could not have had that impact without the permission of the follower. Anthony had allowed it all. Ron had never told him to distance himself from Claire or to hurt Frankie. Ron had never told him he couldn't be gay or that being gay was bad. It was Anthony all along. Anthony had told himself that he couldn't be gay. Wouldn't be gay. It was not Ron who was unaccepting; it was Anthony himself.

His wasted life overwhelmed him. The pain he had caused Claire. Twice. The hurt in Frankie, who died without knowing. The surrendered opportunities, the misplaced anger toward his parents, the self-hatred. The refusal to accept what Dawn, what Claire, what everyone had known. He was gay, and it had nothing to do with Ron. Ron wasn't even gay! And now, at this moment, when he would have proclaimed his true self to the world in order to bring Ron into his life, Ron had made clear his own twisted psychology. It was never about sexual orientation; it was never about emotion or concern; it was *never about Anthony*. It was about Ron's own self-hatred and his own fucked-up and now very ordinary life. Anthony felt bile in his throat. It was awful. He himself was awful. He had ruined his own life—no one could be blamed.

He had to get out, to get away. Ron had drifted off to sleep, oblivious to the catharsis in his midst. Peaceful. Self-possessed as always. As Anthony turned, he spied Moses one last time. All these years, the angry prophet had waited to smash the tablets. Frozen. Paralyzed. *Like Anthony*. Stuck in a belief that things could be better when they couldn't. Believing that his life would have some impact when it wouldn't. Giving up everything for a people who didn't want him. He deserved closure.

With one swift movement, he seized the heavy statue, driven by intolerable emotion. Turning back toward Ron, he brought the base of the statue down on the side on Ron's head. The thud was loud, like a bowling ball striking pavement but less crisp. More dead-sounding. More final. Moses broke in two, leaving Anthony with the torso and head of the prophet, while his legs, still attached to the base, tumbled down Ron's body and onto the floor. Ron slumped clumsily in the chair, and his head, visibly creased from above the temple through the ear and down to the jaw, fell to one side. Blood flowed immediately from his ear and the gash just behind the hairline.

Anthony stumbled backward, bending to carefully set what remained of Moses onto the floor. "Ron?" he asked, knowing no response would come. The country plaid of the chairback was now becoming crimson as blood spread onto the cushion and down the front of Ron's shirt. Anthony wiped a tear from his cheek and looked down at his hand, seeing pink. Turning to the mirror over the mantel, he could see blood spattered on his own face. Looking down, he saw the pattern of a fine spray of red on his shirt. His eyes connected with those of Moses, who lay where placed on the floor. They were still angry, still without full cognition of the impact of what he himself had been about to do. After the deed was done—the commandments shattered—Moses had been forced to return to the mountain to beg forgiveness for his transgression, hoping that all would be set right. Replaced. Covered over. Who would wipe this stain away?

How long he stood paralyzed he didn't know. A breeze finally blew the curtains, the movement snapping Anthony into reality. He knew Ron was dead. He had to be. The blood had stopped flowing, a sign that the heart was no longer pumping. Anthony crossed the room as he fished his keys from his pocket. Closing the screen door behind him, he made his way to his car and got in. As if by instinct, he started the engine, put the car in gear, and drove away. Ron was dead. *Ron was dead.* This was not what he'd planned. He'd planned to be immune. To find Ron impotent to draw him in. In the end, he was completely drawn in and then destroyed. "Who will wipe away my stain?" Anthony murmured as he headed in the direction of St. Veronica Catholic Church.

Thirty-One

The streets were quiet and dark, the parking lot behind St. Veronica's empty but for the Burger King bag that dotted the asphalt. It was nearly midnight when he shut off the car, shaking. The humid breeze was useless. He could see the outline of the rose window but no color. The church was silent. The saints slept as Anthony's mind raced. He needed focus. He put the headphones on and hit play on his Walkman, the strings of one his favorite symphonies jumping to life.

He struggled with what to do next. He needed to see her. To see if she still loved him. To ask her to wipe away this stain. He opened the car door and was startled by the dome light. Jumping out, he locked the door behind him and took off the headphones. As he approached the building, he clipped the Walkman to his belt, shoving the headphone cord into his front pocket. Trying the doors around the rear of the church was futile, as they were dutifully locked. Taking a brick-size paving stone from the path between the church and the rectory, he returned to the back side of the building and broke the small leaded-glass window on the door. His efficiency at gaining access to the locked building was surprising, since he'd never done anything remotely like this before. Reaching through, he turned the handle. Glass crunched under his feet like ice giving way as he stepped into the dimly lit hallway leading to the sacristy. The sound reminded him of the crunch of the snow beneath his feet on the first night he'd had sex with Ron.

The smell of wax and incense hit him first. Sweet and warm. The smell of penance. Of guilt. The hallway was resonant, all plaster and terrazzo. His footsteps echoed hollowly as he made his way twenty paces and then turned right into the room just off the altar where server boys and priests met before Mass each Sunday. He'd been in that room dozens of times as a young altar server, but he hadn't seen it in fifteen years.

Going through the room, he walked quietly out onto the altar, resisting the urge to reach up and ring the bell he'd rung so many times to announce the beginning of Mass as he led the priest onto the altar. The practice ended some years ago when the priests began processing up the main aisle rather than entering from this side room. But the bell was still there. Anthony remembered the sense of power that came when, as the server to the right of the priest, he rang the bell and processed onto the altar from the side sacristy.

The church was lit only by candles and exit signs, a penumbra. A rack of red votives cast an eerie glow on the far side of the space. A candle was lit when a prayer of request was offered. For that privilege, the supplicant placed a donation in the small metal box to seal the deal. Only a few of the votives were unlit, indicating that the needs business had been good that day.

Walking down the marble stairs to the head of the main aisle, Anthony looked up to the choir loft. She was there, as always. Dark and perhaps sleeping. Maybe brooding. Or perhaps weeping, already knowing. But ever vigilant, no matter what. "Who will wipe away this stain?" He spoke the words silently inside his head, wondering now which stain he referred to. In addition to his final admission that he was indeed a homosexual, in addition to his complete failure in relationships—hurting people for decades—he was now a murderer. He was the ultimate sinner. His mind flashed to Ron, slumped in the chair, the flow of blood waning as his life leaked out, taking Anthony's with it.

The streetlamps outside struggled through the saints. James and John were disinterested. Moses was too dark to assess. But Veronica—she faced the street itself and was backlit in a competitive manor. She was quiet—casting her gaze downward, bloody towel in hand. He needed her. Knowing the access would be blocked, Anthony made his way quietly down the main aisle, the center of attention in a congregation of empty pews. The rear of the church was farthest from the candles, lit only by three dim exit lamps situated above the end of the main and two side aisles. The double doors at the end of the main aisle were propped open to the vestibule. As he passed, he dipped the fingers of his right hand into the holy water font and made the sign of the cross. He stopped cold, wondering why he'd done that, then looked into the font to see if he'd left blood in the sacred water. It was too dark to discern.

Through the doors and to the right, he approached the staircase to the choir loft. A gate was drawn across the doorway to the stairs—bolted to the wall on the left, pulled like an accordion across the opening, and then locked in place to block access to the stairs. A key was required to open the gate, which was constructed of metal slats that ran diagonally in a crisscross pattern. The bottom was just a few inches above the terrazzo floor, the top about eight inches below the top of the doorway. Holding fast to the gate, Anthony pulled gingerly. Though it flexed, it was locked tight. He shook it timidly and was startled by the metallic rattle. He stood back and listened to his breathing. Judging that the space at the top was insufficient to climb over the gate, he pulled slowly but fully at the bottom, but it did not produce enough space to allow a body to pass underneath.

He had to see her. He needed her. Veronica. The pass-erby saint. The one who understood living without impor-tance. She could wipe away the stain. Resolute, he began walking across the vestibule looking for something with which to break through the gate. It would be noisy, but if done quickly, it would make only the kind of unusual sound that makes you pause to listen but, since it doesn't happen again, doesn't warrant investigation. On the far side of the foyer was a small room, a lounge where the bride would prepare herself before a wedding. He crossed in front of the steps down to the doors to Haley Street and made his way to the bride's lounge. Windowless and dark, he stood in the doorway searching his mind for what he remembered to be in the room. Turning from right to left with his eyes closed, he constructed the room in his mind. There had been two chairs on the right, with a dressing table between them. It had a small stool—easy to lift but too light to break the lock. On the far wall was a bookcase filled with hymnals and religious texts. In front of it and to the left would be a full-length mirror. As his mind scanned farther left, he remembered the brass and marble plant stand that had been there nearly twenty years before. It was as tall as Anthony when he was young—perhaps five feet. Three brass legs tapered out from a solid marble platform at the top. He remembered bumping into it once when he went to fetch a hymnal for Father Francis. He'd turned in panic to catch it before it toppled, only to realize that the pain in his shoulder indicated the unit was far heavier than it looked.

He walked with his hands out, feeling for the stand. As per-manent as the church itself, it was there. A pot of silk flowers could be felt on top of the cool marble shelf. Setting the flowers carefully onto the floor, he picked up the stand, turned, and returned to the foyer. His eyes had adjusted to his surround-ings, and he could see clearly by the dim light streaming in through the leaded windows above the outside doors. Crossing the vestibule, he wondered whether to use a foot of one of the legs to pry the gate open or make the most of the heavy marble to break the lock. Wanting to avoid the sound of impact, he positioned himself with two legs of the stand between the right jamb and gate and began using his weight to apply leverage to the task. The gate groaned and bent near the bottom, but the lock held. As he applied more and more pressure, the gate continued to bend, but the lock was unrelenting. In frustration, he set the stand against the wall and grabbed the bent bottom edge of the gate and began pulling. The gate was bending farther and farther out and toward him, the noise significant but hopefully undetected. After three final tugs, the gate had peeled back far enough for Anthony to squeeze through on his hands and knees and stand up at the foot of the stairs.

The stairs led him on a familiar path. Up four, a turn to the right, up six, another right turn, up six more, down a narrow landing, the up another flight to the right, and then a turn to the final six stairs. The doorway to the loft was at the top. She awaited him. It was warmer in the choir loft, the heat of the day held in by the brick building. Anthony was panting as he crossed the loft and stood in front of the organ, first facing the altar below. Now that he was here, he was afraid to face her. The gravity of what had happened began to weigh him down. His life was over. Ruined. Ruined by Ron more than fifteen years ago. Ruined by Ron today. How could his only hope be this glass saint or even the real saint the colors represented? Did his power to fail exceed her power to fix? Jesus was failing on the day he was dragged through the streets to his death. Veronica's act may have soothed, but it didn't fix. He went on to die; she faded back into the crowd. The only evidence of the encounter immortalized on the towel. Is that the best she could do? She couldn't actually fix anything; she could only retain evidence of the failure she witnessed. Was that her place in Anthony's life now—to be the final witness of his complete failure? That was, perhaps, her only calling all along. To bear witness to struggle. To failure. To give relief but not rehabilitation.

A car turned the corner in front of the church, the headlights passing through Veronica and bathing the sanctuary in momentary light. Anthony saw the altar clearly for a second and knew she had been awoken behind him. He turned to face her. She was dark again but awake. "Will you wash away my stains?" For the first time, the question was personal. And plural. *My stains.*

The quiet was too much. His breathing screamed. The clicks of the building's joints as the cooling night brought contractions were gunshots. He needed music. Fishing the headphones out of his pocket, he put them on and pressed play on the Walkman. The symphony was one of his favorites—Gustav Mahler's Symphony no. 3. It was written in the late 1800s and was in six movements. A long symphony of over ninety minutes, it is a tribute to the creation of the universe. This was a huge symphony, written for an unheard-of eight French horns, four trumpets, and four trombones. He had seen it performed twice in the past ten years, and it took eighty musicians to reconstruct the entire work. Mahler, in general, wrote grandiose symphonies. But Symphony no. 3 is unrivaled in scale, even by his later works. His compositions, like those of Wagner, often dealt with heavy topics like love and faith. It is reported that the composer wrote his symphonies from a hut he had built on the shore of the Attersee in Austria. The hut contained only a bookcase, a wood-burning stove, a writing desk, and a piano. Each of the six movements presents a story about the universe from the perspective of an aspect of creation. The first movement is extraordinarily long. The music is heavy, filled with brasses and cellos.

Somber chords and an even pace but building continually in breadth and complexity. After an introduction, during which the universe is created, the music of the following movements gives the view of the flowers, then the woodland animals, then humankind, and then the angels. The last movement is entitled "What Love Tells Me." The tape was at the fourth movement, which speaks of humankind's view of creation and features a soloist who sings a poem from Nietzsche's *Thus Spoke Zarathustra* set to music. It was one of Anthony's favorite passages, and he had memorized the words. As he turned the volume to the maximum, the poem howled to the music of Mahler.

The words of this movement, sung by a soloist and choir, admonish all of humankind to take heed and to wake. It goes on to say that while the pain of the universe can be deep, joy is deeper—deeper than any heartache a person can suffer. Joy is eternal, the score says.

Anthony stood on the first riser in front of the organ and watched her as the poem screamed in his head. *Pain…Joy… Heartache.*

"When have I ever experienced joy?" He searched himself. "Pain says: pass away!" His tears flowed without control as the fifth movement began—"What the Angels Tell Me."

What could she tell him at this moment? He held her gaze, trusting that she would speak. But this movement had no words for him. He began mouthing her name as the music resounded in his head. "Veronica. Veronica." Whether his voice was audible he could not tell. The music was so loud, so beautiful, that even if he screamed her name he could not hear himself. He was indeed screaming her name, and the building echoed his rants—"Veronica! Veronica!" No one heard him; even he did not hear his own screams. She held his gaze but delivered no message. No salve to soothe the revulsion inside him. She would not speak.

In his panic at her deafening silence, he considered her brief interaction with the Christ. He was suffering immensely at the point of the encounter and had more suffering to go. She stepped out of the crowd to make the connection. Perhaps he had paused there, turned a weary face toward her. Perhaps expecting more abuse. But she soothed. She did what she could. As he envisioned the moment, he could see Jesus incline his head toward the woman. He made himself available to her. Anthony could hear the angry screams of the guard as he lashed out, striking Jesus for stopping. For falling. For failing. But he paused in spite of the danger, the pain. And she stepped out to meet his feeble approach to her. "I must do the same," he thought. "I must step out. Ignore the danger. Risk more pain."

Climbing onto the organ bench, he stepped backward, out onto the rail. A low, plaster wall, the rail was topped with a wood ledge barely eight inches wide. Anthony felt exhilaration as he transferred his weight, his trust, to the rail and then moved sideways and away from the organ console. As he did, he began to sob aloud. He stood where Ron had stood in rebellion to all that would make this choir conventional. When Ron stepped onto the rail years ago at rehearsals, he had stated that all must submit to his methods, his views. Convention didn't apply to him or to his work. Anthony was a piece of his work. He stood there now, not in rebellion but in submission. Complete submission to his failure.

There was a moment of quiet in his head as the tape in the Walkman went silent, the fifth movement ending. He could hear himself and for the first time knew his desperate calls to her were audible. "Veronica. My Veronica." The sixth and final movement began—"What Love Tells Me."

The final passage of the symphony ascended until spiritual. All of the instruments came together in perfect tone and balance. Horns, strings, woodwinds, and timpani. Mahler himself had said, "This almost ceases to be music." He had once told fellow musicians that a symphony could embody an entire world. Head back, tears running off his chin, Anthony held her gaze. "Veronica!" he sobbed. The music was so loud, so beautiful. His hands outstretched, he willed her to speak, to soothe, to wipe away. "I have stepped out to you!" he called desperately. His eyes closed. His arms still outstretched, he ceased to feel his surroundings, lost in music but present with his own wretchedness.

He could feel her pushing him away. Gently but without benevolence. His toes left the rail first as he drifted away from her. Her gaze did not follow as he floated backward, arms still outstretched, off the rail where his idol had once walked. He had no feeling of falling. Just release. The last vision inside his head was of his own face left there on Veronica's towel.

Epilogue

J udy found Ron when she came home from work shortly after one thirty in the morning. Pants at his feet, shirt brown with dried blood, head creased from the impact of the broken statue. An experienced nurse, she knew at once that he was gone. She looked for Anthony, but he was not in the house. After calling the police, she called Annie. Calls to Chicago went unanswered, and by sunrise, the police in both cities were looking for Anthony. Annie was terrified that he too had been murdered by some intruder, even as she grieved with Judy at the loss of Ron. But Lynn and Judy silently and separately pieced together a more accurate version of what may have happened, even before it was revealed.

Judy and Lynn were there with Annie when the call came. It was a deacon who found Anthony. He was on his morning rounds to open the church for the six o'clock Mass, change the vigil candles, and check the flowers on the altar. The call to the police facilitated the contact with Anthony's parents. His arms still spread, he lay on his back in the main aisle. His body had contacted the terrazzo floor in one impact, his death quick.

Lynn told the police what she knew of her brother and of Ron. She cursed herself for not seeing what was going to happen even as she cursed Ron's return. Articles in the paper appeared for a few weeks as other men came forward to tell of their abuse at the hands of Ron Wilcox during his years at

St. Veronica's. There were some Anthony would have known, including Eddie, the bully who had so often accused other boys in the choir of being "fags." Eddie had attempted suicide twice in his early twenties but had since resolved in his soul all that had happened. He contacted Annie and Keith two months after Anthony's death to apologize for not coming forward when he was being abused by Ron in the 1970s. For not helping.

The church issued statements of shock, although it was revealed by the press that the diocese of San Francisco had paid settlements to two families to clear charges of sexual abuse some years earlier. They had not, however, released Ron from their employ or informed the Milwaukee Archdiocese when Ron had announced that he was returning there.

Annie was shattered by the deaths of these two men she loved. She didn't know whom to blame. To hold Ron accountable for Anthony's death was initially unthinkable. What was being said couldn't be so. She didn't leave her bed, except to attend her son's funeral. There initially had been plans, at Annie's insistence, to hold the two funerals together. But they were separated by a day when the press began revealing the truth of Ron Wilcox. "I will never recover," she sobbed into her husband's chest as he held her. "This is worse than Kathleen. I cannot lose two children before I die." Anthony's funeral was first and poorly attended. His family knew so little of his life that they could not contact those who might have been special to him. The day before the funeral, they gained access to his spotless apartment and, finding his address book, searched for the girlfriend who might be listed there. They called the names of all the females in his book, but no one turned out to be a girlfriend with roots in St. Louis. It was not until a year later when Claire contacted Annie that she was told of his death. He had not put Claire's number in his address book. Bill was not in the book either and, having no knowledge of Anthony's family, was never able to make contact with anyone. The details of the death were confined to the Milwaukee papers, thus he never saw the story. Calling Anthony's office, he was told of an accidental death. Seeing the woman from Anthony's office at church, he learned that two rumors were circulating—one that he had killed himself and the other that he had fallen accidentally and been mortally wounded. Bill wondered about the last hour he had spent with Anthony—the call demanding he come to the apartment, the frantic sex, the quick dismissal. It was clear that something was going on, and Bill concluded that things had gone terribly wrong for Anthony.

Judy was stoic. Her grief was less about Ron's death than about the realization that she knew of her husband's perversion but had not been able to stop it. She felt both victim and accessory. Her life had been painful. Ron's continual fascination with young boys had kept him from advancing in his own life and had, therefore, prevented her growth as well. He'd never finished college and never grown in his career or in his relationships. He had been furious when she asked why the choir in San Francisco did all the same music that he'd done with the choir in Milwaukee. He'd never seemed to grow emotionally from the day he'd left his boyhood home for the position at St. Veronica's. Although she loved him, she'd determined to avoid having children with him and had been motivated to move back to Wisconsin not only for the good of her ailing father but to be near her family when she left Ron, which she'd planned to do as soon as they were settled.

In the end, Annie didn't attend Ron's funeral. She'd talked to Judy about it, and they agreed that while Annie didn't hold Judy responsible for what happened, Ron deserved no more of Annie's love. The funeral was quiet. No music, as requested by Judy. As if to pull any comfort from his final day above the ground, she took his music from him.

In the weeks after the deaths, the two women sought solace in each other even as they felt inadequate to ease each other's pain. Annie's son had taken the life of Judy's husband in 1988. Judy's husband had taken the life of Annie's son in 1973. The two grieved the losses and their inability to prevent either. In a quiet ritual of grief, Annie smashed the two record albums recorded by the choir. It was a formal termination of her respect, her love, her admiration of Ron. She grieved for years, even as she laughed with joy at the lives of her grandchildren and took comfort in the love of her two remaining children. Alan came home more often, and Lynn became closer to her father, whom she'd never remembered seeing cry until the day after Anthony's funeral.

Family holidays changed. No longer centering on the choir years and choir stories, the family forged new memories around the grandchildren.

What would have surprised Anthony was how much the world was changed by his death. Life went on, but its path had been altered. His parents, his siblings, and those who loved him were never the same. Claire never married. Bill became more connected with his faith and reached out to troubled teens through a new ministry at St. Peter's. Anthony's family communicated better and loved more deeply. The people who loved Anthony went on. But they were changed by all that happened. Ron's lies from the 1970s were revealed fully in Anthony's death years later. He had been truly loved and would have been completely accepted if he had accepted himself. His world stolen at an early age, he never recovered. Ultimately, it took his life. It was not Anthony who murdered Ron. It was Ron who killed both of them.

—w—

"The idol is not created by the gilder, but by the genuflector."
—Baltasar Gracián